ALSO BY PETER MENDELSUND

FICTION

The Delivery

Same Same

NONFICTION

Exhibitionist: 1 Journal, 1 Depression, 100 Paintings

*The Look of the Book: Jackets, Covers, and
Art at the Edges of Literature*

Cover

What We See When We Read

WEEPERS

A NOVEL

PETER MENDELSUND

FARRAR, STRAUS AND GIROUX   NEW YORK

Farrar, Straus and Giroux
120 Broadway, New York 10271

EU Representative: Macmillan Publishers Ireland Ltd, 1st Floor, The Liffey
Trust Centre, 117–126 Sheriff Street Upper, Dublin 1, DO1 YC43

Library of Congress Cataloging-in-Publication Data
Names: Mendelsund, Peter, author.
Title: Weepers : a novel / Peter Mendelsund.
Description: First edition. | New York : Farrar, Straus and Giroux, 2025.
Identifiers: LCCN 2024053356 | ISBN 9780374619077 (hardcover)
Subjects: LCSH: Weepers (Mourners)—Fiction. | LCGFT: Novels.
Classification: LCC PS3613.E48223 W44 2025 | DDC 813/.6—dc23/
   eng/20241205
LC record available at https://lccn.loc.gov/2024053356

Designed by Abby Kagan

Our books may be purchased in bulk for specialty retail/wholesale, literacy,
corporate/premium, educational, and subscription box use. Please contact
MacmillanSpecialMarkets@macmillan.com.

www.fsgbooks.com
Follow us on social media at @fsgbooks

10 9 8 7 6 5 4 3 2 1

Blessed are those who mourn.

—Matthew 5:4

CONTENTS

WEEPERS

PLEASE BE SEATED

Lo, here he comes.
—Matthew 24:23

He was here for only a short while: March, on into those last, convalescent weeks of fall. Showed up one morning in the dark garb of our order and stood alone. Me and Chantal were outside the trailer waiting for the calls to go out.

—This the crying place? he said to us.

I nodded and said:

—Union?

—New, he said.

—Done it before?

—Ain't everyone, he said.

Chantal told him how Regis calls the jobs. How paid-up members of the Local 302 get dibs.

—But there is always work these days, I said, and he nodded.

Just then the call came.

When he turned away toward the trailer, Chantal gave me a nudge and a knowing look, but what it was that her look knew was unclear. Maybe it was just a nod to his youth; that we rarely see the young in this line of work. For most, the vocation kicks in around middle age. That's when we figure out that we aren't just your run-of-the-mill types, but real pros; that we have more stamina, and are more able to get right down to it.

I had been named on the job, but didn't go. Instead, I pulled out a brown.

—Smoke? I said to the kid.

Me and him bowed to my lighter.

When we rose, he took me in, his eyes clear as a rung bell. This is also rare. People don't look straight at you so much anymore.

After a bit I took him on over to a spot under the locust tree, thinking he'd want out of the sun. His skin was so pale, and those dark vestments of ours heat up fast. The ease in his shoulders; dress shoes, too big for him; tie, badly done up.

And boy did he seem familiar. Bone structure, posture, something. The feeling deepened.

He kicked the dirt.

Another call, an Episcopal number.

—You're going to get them dusty, I said to him, perhaps a touch too forceful.

Then added, after the silence wasn't filled:

—I'll get you on that gig.

And then went and did so.

After that, for the reason of being unaccountably tired, I went straight home.

———————————

Next day, he was back.

He ambled on over, bottle trailing from slender fingers, and we stood.

—Remind you of someone? he said, just like that. I suppose I had been squinting—but still.

He finished his dregs and lowered his arm into the rusted metal drum we use for trash, placing the empty tenderly at its bottom.

—No, I said.

Reg came out then and said the names. Not mine though—Reg likes to mix it up, and certain jobs require certain people. No one takes it personally.

But the kid was on the list, meaning that his first outing had gone ok; or at least not terribly wrong.

—Good on you, I said.

Bunch of folks began gathering around a van. Kid asked if this was his ride, and I nodded.

—You need any help out there, you just ask Dill.

I pointed.

Dill noticed us looking and waved from across the lot.

WORDS OF WELCOME

Don't cry, you'll rust your spurs
—CountryWesternClassics.net

There's about a score of us weepers in-state. We can recognize a person who works our line from a mile's distance, same as—so I understand it—Masons or vets or men who have sex with men can recognize one another. It is just obvious to those who are similar. Like, there's no secret sign we throw, at least none I know of. But there is a sign, deep in me, in all of us, inscribed by God, so rooted and so indelible that it pretty much throws itself.

And spotting what is out there, tallying up the numbers, our 302 is pretty much it, at least around here, and we are the last of the dodo.

You'd think we'd be more.

It began as a small enterprise, not more than a novelty service—like singing telegrams or birthday clowns—but it had become decent money, relatively speaking. There was a need. In spades. Look around. More need than ever. But fewer every year who can meet it, fewer who have the stomach or the talent for it.

Weeping. Professionally. Weeping day upon day. Clocking in and out, but never leaving it at the office either.

I am a weeper as soon as I awake until the moment I sleep.

For a long time, I kept hoping my disposition might

liquefy right out of me like so much earwax. Or burrow free like a kidney stone. But every sunrise, there I am again, same as before, up with the light.

I got in the habit of waking early long before I wept, back when I tended horses. Though now I could, if I wanted it, have a stay here in my narrow bed, not being so hard up as to need early work.

So I stir, lie there, spavined and dumb, until I roll up to make a Sanka, smoke at the fold-out table, blink, smack my lips, ash, extend a leg, retract it, scratch the back of my neck, etc.

I don't get the paper so it's mostly staring at nothing, biding my time, watch the patch of light migrate along the slowly blanching wall, framing a stain or a crack, occasionally burnishing a centipede.

Sitting until some internal chime tells me to stand. Might as well.

I go to the sink and ream out my cup til she squeaks. Get dressed, always the same. I have appearances to keep up, being the cowboy of our group. So there are the affectations: the hat, the boots, but also that silver-and-turquoise-clasped idiot-string around my neck, which I'm perversely attached to for sentimental reasons, as it belonged to my asshole dad, though, as such, feels occasionally like a noose. Let it be said that one can be nostalgic even for one's old torments, and anything—even the knife in one's own back—can serve as the wrong-headed memento of an unshakable backstory.

Jacket-wise, it is the old-but-still-fairly-spiffy boot-stitch number (black). I admit that I look like a spat-out country-western dickweed, and hell, even my sneeze has a drawl to it, but I long since ceased to give a shit and so no use for my mirror either.

Then there's nothing for it but out.

I stop in the doorframe and narrow my eyes. The world as unchanged by the passage of night as I was, and I'm once again surprised by this, thinking: oh hey, yeah, here's where we're at; like I'm opening a book I'd put down in a doze.

Hello then to the mobile homes. Hello to the red dirt and the endless scrub, peopled with cactus. Hello to the yapping Scotties from the unit next door, the adobes up-ridge, the scattered propane tanks, the bright freeway leveling the horizon. Hello to the sky, scarred with contrails. Hello and big fuck you to the sun's full and disrespectful aspect.

Out and down; a rapid two-step, avoiding the crispy daubs of dog shit.

I catch my breath up in the truck, put the visor down, check the rearview, which is always a keen reminder at how wilted around the eyes I've got.

Turn the knob and summon some crap, mid-twang.

Out of park. Pedal down.

Dirt roads, paved streets, highway.

Pull off, open the old gate, and park in the dust.

The lot. The gang. Chitchat. Boredom's low hum.

Might eat a sandwich, if I've packed it.

Out comes Reg.

If my name is on the clipboard, I'll hit the road again.

The venue. Jesus on the Mount, normally, but we do all the others as well; all the different beliefs. We look equally upon all and sundry, and there isn't a congregation of any sort that does not need our help.

Wherever it ends up being, I lumber in and pop a squat.

Show begins.

Summon that quiet dignity.

And my calling rises up.

Tears. Then the afters. Family and assorted.

Condolences, thanks, gratuities.

The after-afters, in the dark, yeasty corners of the Crown.

Later I'll wobble back to the truck.

Chantal then (sometimes).

Or home again alone, Hi Ho Silver.

Then I'm out.

I wake again in the same role, playing it all over, for more or less the same audience.

The facts on the ground. And you'd think it'd be on automatic. But always atop this, here's me just questioning each and every circumstance and step, for instance: why Scotties? Why the brown cigarettes? Why trailers; gas pumps; sky; pews; chaparral? (Why the kid, and whither?) Why tears; and why do those tears go down, rather than up and out? Why, I say, to the dry breeze distributing heat to the hard-to-reach corners; why do I rub up against the grain of the world like a bow does a fiddle?

This is true weeper stuff here, folks, as I imagine most people take things on faith.

So next I heard was from Dill's cousin Sylvia, who had been trying to fill those rooms above the Bow & Gun for weeks with no success, but it turned out she had finally cracked the nut, and when she described the new tenant, it was the kid from the lot.

—Move-in was nothing, she reported.

—Meaning what.

—Meaning he didn't have nothing.

—Like, *nothing*?

She shook her head in wonderment.

—What is he, some kind of pervert? Sylvia asked me.

I considered that. I thought of the peculiar I'd glimpsed on the boy and then wondered, not for the last time, if I could find a way to sidle up to it. But then thought: leave well alone, Ed.

I had a dream that night where Dad was back, string tie and all. I hadn't had such a visitation in years. In the dream, he behaved as usual: not keeping still, bouncing on his feet. He was always jittering—full of more dark energies than he could tamp—and thinking, as he did, that every problem was just five knuckles away from a solution, would be ready to juke and throw. He looked down upon me—me riveted beneath him, him cocking a jackal head and sucking on those lean cheeks of his in assessment—and he said the words "you won't last a fucking day."

He said it over and over, each time slightly louder.

The following morning, the lot was hot as hell and drier than Egypt. I kept looking up from under my brim, expecting the boy to wander in, out of a shimmering heat cloud. But he didn't. Must have got a glimpse of the lifestyle and not liked what he saw.

I guess I was moping because Chantal gave me a look, and she was bang-on right. And I couldn't help but feel sour. I had sensed, in those days since our first encounter, that he was a marker; a sign of some new dispensation. I could admit that this was horseshit, but that's how I felt, and I've felt stupider things before.

Anyway, the call rang out, and I worked Holy Nazarene with the regulars, as usual and always and ever.

OPENING PRAYERS

The core crew back then was me, Johnnie, Lemon Barbara, Carlos (Hankie) Hanks, Dill Denvers, Peewee Fernando, Sheryl, Chief Clarence, Chantal, the Nguyens, and those eight or so non-weepers we used just to fill out the numbers when a proper crowd is needed.

Occasionally someone like Kelsey Tucson or Abel Moyette would come out of retirement, but only for rare events.

Jeannine also used to be in the lineup, years back, but she stopped.

Jeannine was my wife, now ex, and she was just like the

others. I don't mean "just like my other women," because she wasn't. And I never had many others, and now it's just Chantal, who gets it.

But what I mean is that Jeannine started out like me—card-carrying, paid-up union member—but ended up the other way. Meaning normal.

When we met, she could experience and enact the full range. Boy, I loved Jeannine for that. And she loved me as well for all my funk. Not despite, but because of that ineradicable melancholy. We felt an instant and deep rapport.

—If you think of ending it, how do you imagine doing the deed? she asked once, meaning death. It was that first week of our romance, her eyes shyly agleam, as though we were sharing sexual histories. And it was, in fact, an intimacy. We were both victim to a deep ache, and felt then, if not an alleviation of it, a kinship in it.

But then, after those decades-and-change during which we played at husband-and-wife, she changed.

Amber bottles, pink pills, the hours as smooth as pool felt.

As with most, the sedation was voluntary. Jeannine wanted it. This was partially down to what happened with the pregnancies and partially down to life-being-life and all, and partially (I think now) down to her being married to me.

I just felt enough feelings for the both of us combined. It was simply unsustainable. I guess I knew that too, and I also knew that as soon as she started on her healing that I'd be left behind. That the imbalance wouldn't stand. That she'd eventually want a partner whose days weren't desolation and disengagement; a man who didn't see every fucking state of affairs no matter how mundane as an opportunity to call forth and wrestle his demons.

She improved. I curdled.

The sky bleached, the air hurt my skin. Every gratification was slowly drained of its power. I was unslakable, but couldn't identify what needed the slaking either. The distance between us kept doubling, and seeing me deteriorate like that drove her toward cruelty. She wasn't angry exactly; pills took that away too. But she grew callous; an idle kind of mean, the kind that barely rouses itself. The condemnation of a glance, a calculated, disdainful word here and there—timed to perfection—would gut me. She stuck around just long enough to get some real blows in.

And of course I started noticing the marks on her.

—I bruise easy, she said. And that was true.

But the bruises were always on her pale wrists, a set on each; exactly where someone would grab on if they wanted to hold you down.

After that, finally, at long last and as a relief to both of us: the suitcase; the no-look door-close; the heels on the stairs; the engine's growl, the peel-out. (The enduring silence.) She'd left me for the bruiser.

Sayonara, Mr. Sensitive.

Oh Jeannine, we were doomed. You, anesthetized, me leaking buckets. Though we once held each other inexhaustible, thenceforth, I would appear in your life reduced, a signature on a check; one I'm not sure I ever owed, but which still I will pay.

TESTIMONIAL

Oh, that my head were waters.

—Jeremiah 9:1

Now on Monday, there were two gigs, which, again, was surprising. The first call turned out to be a little ceremony in a funeral home a mile outside of Los Renas. Modest affair, and I got it done early, so after, I went to meet the rest of the gang, who were working the big show. See if Chantal needed a lift to the Crown.

When I got there, the double doors were closed.

So I sat down on the steps outside and watched the street and its movement. Savored a Tiparillo. After a while I got very bored, and went back up to the entrance to see if I could hear where the ceremony was at.

There are different types of quiet which come from the outside of a shut door: there is the dulled sound—gray— then there is the shuffle and cough, the scrape of a chair, interruptions—like a blown nose; there is the low bubble of conversation on a simmer; there is susurration, like a wind. The bored one. The expectant one. There are more.

But this one was pure silence, like God had removed—at a gesture—all sound from the world as if he had decided against it on principle.

I turned back around slow, trying to recall how many swigs there were at my lunch, and then sat back on the stairs.

Eventually the people wandered out. Guests and funerary workers, together.

The attendees looked worked over. The weepers looked confused.

And there he was.

—Son, I said.

—Hey, the kid said back.

Then, all the sounds came back on. A transformer buzzed, a bird whistled. A truck went by and displaced the air. And then people were chatting, engines started, all of it. I made a note to add hearing loss to my litany of ailments.

We hit the Crown. Kid came too.

The kid came too, and I watched the boy a bunch that evening. Like I had a personal stake. Him in a booth with the Nguyens, me skulking.

When he left, old Dill came up. We sat side by side in a drinkers' silence for a bit before he finally broke it.

—The thing today, Dill says.

—Yeah?

—Yeah.

Then a longer pause, which I broke.

—*That good?*

I was designated chauffeur, and had Johnnie and Sheryl in back, Chantal riding shotgun. She was the last drop (as sometimes I dropped myself off at Chantal's as well, depending). She was lifting the black lace and checking her makeup in the passenger side mirror when I pulled in front of her place. Then I stopped, and she opened the door—light clicking on above us—speared the one long, dark-stockinged leg out of the vehicle before turning back.

—You should have seen it, she said, meaning the service.

—Dill said.

—Not a dry eye in the house.

—As they say.

—As they say.

She shook her head slowly, in stupefaction.

We sat for a minute, then.

—Ed, she said.

—Yeah, baby?

—Are you going to escort a lady to her door?

BENEDICTION

I come out of St. Simon. Moved north when ranch jobs got scarce and debt got high.

Johnnie and Sheryl are out of Benson; suburb of there. Chantal's from Weston, though really from France. Peewee moved up from Sepulse after serving his nickel; Dill's from Badger. The rest are Coolidge and Stanville folk.

Back in St. Simon I liked to place a bet, but after some particularly lousy beatdowns, I got right, more or less. Though I like to think, despite the losses, that I have a knack. Not putting money down so much on ponies anymore, but Jesus knows I'm always handicapping, looking for a spot. Saw the kid before anyone, though that didn't take a genius. As I've told it, there was the growing need for our professional services. And there was a lack of qualified to satisfy that need, so most of us had guessed that the time was ripe for something or other. A hole needs filling, and lo, he came round to fill that hole, meaning that I knew he was coming, but not *as such*. Who could have foreseen the true extent?

The kid said he came from out of state, but didn't say where exactly.

—Got any family that's local? I once asked him, early on.

He did not reply to my question and that was that. Because—several beers later, without my ever having noticed the change—he was looking at me with those still eyes and I was the one just gabbing away under them. Told him about Jeannine, and about my cowboy poems—can you fucking believe it? Not shy in the least.

I even told him about my old man, what happened there.

I hadn't told that story to more than a few people, but sometimes I guess things can just feel safer with those you don't know; don't know you. Or it was the booze. Or it was something else.

The kid drank in my tale like he had a reservoir he needed to fill. He got you to talking, and once you were, it became just so goddam hard to stop.

And that silence of his—the way he'd just watch and wait—it made his talent harder to focus on, as it seemed at first like a trick, some sleight of hand; a routine. Whatever it was, it worked. And the working of it made me wonder if he was perhaps born to our path.

Not all who ply our trade are. As with Jeannine, weepers would come through and not hack it. Some stayed a bit, the few with some talent, but eventually they'd hightail themselves out of there, and I suspect that there are more of us who live on the road than those that stay put in a place, as it must be a lot better living as tramps. No one to bog down with your morose ways, just working itinerant, town to town, as mourning the dead is always a sight easier than loving the living.

More often than not folks would come on board for just a single job, maybe two, thinking it an easy buck (it never is). Rookie would find the work surprisingly difficult though; meaning that most people are more out of the habit of tears than they realize. And then coming up short, they'd pretend it was a grift, or a dare, or just a dumb idea to begin with, ridicule the whole enterprise in one way or another, then slink on off and that would be that.

I was always embarrassed on their behalf but wouldn't make a big fuss about it. Though sometimes, we'd recall about them up at the bar.

—Remember that Darlene?

—Her face.

—Couldn't cry worth a shit.

And it's true that the face of this woman was stretched, and also shiny. But shiny: like angry. Like when there's an infection under the surface. Point is, she couldn't move a muscle in it.

—Guy from Ortaloosa?

—Amateur, we'd say, though there wasn't too much malice in it.

But there was that strung-out couple. Reg should've seen them coming and set the dogs on those two. They used vinegar, and made off with a tithing box. But then worse was that guy with an actual lachrymator—pepper spray, tear gas, some damn thing—watered down and kept in a little vial. We took him to Stanville General; him screaming in the back seat like a police siren. And his eyes didn't look right after, said Francine, who was working the shift that night.

Et cetera.

So mostly it was fakers. Normal, but acting sad. I guess a lot of our anger toward these misfits was directed at ourselves—us—for being only too eager to be fooled. We should have known better.

Misery loves company is a thing people say, but also a true thing.

GREAT LOSS

And those who are crushed in spirit.
—Psalms 34:18

Misery loves company but hey, at least we were miserable, which counts as a feeling, and most people these days cannot manage even that, sentiment of any kind, and so it was, and is, and thus we do all the feeling for them.

You saw them everywhere. Wan, blank. All around. More and more of those by the minute; not doing much, reacting at nothing. No expression on their flat faces: not at the Rally's and the Savemart, down in the lots, out on the stoops, at the Motel El Rancho, or at the place that sells local shit (meteorites, Native memorabilia, petrified wood). Not in strip clubs, not on sidewalks. Not at the track, the drive-in, tractor pulls, and rodeos. Not exhibiting anything; not even at any of those places where'd you'd think there'd be a little more emotion on display: weddings, quinceañeras, bachelorette parties, fireworks, so on. It became, for me, and I assume for the rest of the crew, harder and harder to distinguish one normal from another. They were generalized, more than a population of discreet individuals. I felt them almost like an atmosphere, as a mist or vapor. A mildness. A pervasive, barometric presence.

It was Johnnie who really fucking loathed their guts.

—Veal, he would say, and Sheryl would lay a hand on his dense forearm, over that Semper Fi. He would hush then.

I couldn't feel too much enmity myself. I was too busy being envious. *Their easy ways.* And I believe some of the other weepers felt similar. Being us, here, is no picnic. And we are no picnic to be around either.

I had more tolerance, that is. But it wasn't like it was in-finite in me either.

Meaning that they got to me too on occasion. For instance a couple of months back, when that Maureen—copper-top who does the books for many of the concerns in town—collapsed at the Big Box. I had just paid, bagged up, and was exiting when I saw her lying there, puddle spreading out be-neath like she's a popped water balloon; people drifting over, and I had thought they were going to help, get her up again, pick up the cans rolling on the linoleum, but instead they just sort of surrounded her, prompting in my mind the image of a marching-band-of-the-dead, as it might emerge at hell's halftime—single file, then fanning out to form a huge zero, which then would widen as more joined; black trombones,

ruptured drums, the most discouraging glockenspiels . . .
this was the real kicker for me: the slow ritual of it. Their
marble-eyed stares. They simply could not see what I got at a
glance: how much weight Maureen had gained since her
troubles—that hard state of affairs. Her eyes, receding into
her face. Her undone belt—the one that had all manner of
curlycues worked into it, and therefore was made by her husband (who fashioned hand-tooled leather holsters for your
antique six-shooters and fancy straps for your ARs, etc.), the
buckle of which had likely, and more than once, left an im-
print of his drunkenness upon her? Didn't they get how
wretched—heart-and-head-sick—she'd become? Weepers
cannot ignore such things, cannot help but to feel them.

I was very down about that, and so in no mood for what
happened the following morning, which was that one of the
neighbor's Scotties was tagged but hard by an SUV. Dog's
shoulder and one front leg was torn basically off and worse,
and the next-door kids came out, looking mildly curious—
half-lidding it, unplugged from their sockets—their mother
holding the leash of the other Scottie, twin to the first, the
dog pulling hard, which made her look like she's sweeping
the road for mines. She saw me looking and, as if I'd asked
for an explanation, she said:

—We always have two? (meaning dogs) and when I
didn't reply, visibly PO'd, added: Because *the coyotes*? (like
you'd carry a spare tire).

Well, she took one look at the mewling mess beside her
shower sandals, grabbed her vegetative children, and went
back in. I was left alone with the vic, but having had more
than I could stomach, made my own way back inside to look

for my rifle before remembering I'd given it up in disgust after the most recent lone shooter. I admit to cowardice because in the end I called the animal folks instead of getting a shovel and doing the deed myself with its business end. I didn't come back outside again for a while, until I was sure that the pup had been removed, and when I did head back out he was, horrifyingly, still there, sort of alive though very much barely, just tiny palpitations, the small shivering lids, completely alone in its filth and meat. An hour later two men came, and by then the dog was good and truly gone. One of them made me fill out a form. The other had a tranq pistol strapped to his leg, with an air canister hanging off it like a goiter.

—Good stuff, he told me, meaning the tranq.

I didn't reply, but imagined this total gonad with a fuzzy-ended dart in his stringy, sunburnt neck. He carried the dog gently over both arms, which seemed to my eye as respectful until he tossed the body roughly into the van, which was anything but. They drove off then and later I came back out with the hose from my tank to water down the scene and damned if the neighbors didn't watch me do it through their trailer windows like they were put on this earth to pay dull witness—like the seeing of something were just the procedure of looking and counting a thing seen (this being an insult to true witness).

Later still, in town, I saw the SUV that done it. It was outside the package store, parked diagonally across two spaces.

So you see, *there is a theme*: which is that living among them was a chore. Especially in moments such as those I've told above—when it felt like I was dropped among an alien race, one that did not obey the same summons as I did, with their own eerie, flat, and indecipherable concerns.

Though it is also true that—on the rarest of occasions—one of the normal folk might walk by, and recognizing me for some service I had wept, would acknowledge my calling with a slight dipping of the head, a consecrated lowering of the eyes.

It would be from one of them who, no matter how dimmed, still had the capacity for warmth, even if it's just the capacity to warm themselves up at another man's fire. A gesture from one of those who might appreciate what it is we do.

(What we do: 1. Cry so you do not have to. 2. Provide more bodies in the pews and thus prove the deceased was dearly loved and sorely missed. 3. Get things going, meaning set match to tinder; we are tinder and matches both. 4. And perhaps even bring up real sorrow in people who no longer have any. This, our paid communion.)

So that nod; the rare nod. And it helps, that nod. As knowing you are contributing to the common weal can keep you going and everyone needs a reason to be, especially in those darker hours, when, for yours truly, getting up and going to do my weeping work was just a way of deferring the harder and more permanent task of taking the old toaster bath.

But either way, whether they admired or despised or just plain ignored us, we were the exceptions to them, on the outside looking in.

The county's very own, mulleted, mendicant friars.

HIS CHARITABLE WORKS

The last word in lonesome is "me"
—Dolly Parton

—He didn't show again, said Reg.

—Who didn't? I said, nonchalant as fuck.

As with the kid's other absences, I was jumpy—expecting him to manifest at any moment, but he did not.

That day I worked John the Baptist, mourning Mrs. Abernathy. And I felt duly sad, as that's what I'm paid for. Felt sad for the deceased, sad for those left behind, and naturally sad for myself, mostly for having to feel sad, which is a real head-scratcher, though one I am used to. So a lot of sad, but only, you know, according to my own constant manner; meaning *some* tears, muted, nothing to write home about. The kind of light trickle I'd long grown weary of. At the services there'd be the usual humdrum: the droning of whoever happened to have the pulpit, our sniffles, a hitched inhale or two, and generally speaking the other gentle sounds of the professional grief, soft and tender from long practice.

So the good run had ended, and the rest of the week was like blank pages in a diary.

That Friday, I heard from Dill that there'd be some action. I wasn't going to shirk an opportunity for work, as what the hell else was I going to do, but as it happens, I had been to my doctor, having postponed that visit over a span of years. Some things were acting up which could not be ignored. Simply high time, so I got listened to, tapped on, bent over, and in the end got a lecture and a bunch of referrals for my troubles. At least the deed was done.

Then I heard about the boy's being back, and kicked myself.

Went to Dill's to get the lowdown.

Well, Dill hadn't been there either. So we stood there regretfully in silence like the two old dopes we were, until something struck him.

—Johnnie and Sheryl.

Those two could surely testify, and they could only be in one of three places in that lousy town—all of them bars— and there they were, slumped in a corner booth.

—You don't look too hot, I told them.

—No sleep, Johnnie said.

Sheryl nodded.

—He kept getting up to piss last night; he drinks too much, Sheryl said and took a long sip off her cocktail straw.

—Fuck you, Johnnie said to her, politely.

Then he shoved over and I sat. Dill went in next to her.

—Not my fault; I couldn't make it happen. Stood there over the bowl long as I could, waiting. Piss. Piss. *Come on.* Back to sleep. Wake up and back to the head. Repeat a bunch.

Sheryl rolled her eyes.

—It only comes when it comes, I said.

We drank.

—How was today, I asked, having been patient.

He let his eyes drift up, slow and dramatic, and said:

—Wet.

—How wet?

—Shock and awe, brothers.

—Yeah?

—The sluices opened up. Sudden-like.

Then he put his thumb over his beer bottle and shook it, once quick, knocking it down on the table, such that suds spumed out. He looked so pleased with the point he made. By all of it.

Sheryl tutted and begun wiping at that with those thin cocktail napkins. She pushed the sodden bits to one side.

—You meet him yet? she said to me.

—Yep, I said, knowing who she meant.

—Nice boy, she said.

—Sure, Dill said.

—I wanna feed him, she said, like it was dirty.

At that, Johnnie gave her a peeved look and went to the Men's.

— . . . *feed him from my titties*, she said quieter, with a wink.

—You there too? I asked.

—No. I was there for the other one. First Presby, she said, her little red straw: spun and worried.

So many deaths. We were all so tired.

—First Presby, she said once more.

—Kid at that one? I said.

—Yeah, she said. There was a long beat, then she said:

—I fell the fuck to sleep; right there on the pew. You've all done it so get off those high horses.

—Not a crime, Dill said.

—Listen, nothing is more fucking boring than someone else's dream . . . she said.

—Sure, I said, haunted by my own, recent one.

—But still, she said.

She told us. Behind her voice was the music and the bar sounds.

—When I was little I had a window and it faced out to the back meadow—and in this dream I was seeing out to there, though there was never goddam much to look at, scenery-wise, but for that field with the windmill in it. The light was very good and clear, but the windmill dead and rusted still, like it used to be, but here, here, its blades began to creak, then turn once, then twice, then a bunch more, a bunch, a bunch, and then a whole, whole, whole, whole bunch more, she said.

I could then picture that tail-vane juddering all over the place, entire contraption flapping out of control. The laundry snapping on the line, and the thickets of mesquite, bluestem, and sedge going buck-wild; swaying together, apart, together, apart . . .

She looked off past the walls of the bar.

Then Johnnie come up, back from the bathroom. Shook his leg, uncomfortable.

—It's like there's a damn plug up in there, he said.

PILLAR OF THE COMMUNITY

Young man, arise.
—Luke 7:11

I saw the kid around then.

Not too much at first, but more and more frequent. First, I saw him from my truck. He was standing on the embankment of the Culpo, looking out at God knows what.

Los Culpos, our town, grew up around the river, which is pretty much the only reason people settled here in the first place; the indigenous first, and then our lot. Cattle could drink and graze, not to mention that the water presented a way by which those cattle could be driven more efficiently, without hands, or remuda. The Culpo thinned, the ranches teetered, and most of the farms dried up. A few held on, if only by one single toenail, but later droughts took care of them. Eventually the railway barged on through, watering the town with a bit of commerce. The telegraph came too, and then the phone lines followed. After, the highways brought something to the party. Even so, the town couldn't truly compete, not really, not all the way out here in nowheresville, and eventually the few factories we had got shuttered. Bereft of new economic waterways, terrestrial, airborne, what have you, the county won't ever really get a leg up again; and though we do just about get by, there is little here now but that emptied-out *here* itself, meaning the dead land and air. That absence.

Our trickle of river now passes through a nasty concrete

channel, which widens out as it leaves the city limits to about two hundred feet across. Amazing to think, dry as things are, that it was built to keep the river from breaking its banks and flooding the alluvial plains. The site is now enjoyed by addicts, and rednecks buzz the inclines on their candy-colored dirt bikes. And so it will all remain, short of importing new water from somewhere altogether different: the polar ice caps, the Indian Ocean, the seas of Uranus.

I saw the kid there, by that embankment.

I pulled over. Then a few delinquents approached him, then another one, and another, and I thought: here's some trouble. Instead, they all stood together, the kid and those others, in the slouchy ease of youth, no evident menace, shuffling their feet like waiting for a council to reach quorum. It was as if the kid had drawn them in or called them to account somehow. I wished I could've heard their talk, but I was late for my rendezvous with Chantal, and nothing— not even the novelty and wonder of this gathering—could get in the way of that.

Next I saw him walking by the vacant lot, and all I can report from my slow tail is that he passed by all of the dandelions there without kicking a single one of them, which is saying something.

And then I caught him talking to that homeless who always wears those grim pajamas, the one people call Shitburger who set himself across from the diner. (Or I should say—like with the delinquents—the kid wasn't talking, but listening in that way of his.) Shitburger looked like a man whose paycheck had come in, gabbing up a storm and grinning ear to gruesome ear. I sipped my coffee at the counter and watched through a window.

The day of that shindig those from the Rez perform—which is a gathering of nations but also for the tourist cash—I saw him in the crowd. He was watching one of the ceremonies and in this case, saw me looking. He nodded in my direction perfunctory-like, before turning back into the crowd.

Next, I was with Dill and Johnnie shooting pool, as it was a Saturday, and Johnnie had been staring down the barrel of the bridge at a shot that was never, ever going to come off, and Dill had that wry smirk on him which said so. I got tired of watching that cue slide up and down and up and down again, tired of breathing that dry, green air, and so turned away just in time to see the boy darken the backward gilt letters on the window.

—Hang on, fellas, I said, and as I went out through the front door I heard the gentle, woodpecker *tock* at my back.

Once out there, instead of hailing the kid, I walked a ways behind him; far enough back he couldn't hear the quiet crunch of my boots. Protective impulse? Base curiosity? Who in hell knows but he didn't look in any of the windows, didn't even glance side to side as you do, just kept on. He stopped at a light though there were no cars in either direction, waiting patiently like a model citizen. So I had to pause myself and examine some necklace in a shop display for a bit. This meant that Joan Hamady left the register and came out to see if I was interested in getting a piece for Chantal and I quickly realized that—as she was tightly bound up as all the women in this town were with one another—I'd better free up some jewelry funds for later in the week.

By the time I had politely extricated myself, the kid was gone.

Must have crossed the street and turned a corner, but it felt like he had been just plucked on up. And I thought those exact words: "plucked on up."

As I came back in the pool hall, Johnnie looked like the cat got the cream, as he had inadvertently dropped his ball, winning the game. This started off an intense-yet-inconclusive two-way spat over shot-calling that continued all the way to the Crown and after, and even through to the next day at the lot.

The last sighting in that period was when I saw the kid climb down from the cab of a Kenworth semi out by Route 4. Why he'd gone out there to that rest area, who was this truckman that had picked him up . . . I wondered hard about all that. Then I remembered, generally speaking, about how I knew absolutely jack-shit-nothing about this kid in the first place. Who he was; where he came from. It felt like—as he had been *plucked up*—so he had also been *dropped down*.

Out of the sky's white brow.

As I crept by the truck stop, I didn't pull over to offer him a lift, and I missed him at the lot the following day as well as the day after, as, on both occasions, feeling resigned, I had gone on the jobs, and, according to Reg, he kept idling in too late.

HYMN

Roped and thrown (by Jesus).
—*The Complete Cowboy-Chapel Sermons*

—I got the facts, and don't pretend you don't want them, Dill said.

We paused in the dirt between the morgue and the truck. He was on one end of a large and elaborately ribboned wreath, me on the other. The sash across the thing read, in a ribbony script: "Sweetee" (spelled like that).

We lay the wreath and its easel down gently in the truck bed without strapping it.

—Don't drive too quick, Dill said.

—Do I ever?

—Don't start now.

We got into the cab. I waited before turning the key, suspecting that Dill was drawing things out at my expense.

—Well? I finally said.

—The service was for Old McGrath, Dill said.

I knew Old McGrath, but I didn't know him that well, as he was just the guy who ran the filling station down the road from my park. We didn't interact much but for me to pay for what was on Pump 5 and maybe buy some scratch-offs or a wrinkly dog. So I didn't know the first thing about him, really. But what I did know was that he wasn't worth mourning overly, as he was an ornery old turd.

—Mean enough to steal the coins off a dead man's eyes, Dill said, quoting someone or other.

—A *real peach*, I said, grimacing.

—So, Ed, what I'm about to tell you will be a little surprising.

—Go the fuck on then.

—I came to the party a hair late to avoid the front-door widow-greet. Walked into the Veterans of Foreign Wars Hall and the thing was already going. Master of ceremonies doing his bit. Nguyens a row in front, Sheryl and Johnnie on their six. Thought I saw the boy too, somewhere, but lost him in the crowd. I took a moment to decide where I'd park myself to get an ample spread between us, and looking around I caught sight of a guy tearing up, off to my right; he was not one of us, but a guest. So it had begun already. That man crying, softly. Or then perhaps it was one or maybe two other men, Ed, who, I saw, were, there, also, actually, crying, a few of these folks crying, various and sundry, lots of them crying, most were crying, in fact, and ok everyone and I mean *everyone* was crying, that is, definitely *all* crying, the Veterans of Foreign Wars Hall *just packed to the fucking rafters* with crying people, including the master of ceremonies, the (crying) master of ceremonies who afterward (*still* crying) remarked to me (me, also crying) on the strange fact of "everyone crying," and I found out later from the (crying) Veterans of Foreign Wars Hall's groundskeeper that (and this part is obvious pig slop but) even people on the street, as they passed the Veterans of Foreign Wars Hall also began to cry, just by walking on by, as if he and everyone else had wandered into some manner of hazardous airspace, and the time it took to tell it you, Ed, was just about how fast it went down. We fucking killed it.

—Uhhhh . . . I said.

———

So there was that from Dill. A whole lot of tears at the Veterans of Foreign Wars Hall—a place less conducive to genuine feelings you could not dream up, with its used-chewing-gum stucco; folding card tables as cranky as the old bastards who sit at them playing Chickenfoot, Mexican Train, Spinner, and Maltese Cross; that bad light and vinyl parquet—those tears shed on behalf of that one shriveled bastard and what the actual hell, I asked myself.

—Swamp gas, I said.

—Radon.

—Mercury rising.

—Who fucking knows.

—A mood can strike.

And it can. Yet, even in the most loonbats of circumstances—these are not what you'd call an expressive people.

—Strange though, I said.

—Yessir, Dill said.

Strange. And I think that was the most either of us were willing to admit.

Then Thursday I went to the Trembling Hills Convalescent Home, up off I-20, which is getting rid now like there's a fucking clearance sale on.

Mr. Lamont (formerly of our parish) was in there. I had begun visiting him regularly a year or so before. His son was working fulfillment over in Deruta, and Mr. Lamont didn't have anyone close by.

I pulled in and got out, and on my way to the doors, the

kid himself emerges out from the side where the dumpster lives. He was drinking from a 7UP and did not see me.

—Hey there, Slim, I said.

He turned, swallowed, nodded *howdy*, and walked away, which I thought pretty rude.

Did he have someone in particular to visit? When I asked at the front desk about the boy, they didn't know who I was talking about.

Anyway, I got to the room and didn't see Mr. Lamont at first because he was parked in his wheelchair right smack up against the wall in the dark corner. His back was to the door. He was hiccuping softly. He lifted an arm and seemed to wipe it across his face.

I cleared my throat.

—It's quite a thing. Quite a thing . . . he said, without turning.

—What is, I said.

He blew his smoke right into the corner, where it nestled and climbed. Oxygen tank unused beside him.

—You being seen to, I said.

He laughed.

—Never been better, and you can put that on a bumper sticker.

Then the orderly came in.

—Can't even crap alone anymore, Mr L. said, and shrugged apologetically.

It wouldn't be long until I'd have to work Mr. Lamont's funeral, I thought back in the truck, and then I considered about how, under the new circumstances, his funeral just might prove another doozie.

REMEMBERING THE HARD TIMES

You can just imagine what services were like back before we started weeping for folks. I remember one I attended back then, it was for Fred Bodner's wife, and it serves pretty well as prime specimen.

I knew Fred from way back. Haven't seen him since he moved to Chinoa County to work at that industrial farm that employs half their people. Anyway, I went to this funeral as a mourner (doing it *Oh Nature-All*, as Chantal put it).

The service took place at a funeral home; an adobe-faced, flagstone-pathed, succulent-lined suburban tract house, identical to its neighbors but for the hearse in the driveway and the signage out front. Inside was as predictably awful as outside, and once you crossed the threshold, you realized that the joint felt not so much like a sending-off point for the dead as it did a processing area, a dentist's waiting room, an airport without airplanes. Further to this: it smelled like a newly licked business envelope—"bureaucratic mint"—not bad as such, but redolent of desk work and tedium.

We settled, and you could hear nothing but the ping and squeak of the aluminum chairs, the hum of central air, throat clearings, the increasingly epic clack—each one further apart—of a wall-mounted clock. A general tone that brings out the whine in your ears you never had cause to notice, and that draws serious attention to the throb of your pulse.

Only a few folks in attendance. Not enough to heat a room.

The funerary director did the remarks from his Holiday-

Inn-business-lounge dais at the front of his converted living room. He did this as no one in the family wanted to. It was a prefab speech and his voice was monotony.

Widower looked waxen and slack. My right ass-cheek was numb.

Though we were all attired in our best—men in shined shoes, women in their church dresses, all that might be described, on a better occasion, as gussied-up—the scene was blighted by the general blah, like you were seeing the world through cataracts, or through the scratched plexiglass of a DMV window.

Weirdly, at that moment, I couldn't remember a single thing about Fred's late wife. Not the look of her, not the sound of her voice, not a sole anecdote that would recall her to me in a tangible way, and nothing in the speech evoked those either. If anything, the eulogy seemed to drive her spirit from the place. She was the reason for the gathering, but was only felt impersonally, as you'd remember a particular president on Presidents' Day.

And, to be clear: I don't mean to push the notion that a service for the dead needs to be, I don't know, entertaining. Not as such. But no one—and I mean no one—enjoys being bored. I will go out on a further limb to say that of the feelings, boredom is the worst, meaning that pain and sorrow, terrible as they undeniably are, both have what you might call a drama to them, and so come with a direction, and a certain speed; and so it is that we might, even in the middle of our desolation, feel the wind in our hair, even if without us knowing we were feeling that-all. At the bottom of the boredom though is dread. There being nothing in boredom to distract from it. This is the real wolf we keep from your door through our weeper work.

When that service was over, no one stuck around, the whitened carrot sticks and hardened dips got stiff-armed into the trash, the cheap wine recorked for the next one.

People couldn't leave fast enough.

What I am trying to say is that the thing didn't come off, and everyone knew it didn't; knew it wouldn't and couldn't have possibly.

It was what Dill likes to call "weak sauce," and what I call bullshit.

Yet it is important to acknowledge that moods this insipid—a vibe as stultifying as the one in that place, when taken collectively, as they added up—could inspire a community to action, to recruit and enlist the likes of us (draw us to the calling, even). So it was.

Too many events like this one and it was clear that something had to be done.

Because the funerals were killing us.

THE DEVOTED

And something *was* done; we drifted in to do the doing of it, and the 302 came to be. After that, Reg would be hollering out his roll, day after day:

—*Dill, Sheryl, J-Man, Hank, Lemon, Chantal . . .*

. . . meaning a rhythm and routine was established, the

holy offices, and it seemed from then on to me that it would be thusly til forever and a day, which, at the beginning, suited me just fine, until years on it ceased to suit me at all, at which point I thought the regimen might just end me for the sameness of it, and I knew it wasn't going to change ever, now was it.

I was wrong about that.

INEFFABLE JUDGMENT

Slow then. Slow because another heat wave came on down and one day cindered the next.

No one cared to go outside and I did not want to so much as even move. I did have to rouse myself a couple times throughout the days—like when Lemon Barbara called to complain that her breathing had got fitful. She did have enough wind to swear a blue streak, though still I worried—as I mentioned, we had lost a lot of elderly that summer—but she turned out to be more in need of company than actually ailing. I plugged in a fan I found behind the mourning dresses and plastic-wrapped shawls in her closet. It blew hot air in a squeaking arc, diffusing the smell of mothballs and that fruity perfume of hers everywhere. Meanwhile we drank some of Lemon's famous G&Ts. She was in better form after that, though as I was leaving I made the mistake of telling her to take it easy and maybe not smoke so goddam much. She smiled and told me I was a hypocrite and to go have sexual relations with myself.

———

It was too hot to sleep that night and I just lay on my small bed, trying to guess where trains were in their route by how soft their whistles blew. Doing this, I could see the broad, empty scrubland with my ears, as a bat does.

Next afternoon I had to venture over to the Crown, though not to drink. The ice machine was broke, and I said I'd bring my truck by so that it could be hauled off to the shop. Jim, our local fix-it man, agreed to put his talents to the problem, but he stipulated in no uncertain terms that the mountain need come to Mohammed.

It took four of us to move the thing: me, Johnnie, that day bartender with the crew cut, and Sullivan, who owned the place. After we got it into Jim's shop, the two from the Crown took off and me and big Johnnie sat on crates to recuperate. Jawed a minute while the sweat poured down.

—You gonna work tomorrow, Johnnie said.

—Don't see why not, I said.

—I can think of a few, he said, wiping off the back of his neck.

—Hard to put on the black right now.

We both winced.

—You'd think they'd all have AC.

—Expensive.

—Keep the bodies from getting ripe.

—I'll work if my name's up, I said.

—Hard to feel much in this shit. Like it's burnt out of you, he said.

—I guess we'd better be bringing our A-game then, I said.

Came the next day, everything was called off on account of it being an oven out, and that was frankly a relief.

But a couple days on Regis called us back on the job, and Mother Mary but it appeared that there had been yet another success, and another in which I'd once again managed to miss the kid, as if the heavens themselves were interfering in order to tell me something (that something being: mind your own fucking business, Ed).

The bigger thing was that the gang was riding him pretty good.

We do this sometimes with newbies—the ones we believe might stick it out—and it is well-meaning: the kind of banter that's meant to be affectionate while still serving to remind someone of their place, lest they get above their raising.

Lemon was cackling, the Nguyens getting their digs in, Chief ruffling his hair, which Sheryl then smoothed. Johnnie frat-punching his arm; Peewee waiting for an opening.

—C'mon now, leave him alone a spell, I said.

We are all childless—not a single 302er that isn't. So there was something extra at work there in the hazing. Hard to know what flavor exactly, but suddenly I was worried. Kid might take it all in stride but I did not (my pop got ridden like that too, being a skinny boy, and when he grew up and did not shed that skinniness, he decided simply to tan the bejeezus out of whoever happened to mention it or even look at him the wrong way). And that old mourning jacket the kid still had on—hadn't anyone told him not to wear it out in the heat yet? I saw Dill come over to break things up for good and while that happened I corralled the kid over to the side, back to what I had begun to think of, dumbly, as "our spot," where we could smoke in peace, him leaning against the unstrung post of an old cattle fence.

Barren field. Convenience store. Derelict storage tower. Little plosions of light bouncing off of some fuel-truck aluminum far off on the freeway.

I said:

—Been a good run this month.

He nodded.

—Rarely see it. You're lucky, we seem to have hit a seam, I said.

—Sure, the kid said.

—But if it gets to be too much, or you need any help managing, you let me know.

—Ok.

—Make sure you do, I said.

And to make it so he didn't feel castigated, I added:

—Take it from me but this work here can wear you down.

Then I said:

—If you don't know how to regulate.

Nothing back.

—Wear you down, I said again.

Had he shrugged?

—I know a thing or two, I said, defensive, and adding:

—It's been an age I've been at this, so.

I thought then about that: all the stale meals, stale breath, stale spaces, stale homilies, day after day, the dead weight of sorrow.

—An age, I said, quieter.

And just like that, I was lowdown and wretched. It landed on me all at once. A surge of self-pity near-on sickening. I crouched down in the dust.

Spat.

Got up again. But slow.

—Dizzy, I said.

There was much about the kid I'd yet to see clearly, but at that moment I felt something, oh Lord. Something on the loose. Took it in like a breath at high altitude. The mind still has a way of not wanting too much bewilderment all at once. So I reached into my shirt pocket for a smoke, then watched as Regis's work bus lurched into the lot, churning up the dust, ready to take the chosen out to their ministry.

When that spell of morbidity had lessened, I thought: I should take the advice I gave Lemon Barbara, meaning I should smoke less, drink less. I should worry less. Take my pills regular. Sleep more.

Then I thought: he is too young, and there has to be easier ways for this boy to make a buck.

Later, I spent a portion of that night haunted by the idea of radiation, and those people close to it who got poisoned by having their atoms moved around inside them.

———————

That Wednesday, I was filling in for Reg, being a senior member in good standing. I had the day's names on the clipboard for whatever might arise, and, selfish, I did not put the kid as one of those, so that we could stand together again under the locusts.

Which we did.

—You sure you want this? I said, nodding toward the lot, the rest of us.

—*Horses for courses*, he said back, unsurprised by the question.

It seemed like he knew something about me I hadn't told.

—That's the crux of it, all right, I said.

Even from there, I could hear the phone in Reg's trailer ring out like a knell, and so I hurried off to answer.

TESTIMONIAL

Bubulcitate (verb): to cry
like a cowboy.

—Hayward and Blount, *American English Dictionary*, 3rd edition

Horses for courses.

So, as I've mentioned, I fancy myself a bit of a cowboy; or anyhow that's what Jeannine used to say ("You fancy yourself a bit of a cowboy"). There was some truth there—that I fancied myself that way (as a cowboy). When I was a teen, I worked horses down-ranch in Dolores, money problems having got urgent after Dad went south. Ranch work was work all right, but I liked it, and continued the practice, working as a stable hand, a groom, a trainer, mucking stalls, carrying buckets, exercising ponies on the ends of lunge lines . . . worked every job a self-fancied cowboy could work, until that

time when I tumbled down the slippery slope between ad-
miring horses and wagering on them. I've always had some
deep kinship with our long-faced cousins, and I felt, often,
when I'd go down to the stables—especially late at night, especially when drunk, especially when I could not abide the
recriminations of my newly half-empty home, with the stables smelling close and vegetal—as though the horses and me
could almost join up the boundary betwixt us. Bridge it.

On these occasions, I would talk to them. Confess. Blub-
ber. Recite a few lines. (The love of language being inherited
from my mother, result being that I also now "fancy myself"
a bit of a "cowboy poet." And I am that. Albeit with mixed
results.) But when those ponies didn't say anything back, not
even to my bawling, I'd just talk and cry at them some more.
I will say that weeping in front of a more or less impassive
animal really brings one's self-loathing into sharp relief.
Though it also can be oddly refreshing, as sometimes a man
just needs to squeeze a few tears out without having to pro-
voke something in someone. (And here's an image I just
thought of, which is that I was, back then, like a cow didn't
want her milk drunk.)

So them being just about mute and all was a great boon.

Though sometimes I would scrutinize those caviar eyes,
put a hand down flat on their twitchy, muscular, tight-as-
sausage bodies, hoping for a rhythm which might signal
some specific; a specific of feeling or belief—something like
mournfulness or love, once it was all translated out of horse.

They'd whinny a bit, maybe toss their head, but that's all
I'd get for my troubles. Pretty sure that they could cry in
their own way though. Once I saw a mare in bereavement

over her dead foal, waiting and waiting at the gate, head held low, and it was a terrible thing. But there you are. Anyway, having that captive audience to cry in front of was perfect training for my future work.

And though that is my ten cents on the cowboy and horse and poetry thing, my broader idea here is that we all had a part to play at the Local 302, and "cowboy poet" was mine.

Chantal had her role and it was just about what you'd expect and it was "femme fatale." She has the beauty for it, albeit a tad faded. She's got the wardrobe, the lipstick and thin cigarettes. Nobody runs mascara like her neither. When it comes to black-rimmed eyes and dark rivulets dried up on cheekbones, Chantal has you all beat. This is a specialty in our line, meaning those men who'll pay for the mysterious mistress to show at their future wakes, and these are Chantal's highest-earning gigs.

Now, Dill, he is the old, friendly neighbor of the bunch; the guy who will help out in a pinch; the Samaritan. Best pal.

Johnnie is our soldier. Was. He's old now like the rest of us, but once he ran with a division in one of those desert ones, meaning that Johnnie was in the worst of the action and uses this in his work to good effect.

Lemon Barbara'd be that old matron who'd drink you under the table and steal your wallet, kicking you for good luck once you were down there. Course you'd never know this when she's on the clock and the portrait of your beloved Gran.

Chief Clarence is, when he works, not so much a man as

a symbol, a potent one, and he weeps for the land and what was taken. (Chief is a local elder, and of course "Chief" is not what he started out calling himself, but then he did for commercial purposes, and though the term made us all itchy at first, eventually we all forgot he was ever called anything but. Chief was the first of us, very first weeper—at least in-state—so he's owed a thing or two, even if it's his own inappropriate nickname.)

Peewee is chastened; the Nguyens: outsiders. Hankie's a sour-ass complainer, though even this comes off as grief of a sort.

You get the picture. Horses for courses.

Every gang needs its types, and we filled out these parts, a further point perhaps being that if you were to scrape just a little, behind the greasepaint you'd find a perfectly apposite story of woe.

And him: he was just "the kid."

Looked the part, as I've said: about five ten, five eleven, I'd guess. Slight. Narrow-hipped as the devil himself, and in that inbetweenish period of a man's life when there are contrary indicators everywhere. Strong forehead, but some fat on the cheeks. Muscles in his arms like baseballs tied up tight in a tube sock, but also he tended to blush. A man-boy. He slumped when he stood. Sweat a lot, but didn't smell bad. There was a constellation of tiny brown marks on his neck, and some on his forearms. He often looked at you like he was scrying your face (though as I soon learned, when he was working, those same active eyes of his went dead as nickels). When he sat, he seemed to be all legs. He didn't ever wear a hat, even out in the sun. His hair was parted nicely, though. And he dressed like he was only granted access to some great-grandfather's wardrobe. The dark clothes, thinned and shiny. The shoes. Laces knotted up like no one had taught him.

If there is some form of line we must travel, surveyed and determined from the beyond, he was, as much as I tried to steer him otherwise, destined to be a weeper. Or an undertaker. From the outs. But a perpetually young one, like that kid doctor who used to have a show on TV.

A child undertaker. Picture it.

Horses for courses: the strangest thing.

MUSICAL TRIBUTE

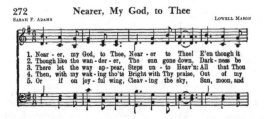

The calendar kept on flipping and there were more races to run; more dead to mourn; illness coming through regular.

Along it came. And at the end of that slate was the service for Mr. Lamont from Trembling Hills, the gentleman whose death I had so recently predicted. As it happened, Mr. Lamont had made his own prediction and taken matters into his own hands. When he slipped off into oblivion, it was on the day of his choosing, on the wings of a high-octane euphoria, pupils like pinpricks. We all wondered where the narcotics came from, but in the end what did that matter. His way seemed the best way to go, shy of the sleeping one.

Anyway and all this aside, his funeral was a dandy.

Mr. Lamont didn't seem to have that many people in his life, like I said, at least none who would visit him in those declining years, yet the place was—if not packed—more folks than you'd reasonably expect. Who were they? But from right out the gate, the emotion on display from these mourners was heartfelt and spirit-raising (this was, after the last few weeks, not totally *unexpected* either). We sobbed through the reminiscences and sobbed more through that crackerjack homily. Also we sang, ragged through the tears. "Nearer, My God, to Thee" and "Jerusalem," the latter which I've always loved, mostly for its indecision on the point of whether to be a major-key tune or a minor one, but also for its inclusion of the phrase "satanic mills," which, when I was a child, raised far more questions than it answered.

I know all of those ditties by heart—the hymns, psalms, dirges, chorales, requiem masses, songs of remembrance—having had some fair experience singing them, and have compiled my own informal, personal, funereal hit parade, the ones I'll sing out louder than normal with my pitchy, quarrelsome baritone. Though mostly it's just sitting and listening; often to the really bad ones; your "Danny Boy(s)," your "Candle(s) in the Wind(s)" and the like—songs which tend to throw cold water on the spirit of my performance and keep me from getting into the mood of it. But at this one, all the tunes were affecting; yanked hard at my single, fraying heartstring in that way only good music can.

And, and . . . dear God but there was the boy, plying the trade at last before my very own eyes. One pew in front, just off to the left.

Throughout the show, I could not think on another thing, and studied him. I studied him but hard.

He barely moved throughout the ceremony, not to itch himself or yawn. He didn't move to wipe away a tear, as he didn't shed any. And, as everyone around him lost themselves in sorrow, I lost myself in wondering what his strategy was, or even if he had one to employ.

Was he contributing at all? I thought he wasn't, and then I thought that yes. Maybe. Yet, if so, I could not have put my finger on how. I went back and forth, chewing on this for a while, then shook several theories from my head.

He was still. So still.

His work—again, if there was any—did not register, and of course, if done right, our services shouldn't be registered, not overly in any case, and virtuosos are those who make a thing look easy.

Him, he just gathered himself into his coltish body and that was that.

Nothing gleaned. A boy in a church. Period.

And you just could not touch him where he dwelt.

PLEASE JOIN HANDS

That critter labeled Worry is the orn'riest of the herd.
—Arthur Chapman, Cowboy Poet

Where he dwelt on the first Saturday in June was the hospital.

I was out helping Dill set some fencing on his property when Sheryl had pulled up in that inappropriate car of hers to tell us that the kid was there.

—I was up seeing Francine when he came in. Wasn't no one else to call and I wasn't about to call Reg, she said.

(Were we two old fools really as near to next of kin as could be rustled up? How could that be.)

—He's ok, dinged pretty bad, but fine overall, said Sheryl.

I went to the truck, Dill hiked up his trousers and followed.

Kid was sitting there in the waiting room crouched over a magazine. There was a bag of ice on the seat next to him. When he looked up, I saw that there were two ugly holes around the left crease of his mouth where it seemed like his teeth had come through; each wound with a brown halo of iodine around it. His forehead sported a square bandage. One eye bloodied.

—What happened, I said.

Francine stood by, eager to hear if the kid would divulge to me what clearly was not given to her. Francine was that day's duty nurse. I knew her. Her face had been broken at some point, but that only added to her charm.

—Guessing there was a tussle, Dill said.

—Who did this, I said.

Francine went away and came back with a small paper cone filled with water.

—Thanks, I said on the kid's behalf, and went to the desk to collect the clipboard.

—Insurance? the man said.

—Supposing not.

I filled out the blanks on those forms best I could (the already filled-in parts being where I first learned his name; his true one). Then I paid and they discharged him.

—Real pugilist, you, I said to the kid on the way to the truck.

He kept on walking.

—Should I be calling your parents? I said.

—Parents? he said, turning to face me.

Which could've meant: why would I do such a thing as call his parents; though it sounded more to me like him asking what the hell parents were. I didn't follow up as I didn't want to smother.

When we got to the Bow & Gun he got down out of the cab and headed straight for the door. I reached into the glove, pulled out a bottle of aspirin, got out myself, cleared my throat, and tossed it over. He made no move for it and it rattled on the sidewalk. Then he picked the bottle up and walked around the truck, handing it back to me in silence.

———————————

I never found out the story on that tanning of his, but several days on he was at the lot again. And because of that moment in the hospital—my fearing for him—I began driving him places. Took it upon myself.

I'd pull up and push his number in that vestibule beside the entrance. Stand there, expectant.

He never buzzed me in, not once. So there's me, waiting like a stooge, leaning against the truck, not having a number to call him on. Eventually he'd come on down.

I wondered then about his place and what it was like up there. I had constructed a home in my mind from scratch, but I had no idea how to furnish it. Did he read books? (*Reader's Digest*? Louis L'Amour? Dale Carnegie? English as a Second Language?) Did he buy himself a poster to put on the wall? Of what? Lady in a bikini? What about a lava lamp, television, beer can pyramid, statue of the virgin mother? Would plants thrive on his sills or would they curl away from him like burning paper?

Who the heck knew. (Though I did know in my heart that it would be blank walls and barren floors, a night-light inherited from a previous tenant, a Solo cup on the bathroom sink, a fitted sheet over the window, attempting to be rectangular. The cruel borrowedness of a motel room.) I presume that he had taken girls up there, if that was the way he leaned, but I wasn't even sure of that honestly. Because that Sylvia had clammed right up on me, ceased her gossiping and discovered discretion for the first time ever, and from thenceforth whenever I had a question she'd say:

—Ask him yourself.

Sylvia would not even gab about the kid with Dill—her own kin—like the kid had gotten in there, won her over, and gained some secret loyalty none of us could imagine her granting anyone. I doubted he'd needed to raise a finger to acquire this loyalty either.

So I continued having to guess at everything.

Either way, one day after another I hit that buzzer and there he'd be.

I'd grimace a little, smack my gums, and feel strangely self-conscious at the sight of him.

—Ed, he'd say, and then go hop in the truck.

On the way to the lot, he'd put his feet up on my dash and I wouldn't mind.

He was silent as we drove, so I was too. But—blended in with the sounds from the truck and the honks and the blinkers' yakety-yak—I would hear him breathe, swallow, scratch his scalp, give out a genteel little belch. I could smell the bad leather of his overheated dress shoes. I'd catch glimpses of him from the corner of my right eye; the fine hairs on his forearm . . . and generally speaking I would take in the diffuse feeling of a genuine, human presence. In those times I would know he was an actual person; a thing I had begun to doubt.

He would stare away out his window.

Then we'd go earn our keep.

Cry, get paid. Boy did we. Like the community had sprung a leak. And what Johnnie had said was proved true beyond a reasonable doubt: it was real.

ATTENDANTS

One can be hired to perform a
variety of tasks during a funeral:
placing the casket in a parlor or chapel,
arranging floral offerings, directing or
escorting mourners, weeping.
—*Exploring Careers in the Funerary Business*

—Full house, Reg said.

—Where we working at today, Sheryl said.

—Lamar Episcopal, Reg said.

We moved to leave.

—Don't you idiots thank me all at once, said Reg to our backs.

It was real and I wanted it to last and last; Lord willing and the creek don't rise. It was real and the days kept providing; we kept profiting—getting that for free; as a gift. It was real, our newfound success: this pocket of ease from out of nowhere.

The 302 barely had to lift a finger. No need for conjuring big, bad memories in order to spur the tears. Which meant everyone was able to handle more, make more money, and I was actually paying off all of that outstanding debt I owed on, and began to resent less the payments out to Jeannine. Down at the lot Reg was wearing the sly grin of a man who'd just seen a gold glint in his prospecting pan.

The very second we crossed the threshold of a church, funeral home, crematorium, whatever the fuck, people would start totting up their losses as we would our earnings. All we had to do was show and sit.

How could we not congratulate ourselves on what we'd achieved in the region to date? Us, having staved something off; such that sorrow and its sentimental siblings might not indeed pass altogether from this earthly realm? Our cumulative effect? That the flattening, the deadening unto death wasn't destined to continue? That it was not too late. For the community. (The world?)

We must have been doing *something* right; meaning that we felt we had—apparently, finally—broken through. On the evidence.

That such a moment could arise! Thundering Jesus.

Unbelievable.

We worked every damn job we were handed; which was a fair number back then. Not just Los Culpos, Badger, Sepulse, so on, but the greater county and environs.

Word got around about our streak—and a man wants what his neighbor has, even if his payday only comes after he's not around to enjoy it.

And the kid would then be in attendance there like it was a usual thing. Though the strangeness of him did not become a usual thing—him: unmoving and unmoved. A blank in the middle of it all, as if someone had cleanly erased the shape of a boy from an otherwise crammed composition; only the paperwhite left.

He had more or less become a real fixture.

Occasionally he went AWOL for a day or two. There was no pattern to it, and I sensed he wasn't ever going to explain himself. He could've been out wandering the wilderness, the byways, sleeping rough under the stars or overpasses; he could have been percolated, or burnt, his ashes drifting down over the land; he may have been subsumed into the mean heat that cloaked us all, or simply holed up in that place of his. Still, once in a while then, unable to stop myself, I'd ring his bell in the morning to no answer, he'd not come down at all, and things would cool down for a bit.

And then, without fanfare, he'd be back.

———————————————

One morning I was in Regis's trailer out on the call lot; it was still early, so me and him were laid out in front of the TV. The place smelled like Lysol, cheese, and beer. Game was up there in inning three. A knock rattled the screen door.

—Come, Reg said, and the kid loped in.

Reg didn't turn even to see, but I levered my ass out of the chair.

—You looking to get on a job, Reg said.

—Yessir, the kid said.

Everything was on the rise, so the fewer Reg had on the

rolls the bigger Reg's cut. In that moment—the early days—kid was a charity case far as Regis was concerned.

—You want regular work, you gotta work regular. Can't come and go as you please.

Kid shrugged, rolling up a smoke.

—Not in here, Regis said, holding his spit-cup at its usual dangerous angle.

I nodded a greeting at the kid, he nodded back, my cigarette dangling unlit. We stood in silence watching the players move around the diamond like hands in a backward clock.

He wasn't going to say thing one and I knew that.

—Either sit down or fuck on off, Reg said.

Kid and I looked at the tube for a beat longer, just on ceremony, then I guided him out the door of the trailer and down the two steps to the lot. Dust clouds and crunching from the first couple of weepers to pull in.

—You heard Reg, I said.

The kid lifted his untucked dress shirt and scratched his tidy, hairless abdomen.

—And it's good to be of use, times like these, I said.

That was, after all, our job: to be used, like is the case in most jobs, and used is in some ways the meaning of job, in the sense of "being of use." Though in fact weeper work is more being used in the other, bad sense than many other professions; save for maybe prostitutes like that Brenda out by the tracks, and maybe also those folks who are paid for someone to do medical experiments upon them. Still.

I'd tried to get him to quit, but if he was determined to do this thing, he could at least be consistent in it.

—You want to work this funeral with me, Dyer City, I said.

—Yep.

And we did that.

And we did that, we sat that job together. I was hoping that he'd ham it up a little bit, and he should have. At least tried to. There are those who might begin to feel he wasn't earning his portion of the pool.

But as was his way, he did not; still did not lose a single dram of his tear-water.

Had he ever?

When he skinned his knee as a tot, would he pick himself up, mute, unaffected? It was not hard to imagine, in fact.

And I could well imagine on the day of his birth, the doctor smacking his rump and him not giving so much as a complaint and the confused and worried looks on the faces in that hospital room. For such a thing as that is very unnatural, and a baby who does not cry upon entry is either a miracle or else in deep trouble.

Maybe both.

But now another thought here, apropos of not crying:

Namely, I wonder how, if you can't cry about a thing, do you know you've mourned it? That is: what if everyone you lose just hovered around in spirit until you felt wet-sad? If this were the case—that the dead need our watery blessing to leave this realm for the next—it would mean, given the dry state of stuff and looking around the flat faces of those Norms, that the number of ghosts in the world must be increasing, and that our spirit realm may just have an over-population problem.

I am joking, but not entirely. I hadn't much thought about it this way, but after doing so, I felt, all of a sudden, freer. It seemed obvious that (unforced, unpaid) tears go a great distance toward letting the dead die, and I wondered: if I just concentrated harder on that kind of crying, could I get my old man's apparition to just fuck on off for well and for good?

Following Dyer City, I ended up helping the groundskeeper by hauling a pile of cemetery crap out to the dump.

Trash from a happy event is not so different from that from a sad one. The difference is that after a funeral, the trash needs to stay awhile; it being disrespectful to the dead to remove all the tributes, gifts, and remembrances before (. . . before what: before the deceased have a chance to notice and enjoy it all?). So it lies there and molders. Flowers, obviously, plastic and actual, single ones as well as bouquets and complicated wreaths, fronds too, crosses, signs, toys, little windmills, handwritten notes, edible arrangements going bad. Mylar balloons sagging down from the stones like old breasts.

But eventually it all has to go.

The only thing that remains, even months after, are the little rocks folks place on top of the headstones. I was never clear on what this meant, but people do it as if someone told them to do so. And I like that; the unconscious act of ceremony, like those inscrutable piles of shiny objects magpies collect.

When that task was over and done, I stopped for gas, clocked Sheryl over by the pump. She was spreading a gray filth all over her windshield. I got the guy to fetch out some fresh water.

—Here, I said, taking the squeegee and cleaning it all up.

—Such a fucking gent, she said.

—Sure.

She watched me put the squeegee back.

—He on the job today? she said.

She narrowed her eyes and nocked one side of her mouth.

—Yeah, I said.

—The kid is . . . *the kid*, she said as if that settled the matter.

And then she too shook her head at me, just as everyone had begun to, and I'll say that there are certain people for whom there is—not a stock response exactly, but some personal aspect which is so significant and undeniable as to take over the way people speak on them. Johnnie, for instance, is what you'd call a big boy—an unusually large sonofabitch who just sort of fills out the frame—such that when someone is talking on Johnnie, they expand, bulk themselves out like his size is contagious. No one means to do it, but it comes as part of the telling. Way back when, when mentioning Dad, people would narrow their eyes. But they would smile and lean a little forward when talking about my mother, and their voices would lower: her being so gentle and smart, etc. With the kid, it would always be that same shake of the head. Like the way you'd acknowledge the unexpected sanctity of a thing, or perhaps ward off the unnatural, and it would be unknowing as a habit.

—That he is, I said, and smiled.

—Thanks for the cleanup, she said through the open window and peeled out.

WORDS CANNOT EXPRESS

For a good while then there were no more gaps. He stuck around and stayed.

I performed my daily duties: transporting him, attending to him, watching over him. And there he'd be, him the new variable, him the still hub of the flying wheel, innocent in his grown-up clothes, set there, silent, inanimate.

And after, the Crown. But now he'd insist on leaving alone; leaving the bar earlier than the rest of us. I'd put up a fuss but he'd simply hold a hand up and then just lope off alone, down the street. Gone for a moment, then back again under the light of the gas station island, followed by a slow fade. In all honesty, though I worried on his behalf, I used to like watching him leave like that. Diminishing into the murk. I'm not sure why, but this awoke some plangency in my heart, almost as if I could hear the words "there goes the kid, into the night" in my head, and see the line descend over him like the final credit of a film.

Then I'd go back in, and there we'd all be. Music wheezing, sawdust, the beer's urine tang, stray wisps of sex, anger, turpitude, all drifting ceilingward to mingle with the smoke; neck bones surfacing as heads slump, sleeves inching up as glasses raise, revealing biceps that have seen better days, and bearing the murky pastel of old tattoos. Feeling the close fug of camaraderie and fatigue. Of course, we'd pick ourselves off the floor eventually. We'd pay the tab, steady ourselves for the trip home, mutter goodbyes, prepare for the dry-out.

The next morning, down at the call lot, we'd all look like soured mayonnaise, and there he'd be again: he'd appear, fit as a fiddle and ready to put shame to the rest of us.

———————————————

Who was he, really? I asked Dill much later, after it all ended.

—It's a stumper, and some things you just can't ever know, Dill said that time.

But what did it mean? What?

And why all that tragedy? At the close?

Why did no one care?

Who weeps for the weepers?

DEDICATION

When words are empty,

tears are apt.

—AffordableUrnsOnline.com/condolences

—He's up to something, I said one evening to my Chantal.

—Who, she said.

I was dandling her on my dandling knee. She got off and went to the fridge.

She popped a spigot in there.

—He's, like some kind of . . . ET.

There was mouth-smacking behind me.

—It's awful this wine, she said.

—You listening, Chantal? I said.

—I am, you said *eetee*. Like: small.

—No, like an alien. From outer space, I said.

—Not again, she said and sat on a chair this time.

She blinked her eyes slowly at me. Once. Twice.

—This one's different, I said.

Couple of years before I had been going on about a man, the unusually tall and gentle one with the beautiful singing voice. Turned out to be an occult extremist (if a right-talented tenor). He seemed so special at first; I would harp on. How well he cried. His unusual grace, innocence, dignity. This was all before he started in with everyone about the forthcoming race war, before he left his boarding house and went off to a compound with likeminded loonies to prepare for that-all.

—I guess I'm lucky you put up with me, I said to Chantal, trying to recoup some dignity.

—Pfphh, she said.

Yet fuck me for a simpleton, unlike the rest of the 302 who kept him on as son or mascot, I myself simply could not shake that there *was* something extra-special in the boy. And because of this "special"—the power and puzzle—I could not leave off wanting to learn more.

Was there a pledge, turn, and prestige to unlock? Might I cotton onto some special move or procedure that would help me with my twisted mainspring, my faulty escapement; fix my faulty innards? I wished then, badly, more than ever, given the deterioration of my health, to plumb whatever mystery there was to plumb, and thus be so supple again myself; slender and equal to life, at play in the fields of the Lord.

Now, what I should have done was think more deeply upon the recent uptick in feeling.

Gone over it each night as in a liturgy, given it was so new and unusual, so out of fucking nowhere, especially given how people are not just deadened, but ripe for anger, inches from it, everywhere and all the time, as the world these days seems to be filled up with those who will cut a line or those who will not let you merge on a highway; your arm-crossers, fist-shakers, bird-flippers; your daily dirtbags, and even a faint breeze will push them over the line toward a killing mood—and I suppose that if you open the paddock marked "tears" it can throw wide the doors to *all* the enclosures, and something worse than run-of-the mill shittiness is bound to get out.

But who would've wanted the numb times back—not me, no way. And so instead of expending my waning energies upon the larger thing, I merely took the kid's measure, puzzled over his dry, dry ways; tried to follow the money-card, and basically did jack shit.

<u>Whoever owns a green Chevy Caprice,
it's being towed.</u>

HIS PASSING LEAVES A VACUUM

There are a few things I've picked up over the years doing my work. One of those is that no two weepers will weep exactly alike, each have their own spin on it, and every weep from every weeper is the result of their own distinct temperament.

For Chantal, weeping is slow and patient work; and when things work right for her, it is sincere, and wells up from deep. She is nothing if not genuine.

For Dill, say, or Peewee or Hankie—not to disparage—but they each rely on a routine they cleave to, and that works in its way. For those like them, weeping is mostly about procedure, making ritual out of whatever done the job before and getting the most out of it.

Johnnie muscles his way through. I think with Johnnie it's as much about rage as grief. Or rage which brings on grief. Either way he gets it done.

Sheryl works with that small piece of ribbon, which she threads through her fingers a bit beforehand to warm herself up. When she does this she looks concentrated, like a ballplayer swinging his three bats before coming to the plate.

In fact having a talisman is not uncommon. Bunch of us have different props that way. Stuffed animal; dog tags for Johnnie. Could be an article of clothing, as for that old weeper Abel Moyette who had that young man's football jersey he'd pull out, which gave me the willies, though I too used to carry that little dictionary of my mother's. It brought her voice back to me; the old, teaching one, that sounded as if she was handing me something fragile. I'd remember how she'd point out a phrase in a book, or a small, bright word; her quizzes and soft admonishments. How she'd turn a page, pinky up before wetting her lips to begin anew.

But after a while I stopped with the dictionary, I'm not sure why.

After that, my dad's tie did the trick (albeit differently).

But it should be said that some—some weepers—need neither preparation nor prop. These are the real artists.

Real artists, and they tend to be emitters; and have a blast radius.

Some of this type sympathize, feel what you feel and send it out wider. Some are sufferers themselves—the wounded, life's martyrs—who, since the dawn of creation, have walked the paths of sorrow and just happen to be good at telegraphing out their particular ache. Either way, such weepers are your all-stars; pulling pain from you which you didn't in fact know you had. Sometimes this isn't so difficult, and the groundwater is close to the surface. But sometimes it is deep down beneath all the rock and limestone, and only a few can dig that far.

Obviously, all of this is done through tears. And though the weeper, as it says on the label, weeps, there are exceptions to every rule, including this one about tears, and that lissome strangerboy was one of those. Meaning, as I've said, his never having shed a single one in my presence.

So if he did not weep, what was it he did, and how did he do it?

———————————————

I recall one afternoon once, biking down to the bar to get Dad on my mother's orders. The boss had called wondering why he was not on the job. I did not want to go, and said as much, but I went, and I found him there as you'd think. He was hugely crapulous, in no mood for me, though the bartender made a show of having me pull up a seat, young though I was at the time.

—Get out, Dad told me, but I did not move to go.

I said to my father what my mother told me to say.

I don't think he took in a single word of it, and once I was done, he began telling a rambling and loud story at the bartender, hard to follow, extolling the virtues of a "life on the plains" (which was pretty rich, him having been a poor rancher even before the foreclosure; a half-assed one), and then denouncing, in the worst language imaginable, the salaried world, especially the low-salaried one he had been forced to endure. The message to everyone within earshot was: "I am no man's slave," or some melodramatic garbage of that type.

I just stood by the yellowed glass of the cigarette machine and waited for this humor to wear off him, which took a while.

Eventually, when he decided enough time had passed such that he could seem to be walking out of there of his own volition (or realized no one was listening or gave two shits), he grabbed my shoulder—half yanking, half using me as a crutch—and we left. Went to our car and got in. I was worried about him driving, but when he turned the key the engine sputtered and the car was dry of fuel, which was a blessing. He hit the steering wheel with both his hands, cursed awhile, but then, abruptly, something changed, and he turned all warm toward me, which was bad. Said he'd teach me. Teach me "something important." He looked like we were about to have a father-son moment to remember. Terrifying. He stank. He put a hand on the back of my head, as if to tousle my hair, but instead just grabbed it with both hands, hard, palming my ears. His rheumy eyes.

He broke the whole menacing spell then, lifted himself up and got out, went around back of the car, and I heard the trunk pop and after a moment slam closed, and when he was back he had a small length of hose out. Showed it to me. Then he got behind the wheel, put the car in neutral, and we pushed it such that it was alongside another. I knew what was up as I wasn't stupid. He screwed open that man's gas cap and let it clang to the pavement, stuck the tubing in and gave a suck, and spat and swore some more, then put the other end into our tank.

—Just *borrowing*, he slurred.

Finished up the rigmarole. When our engine kicked back on I told him I had my bike and he cuffed me once, bad, and the world was no longer level for a bit. So I did what he told me, leaving the bike where it lay on the sidewalk, and we drove back straddling the double yellow like a monorail, a miracle we stayed on the road at all. He could barely find the door when we got in the house, and he had words for Mom and maybe more than words, but by the time they were downstairs again she had talked him down as only she could, or he had just spent all his fury, and I saw her put him in front of the hall mirror and slick his hair from behind. Straighten out his tie. Then she handed him the phone to call his office.

Anyway, that thing Dad did with the hose?
Just form enough of a vacuum to get it going, and out she comes.

Out she came, and things going as good as they were, our Local 302—we'd look like we too had been in a brawl. Our faces raw red and puffy like that. And the solidarity of it, like we had stood down some fuckers in a punch-up and could, after the adrenaline and fear had faded, drink out of relief and from the love of life and of one another.

We abetted in a bunch of crying, and I never once felt the stage fright or the dryness in the kid's presence. And when I'd get in the truck to head to work, I'd catch sight of myself in the rearview as always but I'd see something different—that I was marshaling some force to tamp down my keenness.

Then—one morning in bed, levering myself onto an elbow—I marked as the moment in which I acknowledged my life was finally beginning—so late—to have a clear heading; that it was finally taking on a particular shape and style, and might yet become a story worth telling.

Still I knew who the protagonist was, and it wasn't yours truly.

But what was the kid to me, I wondered. Or I to him?

I was not his friend or relative or shepherd nor sheep nor official chronicler. Of course old-fart-teaching-young-greenhorn-the-ropes did not describe it at all, because of who wanted what from whom, but I will say that my friend Rev—and more on him later—told me once that the word "compassion" in its original means to be "suffering beside," as if those of us cursed with our particular sensitivity have no choice but to be along for it.

And so we worked the funerals, mismated but yoked together—the county's suffering being our gain—and for each of these, we all wept copiously, except for the boy, who did not cry at all.

A REAL TRAGEDY

If one suffers, all should suffer together.
—1 Corinthians 12:26

The end of that week came another shooting spree. The less said about this the better. Reg chained up the gate, and I stayed in my place. I didn't hear from Chantal or Dill, and didn't inquire what the kid had got up to. I burrowed in deep, as we all did, and only came back on duty when the flags began to raise all the way up again. The mourning of children is unlike any other form of mourning. And we steer well away.

We learned our lesson from that massacre up in Badger a while back. Your basic-if-terrifying Caucasian, male lunacy; guy opening up on kids who never knew what hit them. Back then every weeper in-state was called on to attend the big thing in the two-headed, red-and-brown brick Catholic monstrosity on Main. I had spent the time on the way there imagining, as I often do, the state of mind of those left behind and tried to prepare myself for sorrow-beyond-sorrow. But when I pulled up, there was a big protest underway. Pale guts spilling out of patriotic tees, scrubby beards, ammo vests, semiautomatics held downward, one-handed—placards, beer. One man had a neat row of jowls that put me in mind of a conch shell. He, like everyone there, was screaming his fucking brains out. We had to run a gauntlet to get to the front door, like women needing abortions.

Anyway, the gun-nut/fascist fanboys weren't even particularly mad at us weepers, reserving their venom for the bereaved, who (their thinking went) had enjoined in an argument with them about their weaponry, purely by virtue of those parents' losses.

By the time those little angels were buried and we were safely home again, I had decided that was the last of those ones I'd ever attend. Later I learned that we all—all of us

302ers—had come to that same conclusion independently. Even Regis, despite his loss of income.

These things are too ratcheted up, too full of pain, incomprehension, and rancor to tamper with. What I mean is that there are funerals, and there are *funerals*.

A TIME TO MOURN

The first one I ever attended was as a boy, and it was for my father's father . . .

Bowed heads. We don't really do this now, but back then it was usual.

Two phrases I did not comprehend: "forever in our hearts," which at the time I took in the anatomical sense, and the expression "will always be with us," which I took to mean zombies.

The long recitation of the old man's CV, meaning his biography, I guess, though that was mostly made up of a literal CV, as in: "laid pipe . . ." "seismic drilling in . . ." "air freight for . . ." et cetera.

A few testimonies from his codger buddies, one of which included a line about Granddad always being found in his scrap pile of iron, wood, and machinery parts. For some reason the adults thought this was hilarious.

There was another bit next I perked up for, about Granddad jerry-rigging a self-hitching bale wagon, which I loved. Like many a young boy I could enumerate every species of tractor, truck, and heavy equipment under the sun. So learning that old Granddad knew all their nuts and bolts brought out my familial pride.

Then, there was the closed coffin, set on a bier right behind the celebrant (him and it forming a horizontal exclamation point). And boy did I have a slew of questions about what was going on inside that box, as it was forever closed to me, and thus was completely and totally mesmerizing.

The desire to see in there was simply tremendous. (Not anymore, of course. I've seen what there is to see by now. Many times over.)

Then came the "time to kill; time to heal" thing—another brainteaser, as I didn't know what a "time to kill" could possibly be and settled on the siren from the slaughterhouse up on El Camino which you can hear for miles.

There was the priest announcing that we were going to listen to a hymn, and then going over to press play on the stereo's tape deck.

It was "I'll Fly Away." And all I could think of in this regard was about the flying and how it was supposed to go down given that Granddad's body was secure in its container.

Then we were standing, and the priest crosses himself and so does my mom, who looks down, irritated at me not doing the same, and seeing this, Dad yanks my hands out of my jacket pockets by their slender and welting wrists (I think now on Jeannine . . .).

The priest kissed the coffin, *actually kissed it*, and then exited through a frosted-glass door beside the altar.

Two attendants came up and wheeled the coffin away, smooth on its gurney, out through that same door.

So, the "flying away" would take place out back, I guessed.

They'd open the coffin like the door of a birdcage and out he'd go. Later we saw Granddad interred. So, consider that another lesson taught and learned.

So this ceremony was pretty much all confusion for me, that is, though it made its mark all right.

POETRY READING I

MISERABLE COMPANY

It's not just a question of avoiding their eyes,
not circling them too quick on my horse,
keeping them bunched up tight.

The old cowboys will tell you: it's
how you *feel* that affects the herd most.

"So don't be skittish.
And don't get too down in the mouth."

And I say to those veterans of the long trail:

"That is one huge fucking ask,
as I am just as much what I am
as a steer is what a steer is."

A dumb brute.

Still, they have a point—if I'm down
in the mouth,
the cattle will also get
down in the mouth,
and then the cattle will,
in turn, make me even more
down in the mouth,
and so on, until such a time as all our mouths have dropped
right off our stupid brute faces.

Nevertheless, over many years,
I have learned to not get jumpy.

Not yelp when I see a rattlesnake,
or worry too much about sandstorms.
My hands are steady on the reins.

But Jesus Christ I'm not sure I could make myself cheery,
even for a lifetime of trying.
And neither am I convinced my herd would
become any happier
or feel any more warmth toward me
even if I could.

Meaning I'm still as down in the mouth
as I am long in the tooth.
I'm fine with it. And just look at them over there:
taking a dim view of everything.

E.F.

PSALMS

208
467
599
162

More then; more and more. Services, wakes. So forth.

And it was given to me to be privy—to bear witness. Such a fuck-ton of witnessing.

And though I will tell you now that, even when all was said and done, during that "Time of the Kid," I did not gain a thing in understanding how he did what he did—not clue one—I did, in fact, finally recognize him for what he was. One day everything changed. The dime dropped, simple as that, and once a dime drops, it can't be un-dropped. Fuck but it was raining dimes.

———

I'm a goddam idiot, sure, but that it took so long for me to reach that moment of revelation and conversion was understandable. As we know, he concealed his ways, used them offhandedly, without fuss or show—kept them hidden beneath the foot-shuffling, aw-shucksing, shrugging, ground-examining, straw-sucking, yawning, knuckle-cracking, etc. It all could be missed by the naked eye, or passed off as something else entirely. His work seemed to vanish upon being writ. A gesture, a manifestation, a slight change of temperature or degree; subtle, the color of air; the weight of it too. Nothing that could be pinned. Nothing in the open. His eyes continued to be a closed account and he still, rarely, if ever, opened his parsimonious mouth. That Adam's apple did not move but for the swallowing. It was clear that he wasn't in it for the seeming, but onto deeper currents, and perhaps that annoyingly complacent look of his was the look of someone emptied out of everything but the doing. Even as folks around him turned heavy dismal. But as we went about our weeping, there was no denying what was what.

I badly wanted to herald him. Me; my flaccid trumpet. "Prepare ye the way," etc. But—as Chantal so pointedly re-minded me—I had lost all credibility, though even if I hadn't, people are only ready when they are ready and some things should not be rushed or taken lightly. So I managed not to say a peep and kept what I knew close.

I saw it all, as I was there when it all went down—not knowing what to do or say; trying not to gawp. I decided to adopt a professionally serene demeanor, like a doctor looking at your down-belows, having spotted a bad sore in an even worse location; neither shocked nor embarrassed—*simply doing my job, sir.* This, as the wonders unfolded.

Wonders. True ones. And here are merely a few more examples.

(These I later thought of as his "good works." Some of which were official, some of which were *un.*)

He and me were up by the kennels in Wiskitassas after a job because the crazy idea had come to me of buying Chantal a puppy.

The woman who ran the joint took us through two rows of cages, aisle in between, that astringent smell, and piss, and fear probably, and I suppose that those hounds will normally go off when someone goes in there but for us it was the dead opposite. They were braying to high hell before us, and when we walked in they all came together in a single long whine like a women's choir. Then: dead silent. On top of that, they all then lay down as one.

—Never seen this, the woman said.

I didn't take one of those dogs because I was spooked.

Of course there was that time we were at a tavern nearest the LDS church, on that street which forms a gulley. The bar had a red-lit sign, and we were drinking our longnecks outside of it on the pavement, despite the mosquitos, and those men came up, calling him "pretty boy," and me "fag." Sometimes people can see the soft on you.

—I beg your fucking pardon, I said, as I was drunk and not feeling generous.

—You old *pussy*, the man with the backward cap said.

The kid watching, very constant.

The moth-bothered light.

And when one of them stepped up to do something, the kid moved in between, and then the man come away like he'd been jolted. His head was in his hands, so it was hard to know what he was about until we heard the sobs.

—Kind of bullshit? the other man said to the crying man.

I don't know what the kid said in that split second—though it was clear that this peckerwood was drunk enough to be already riding the fine line separating belligerent from self-pitying—but it all turned so fucking fast.

And now there are moments when I feel as though I never saw anything so remarkable. The sorrow of those men, in that gully, under that red light.

They bought us both a round later, inside. After they had got the grief out of them.

You could call such matters "small things"; small things, small things, but also big—big ones; so big it was as if there was wormwood in the water table.

Hallelujah, day by day by day by day an indisputable, un-diluted, unprecedented sadness contagioning its way through the county. A dirge, rising above us like the moon.

We saw it at the services, as I've already chronicled. Those astounding services.

But astounding only when he was set there.

Though it is the one-on-ones that stay with me most.

I'd see them happen at receptions: kid and some man by

the coffee urns. Kid would have raised a hand to the man's shoulder; then the man rattling his cup, not loud, but the quietest sound of china on china, then the man would put it down so as to grab a napkin from a stack and slyly wipe an eye. More of the kid, then, and after that the man might put both his hands on the table to steady himself and heave out big sobs.

Or sometime it was him sitting next to a woman, in a pew up front, his head turned toward her, listening, and then, when she turns, her gaze so beautifully full; lustrous with sad.

So those as well.

I saw it all, and from then on knew clear as day. Nobody I'd ever encountered could bring up sorrow like him. Holy mother do I whistle in amazement.

His power probed a room, before drawing out what needed drawing, getting from people something they could not get to themselves, but making them do it in an unconscious, if instinctive fashion, as when you are watching on TV an outfielder stretch to reach a high fly, and you, sitting on your couch, will extend your neck and shoulder muscles, reflexive, to help him do so. Like that.

Like that and he could agitate you, like that shaking hand holding that saucer, which shook that cup. Excite a thing, like. But I suppose he was an agitator in that other sense as well. As in: one thing troubling another. This too.

And given what was going on—the historical moment he had (I now knew) single-handedly inaugurated; the intensity of it all—I began to wonder, did he have a tap he could turn on and (more importantly, off) when necessary? Blow some of that talent of his out an open window?

But then, looking around at the people he sat amongst, red-rimmed and streaming, I thought that perhaps, no, he did not. Perhaps he had no more control over it than one of those sorry folks like Shitburger who blink a lot and twitch and swear too much.

A TIME TO HATE

And still with the strange sightings.

The one where there had been a twilight for the ages.

I remember this. A celestial show; one of those tie-dyed catastrophes that make God Almighty look like the hippie king himself. And whenever these descend, I am likely to put out a lawn chair somewhere in the trailer court and settle in to watch it all explode and fade. On this particular occasion, Chantal was there beside me, Dill on my other side; comfortable in each other's silence such that we could hear nothing but the night music. Wind, chirrups of desert bugs, and the light snores from the highway up-ridge.

When dark had finally shot through it all, Chantal let out her little yawn and took away the empties over my protestations.

—Stunning, Dill said and hadn't meant the sunset but the action down at the Redeemer.

(Stunning. It all continued to stun. How we had put all those dreary, washed-out ones behind us, and now had these new services brimming with life.)

Bullbat came out and swept the sky. As it dove, the little bird sounded like a truck grinding down its gears. It was gone.

At the end of the night, Chantal decided not to stay at mine, wanting the alone time, but I insisted on dropping her, so we hopped into the truck and when we got to hers, she laid a nice kiss on me.

On the way back, I exited the highway for a scratch-off and ended up buying way more of them than I should have. As I was being rung up I looked down at all that shiny, colorful paper on the counter—which put me in mind of a variety pack of condom sleeves—and grimaced.

I stopped out by the pumps, fished a quarter from my pocket, and was scratching away like a prairie dog when I heard someone coughing up a lung. I looked up and out by the restrooms and coolant were two men. One of those I knew to be the kid. Something passed between them.

But when I went over, there remained only one man. He was bearded, thin, yellow, and fucked-up as a chewed pencil. He coughed, and continued to cough, and when it was done he settled into a stupor. I apologized and retreated back to the truck.

Next day me and the kid were driving, bum tickets strewn around the seats.

—Go out last night? I said.

—Naaah, he said, picking at his teeth with the corner of one of those lottos.

Now, despite my late physical difficulties, my eyes are still like a teenage falcon's. I have lived my entire life in this low-rent state; one of the benefits of this being that I can see clearly, almost everywhere I look, one hundred uninterrupted miles. Even now, rotating in a slow circle out on the flagstones, the land is pretty much flat all the way from here to where it quits; to where cold, outer space may as well take over.

Later in the week I had been drinking my night rounds and after took the small roads home, driving slowly because of the booze. I knew that as I thumped over the railway tracks I would see that Brenda, sad case, working her corner alone.

The improbably named Brenda Walker was what my grandfather called a "sporting woman," and what my father called a whore. And I'm not sure which is a poorer word for it, but sometimes I'd maybe pull over by the depot and she'd smile her busted smile at me. I'd offer to get her a cruller or a bear claw and maybe we would exchange a pre-written pleasantry or two, which was all that ever was of course, all of the polite flirting covering up my concern, that being more risky to express and receive for some reason, but if she wasn't there at the junction it meant she was plying her trade and I would wonder what made me feel more abject, seeing her out there alone in the dead of night in that fur—spiky and pilled up as her hedgehog hair—or *not* seeing her there; her actively on the job. And I could never keep myself from imagining the shittiness of all that, the roughness, the rank intrusions, and as much as I've been complaining about my own lot, many folks, obviously, have it truly far worse—far, far worse—and as I drove by that night, skinny little Brenda was there, and so was the kid.

Before I hit the tracks I peeled around a next corner, parked behind the depot, army-crawled through a back lot over a bunch of pallets (an awkward and painful thing, I'll tell you). I kicked through some bags until I was over in a dark spot. Crouched, and I could see between buildings. I couldn't hear them, though they were talking. Brenda was rough and worn as ever, but her, next to him in his getup, never looked more like a small girl in a grown-up's clothing—night-town mirage—the two of them, waif runaways.

They stayed like that awhile. Then there was a turn.

She looked at him mistrustful and sharp, as if learning of something new and perfidious, and her face twisted in that betrayal, real or imagined, and then she began to lay into him. Boy oh boy. She was letting him have it both barrels. Shouting, and though I still couldn't hear the content of it—just violent little sounds, as like if you squeezed a songbird in your fist, bursts of high noise—it must have been fucking terrible given the expression on her. Then she went full bug-fuck, stabbed a hand out, the kid turned and ran. I thought Brenda was packing that plastic, orange box cutter I'd seen once poking out her little purse. But by then she'd probably got herself a proper weapon; kitchen knife or some such. Either way, the kid was gone, and there was Brenda alone again, hands on hips, huffing, head on a swivel, glaring out into the night.

I hustled out in the direction the kid had gone and couldn't find him anywhere.

Brenda was after that gone from her spot and the town as a whole.

And another, and another, one of which happened at Vince's Embalming, Headstones & Remembrances.

If the day is a series of pulses and weights, and we enter some atmospheres like walking into a smell: this was a bad one. Vince just rubbed everyone the wrong way. The kid and me had walked in and the doormat had dinged. Vince came through the back curtain whipping off his Harley do-rag and grinning, but when he saw us, he lost that glossy, for-the-customer face—the one he wears when he's taking them through his catalog of stonecuts, urns, fancy marble varietals, and wreath types—the expression just fell off him like an avalanche.

—Vince, I said.

—Here for Winona? he said, tying the headpiece back on.

He meant Winona Purlieu's headstone, which we were due to deliver to the gravesite. Reg had a hand in everything funerary—accessories included—and he had gone in with Vince on this particular venture, knowing as he did that death was on the air, and that there were benefits to be had in conglomerating.

Me, I had a free truck bed, so Reg would throw some money my way for transport. Though I didn't balk at this work in the past, there, then, with the boy by my side, it felt demeaning. Beneath the boy's station and somehow dirty and wrong.

I presented the yellow sheet, which Vincent tore from my hand.

—Wait, he said.

We did that.

Kid wandered the aisles looking at the merchandise while I stood leaning on the counter. I watched him look inside a casket, which was padded as if for shipping fragiles. He picked up a plastic flower, turned it over in his hand, and then put it back. Ran a white satin ribbon through his fingers. Squatted down to read an inscription. Christ on a cracker, I thought.

Vincent was taking an age in the warehouse, so I went out for a moment to smoke. When I came back in, the kid was nowhere.

—Hello? I said.

But hearing something behind the curtain, I went there and drew it open a tad, and there was the kid, standing alone in the half-light of the embalming room. The smell almost knocked me down.

There was a corpse upon the steel slab, looking the way they often do before being dressed and make-upped, meaning: swollen, and mottled like wine cheese.

I looked on as the kid walked up to the table. He reached out slowly toward the cadaver and touched its cheek. Tenderly? Pushed the skin to see if it would resist? And had one tear then traced the body's waxen face?

I was all attention, like my view had zoomed up so as to see only the tip of the boy's delicate pointer finger on that dead flesh. A hush, and I was in thrall to it.

What was I expecting would happen next? What species of miracle?

The kid pulled his hand back slowly as if thinking better of whatever he had planned next.

—You'll want a mask, I said.

He turned.

Vincent then crashed in pushing a hand truck with the stone strapped to it.

—What the fuck you up to, he said.

We all went out front and hefted up the headstone, which

bore an engraving of a lifelike dove; one I'd definitely seen before, maybe even in the same graveyard this one was going in. Like two people wearing the same dress to a party, I thought prissily—and wondered about this notion of having your lasting emblem chosen from Vincent's shitty binder like a cheap tattoo from a flash basket. The words "Winona Purlieu" were written on it in a wedding script. After the lifting I was tired and had to rest. Hot, with maybe one of my mild fevers. I recovered quick though, the kid took the hand truck from Vince, I signed the form for it, and the whole event made my gorge tickle.

———————————

There was then a prison pickup.

I was at Dill's when Regis called. Cops had called Regis because of the union card the kid had on him. Dill stayed put as I told him it was my job and duty, which is how I felt, and I ignored the look he tried to give me as I hustled out.

—Wasn't there so I can't tell you, said the cop at the desk.

—Has to be a charge.

He shoved a paper at me. The form was smudged, writing blurred as if rained on.

—Not yet. But there's a record, he said.

—How's that.

—Priors.

—Ok, let's have it.

—You his lawyer?

I could see through to the holding cell. Kid there. Also

an unusually big-ass man in a too-tight brown tee. Man was smiling, but the smile was all wrong.

Eventually the boy was led out.

—I know, he said to me; nothing more to add.

We walked back to the truck and I saw his black fingertips. Jail time would explain those missing days of his.

Next afternoon I went back to the station. Kid had forgotten his mourning suit and other things and I said I'd collect the stuff for him as he seemed nervy about it.

The man in the cage pushed a tray through the window. There, neatly folded, was the kid's black jacket. Beside the jacket there was also a crumpled pack of cigarettes, a plastic lighter, a safety pin, a straw, a pocketknife, and some breath mints. On the top of the jacket was a small notebook.

—Send my regards, the guy said.

I left.

Jacket over my arm, rest of it in my pockets, but the notebook I held. And it wasn't until I got back to the truck that I noticed how red and fiery my palm had got. I had been clutching that little book pretty hard.

WONDROUS WORKS WITHOUT NUMBER

> And great grace was upon them all.
> —Acts 4:33

It's quite a thing . . . of course it was. It was quite a fucking thing.

Mid-June, after another one of those famous successes of ours. Another recep:

—I believe that we did pretty good, I said, approaching the kid with a drink in each hand, stating the obvious.

He was standing in front of the chafing dishes, the Sternos, urns, and casserole tins which represent the final act in ceremonies of grief. (Though I gather that there can be a lot of fasting around a death overseas, here in our place I suppose we subscribe to the notion that food in excess numbs us when we most need the numbing. It's that or simply an opportunity to get stuffed on someone else's buck.)

Anyway the kid mumbled something to me, lifting his face up from his plate for a moment and stretching out a hand to take the drink I proffered.

—Slow down, you get a cramp.

I took a drumstick off his crowded plate, sat down on the sofa, and sank into its cushions. He sat opposite.

I held that chicken leg and watched the kid chew.

It was just beginning to become (if mildly) bothersome to me, not the chewing, but him never having nothing to say for himself; especially after the wonders, all those, which, it seemed to me, would eventually become quite impossible *not* to speak on.

Hunched over his meal like it was the last he'd ever see.

I am patient, ask anyone, but not infinitely. Fuck, I thought: water from a stone.

Bunch of people came by the couch then to pay more compliments for what we did, then left us again.

Look at him, there.

His weird eyes.

Sometimes I'd think they were vacant, evacuated of content, but looking closer, I'd consider that they might just be so full as to appear empty. Like those natural wonders—mountain ranges, deserts, open oceans, so on—which are so large, so unavoidably present, heavy with existence, so teeming with detail that they come at you as but a single thing.

I was startled to find him then looking at me back.

—You staying out of trouble? Generally speaking? I said.

The light was going down outside and no one had put on the lamps yet. It was all melancholy. I thought of how lonely a boy that age must be: seemingly no loved ones, no real home. Not that he seemed lonely. Eyes aside, his face did not have a particular cast to it, but to me then, in the half shadow, it suddenly looked like a death's-head.

We sat like that in the heat and growing dark as guests started to file out. I was going to rise as well, but saw that my dad was set down too, next to the kid, perched on the arm of that ratty old lounger. Dad looked at me. I laughed; which turned into a quiet, staccato little sob. Shit, I thought, get a hold.

Dad looked at me like he did when he used to give me thick ear.

Kid looked at me as if to be reading my mind.

Dad flickering in and out for a moment, like a bad bulb, like the gray flashes of heat lightning fizzing off in the night, out the window behind the couch. Then he was gone. And then the bereaved family came over with our winnings, handing the thicker-than-usual envelope on down, just as I caught the curious face of Dill.

———————————

Then:

- We did a long Catholic show in the place down Badger, and the priest broke down and could barely get through a Lord's Prayer.
- A Baptist one, where the son of the deceased tried forcing a bunch of bills into Dill's hands representing twice a normal fee (he refused, but the tips that night were, like the tears delivered, exorbitant).
- One happened after the reception where afterward a man said to me that he had "never felt so seen" in all his life.

All slam dunks, though the kid himself never appeared to care or to even notice.

Often my dad come back around to me, as if he'd learned I had a spare bed.

It went on.

Couple weeks then, and we are driving out; the kid gone into his silence.

Bored and left to my own devices, I looked out the window at subdivided ranchlands. It's all white squares now, I thought, like God's tiling a restroom.

—Son, you *ever* going to learn to speak? I said. The

ensuing quiet only deepened. So I just kept driving and staring out.

The land used to give a fucking impression, I thought. Could be felt. No more. Not out on the multiplexed plains, down the shopping-mall-ed canyons, not up the blister-packaged hills, on the office park's greensward; neither in these drainage hollows nor on our faded, emerald courses . . .

The kid stuck his head out and spat a loogie backward.

—Please, I said.

He wiped his mouth on a wrist.

—There are times when I believe you must be a deaf-mute, I said.

—I can talk, he said.

(This was true; though it was a close thing. What I mean is that he didn't say *nothing at all*. He was a penny-pincher when it came to words, sure. That much is real. But there still was, on occasion, a small expenditure of language which could be freely sprinkled around the rest of my telling like so much salt and pepper, for instance: *This the crying place?—Ain't everyone?—Nah.—Tomorrow I might.—I don't worry about it.—Pass me one.—Ok, maybe.—Hope that don't lead anywhere.—Ma'am?—Four fifty.—Horses for courses.— Sure, sure.—Ketchup.—You know that, same as me.—Not done.—Who lives there.—Can I? Can you? Forget it.—Huh.— I'll be right back.*)

The silences could last hours, and there were examples of whole days where he didn't open his mouth and I never really understood how he got away with that. Though seemingly polite and unobtrusive about everything else, he had no problem blanking you when you asked him something direct. And because of the other compensations I—and I suppose all of us—more or less let it slide.

I was thinking about this as we passed through the toll and swung onto a smaller access road. I looked out at the steeple of the church in the distance, straight off on the plain like a pin in a map.

—You are piss-poor company, I said, as it was really starting to chap my behind.

And when we stopped at the light, he reached out and put his hand down on my shoulder.

I jumped in my seat.

He removed his hand.

The car behind me honked.

I pulled out and we got to the parking lot without another word.

Well I'm still not sure what he meant by that gesture, but when it happened, it was like when you turn the ignition in your car but forgot your radio was up full blast.

A frantic scramble to find the volume knob.

Maybe it was just how tightly strung I'd got since his arrival, the uptick in Dad's drop-ins and drive-bys, the periodic fevers I'd been suffering, him sliding those dress shoes upon the rubber vehicle mat, or simply the unexpectedness of it all; it was, after all and in fact, the first time we had ever touched.

I knew what it was though. I knew it, and knew the jolt as a sign. And as we sat down in our pews to weep that day, I believed that I understood why this boy kept to his own.

———

Anyway, two days after that, he was gone again. For a bit.

And when I saw him next down at the lot he had two fresh stitches in the side of his head and would not say a single word about that.

AVERT FROM MEN GOD'S WRATH

> There's a tear in my beer
> —Hank Williams

Selective mutism: Francine from Benson County General gave me that. And I suppose if I'd bothered to go to the library there'd probably be more of such. Anyway if there were names for those things, for that behavior, fine. Ok then. But was there a name for his power? His power, though.

What are the words to explain how everything changed because of it. What gifts that power bore. Sure, there was the *ominous* that hung about him, the dark what-ifs, the uncanny undercurrents . . . yet those gifts he bore were much-needed ones. Ones we all should've been grateful to receive. His various run-ins, I decided, irrefutably, were merely the price paid for that very "bearing" (his being the "bearer" of "gifts"). And I was furthermore furious that the "gifts" he "bore" were beginning to be met with anger or disbelief.

(Which, also, for me, only served to confirm his blest and true abilities; knowing—from the stories, annals, accounts, and ballads—that where there are miracles, martyrdom lurks. And of course martyrdom and victim status are the ones I most identify with; and to a nail, everything is a hammer.)

———

But it began with resentment, and nothing worse.

—Horseshit, Hankie said.

—Why so pissy? I said.

—Yer boy.

—What'd he do to you.

—Coming in through the side door.

—Came in the front gate just like everyone else.

—Sure he did, Hankie said.

—This isn't some cheat.

—You positive about that?

—Not like the others. Seen it yourself.

—Don't know what I've seen. Neither do you.

—Come on now, you'd have to be blind.

Hankie had a reason for that constant bad attitude of his as he'd long ago lost a leg at the knee. But this here was not that but instead jealousy, pure and simple. Hankie was a mediocre weeper who did not believe in such a thing as talent, as he himself hadn't a lick of it. So he was always going to have a sulk.

—I'm with Hank, Ed. I don't like it either, piped in Chief Clarence.

—See? Hankie said, as if Clarence's corroboration sealed the thing.

—He doesn't even fucking cry, Clarence said.

—I don't see what that has to do with the price of gas. He's like a . . .

—Yeah?

— . . . a sad presence, I said.

—A *sad presence*? he said.

—Can it, Clarence, I said.

We were all riding out to the cemetery in the bed of Dill's truck, mine having been up on the lift that day.

—I'm allowed my opinion, said Clarence with his trademark flat baritone.

(And sure. If anyone was allowed views on a white man sidling up and moving on in, it was Chief.)

—We should kick him to the curb, said Hankie.

—Hell if we will, I said, thinking on how threatening the boy's gift was; how it allowed him to just fling wide the doors to another's house and stride in like an honored guest.

Thing is, people come to resent their guests. And it doesn't matter in the end how warmly welcomed these guests were in the first place. Eventually, given enough time, every stay begins to feel like a trespass.

—Well don't have a goddam piss-fit about it Ed, said Hankie.

—We should put it to a vote, said Clarence.

—All of you shaddup back there, said Dill through that little window as he drove, after which he cranked up the tunes to cement the point.

POETRY READING II

UNBRIDLED

When I took his bridle off, my palomino hit the
    trough; his liberated muzzle
sunk below the water that he drunk. After that he
    went to graze
and passed one of his gentlest days. Later, placid,
in the stalls, he kicked the new boy in the balls.

E.F.

MAY HIS MEMORY BE PRESERVED

Then came the gig which was out at a little mission, sitting like a headstone in the middle of all that yucca; perfect blue sky at its back. The event was presided over by that old pal of mine I already mentioned, Rev, who also used to weep Local 302, but now works the other side of the altar. He and I still drink together on occasion, usually after I work his territory, and so was planning on a lengthy postmortem when we were (truly) post mortem.

Service was classy, and our work was flawless, deeply affecting. After, the kid hitched a ride with Dill, and I hung back with Rev. We waited til the son (banker) of the son (dentist) of the deceased (farmer) paid us, then Rev doled out his two-handed goodbyes and blessings. Rest of my gang got in the van and left the lot. Then me and Rev humped into my newly repaired truck and went off to Larry's Rest up on Simpson. Couple of pints into it before the Rev says anything.

—You hearing rumors? he began.

—Which would those be, I ask.

—Down from Salvage, and Badger?

—Can't say I have, Rev.

—I work those regions.

—I know you do.

—People calling it all kinds of things, even over the state line.

—Calling what. Say what you want to say.

—Bad goddam shit, Ed.

—Sure.

—Rest stop. One down Culpos Paintball. Something after the truck rally.

I did not know specifically what he meant by that, but did not want to go down the road with him either.

—Climate these days, I said, wiping the foam off my famous mustache.

—Except the ones I'm talking about here, was always some youth come around when things went belly-up.

—What are you trying to say, Rev?

—What's your best guess, he said.

—That my kid is disturbing the peace? Don't be ridiculous.

—Keep an eye out. I clocked him out there today at the show, down in back. Something's not quite right.

—He's a whole new generation, Rev.

—Doesn't that frighten you?

—Maybe we have a thing or two to learn, old men like us.

He put his chin down on his fist, looked at me all solicitude, and said:

—I believe that you know enough already of sorrow, Ed. Most do, without having to go chasing more of it.

Rev was a reverend for a reason, all right, but still: I always had such a hard time knowing when to quit something, and I have the gambling debts to prove it.

Next day I was in town passing by the Wash-o-mat. I had seen the kid through the window and gone in.

Nancy Nguyen was trying to ream a slug out of her broken soap dispenser.

—Animals, she said.

Liem Nguyen must have been in the back, as I could hear that pop music of theirs coming from the other side of the staff-only door. Both Nguyens were weepers and had been running with us for years, but also carried several other jobs as some must. Laundry was a main source of income and must've done decently for them. Folks came in all the time from the RVs in particular, and the more hard up people got, the more people moved out of real homes (the kind with foundations), the more cash the Nguyens made.

On this day though, the place was empty but for us and Minnie—Tom and Marlena Spafford's oldest daughter— who was over at the folding table.

It was the day before the Fourth, and I guessed people were preparing for their cookouts. I myself had a bag of Roman candles, fountains, M80s, and Big Bursts under my arm, as I always do this time of year. Dill and me have a tradition of this going back to our teens and we keep it up.

Nancy, seeing my stash of armaments and projectiles, tutted at me angrily. She had gone behind the counter and was paused from her work setting up a neat row of little flags, stood as a cordon in front of the register like in a veteran's cemetery. The admonishment from her seemed harsh, until I recalled that the Nguyens left town every year on precisely the evening of the fireworks, just as surely as I always attended them. Loud noises must spook them, I concluded, even so many decades after the war that sent them here.

I smiled apologetically and she frowned on back, so I plopped down in a bucket chair next to the kid and put my munitions on the floor, feeling shamed.

—What's new, I said to the kid without hope of an answer; as you might greet a doorknob. He watched his whirling clothes.

Minnie side-eyed us, her folding almost done.

Eventually, the kid pulled his meager pile out of the dryer including that black suit of his, which he really should've been dry cleaning because it was puckered as old elbows. We said goodbye to Nancy Nguyen and left. But we hadn't gone a block down the pavement when Minnie came shouting after us. I thought he'd left a sock or some such, but it wasn't that.

—Minnie, I said.

—Need to talk to you, she said to the kid, out of breath and mad as a hen.

I stepped between them without thinking to.

—What the fuck was that last week you somebitch, she said to him, pushing me aside.

Her mom had just passed. 302 hired by the other daughter.

—That what we paid for? Your fucking idiot face? she said.

—He does the job his own way, but I assure you . . . I said.

—Or he doesn't give one shit. Practically dead himself, she said.

—You on the anger stage of grief, Minnie? says I, instantly regretting it.

—Ed, you might want to reconsider those words and then apologize for them.

I did that.

—You were there, you saw him, she said, insistent.

—Sorrow drives us to deep places, I said.

She furrowed up her brows.

Then, the kid slowly reached out as to take her hand. She moved to recoil but he was too close to avoid.

He laid his fingers, soft upon the top of her hand. Didn't grab her. Simply placed two fingertips down there. A sign of understanding—there, there—or like the taking of a pulse.

Either way I could see the slackening in her. He moved his hand away.

She looked long at him, then me, and then back over at him, then me again. Eventually she said:

—You vouch for him, Ed?

—That I will.

—It's been a lot, she said.

—I knew your mother. Never an unkind word, I said.

—I don't want her memory disrespected.

—I thought it a remarkable service, I said.

—Yeah, she said, and added, more soft:

—Sorry, Ed, she said, and saying nothing to the kid, turned and left.

We walked toward the truck without a word, as if Minnie never happened.

Looking at him then a doubt appeared, one that was later to cause me shame. What if he was just stupid.

Plain stupid. I'd picked myself up a fuckwit as copilot, and what I took to be genius was just run-of-the-mill dumb. What if I'd been completely buffaloed. Could be that. Chantal thought as much. In a way, that would sit easier. Easier that I put all this on him that wasn't there.

But the moment of doubt passed as soon as it came on.

That magic touch. I'd seen what I'd seen!

I drove him toward home, but as we'd both pounded a soda each while waiting for his clothes to dry, we had to pull off the road, walk through the scrub, and take a leak.

We stood at the requisite distance, each facing off to the chaparral. When we'd zipped up, we went back to the truck without speaking. Three miles on we got pulled over.

—Taillight, I said to the trooper, though it could have been anything on that piece of crap truck.

—Come down, he said, and I made to.

—Not you.

—Him?

—Stay put, sir, he said.

The kid went out and walked around the back of the truck, then walked over to the squad car. I could see the Statie looming above the boy in the rearview.

The cab was heating up and beginning to smell. Guy had those tight, gloved hands on his hips. He'd pause his talk, then start up again. His hand dropped to idly finger the top of his holster. Fly buzzing around me. Cop looked in maximum authority mode and pretty pissed.

I waved the fly out a window and so missed the next bit

but the kid came back and got in. Statie took a long, stern look back at both of us, slid into the squad car, and plumed out onto the road.

Kid sat there.

I left the engine off.

—Nothing? I said. We drove in an even deeper silence than usual.

But three days on he had his arm in a sling and who the fuck knows. This, after all he'd done. Call me ignorant (I thought then, arguing with no one), but where is it forbidden—in what charter—that a man should not do his job *too* well. Where? That's no federal offense. And if we take to blaming the kid, I thought, and go down that particular road, let me ask you: where does it end? Each of us only doing all our work half-assed? Quarter-assed? Using one eighth of our ass? And how good then is 'too good'? I was raised to believe that we all should aspire to do the best we have with the gifts God gave us and that no man shall keep us down or raise impediments to our pursuit of professional excellence.

This is America still, is it not?

VIEWING OF THE BODY

> Even at Horeb you provoked
> the Lord to wrath.
> —Deuteronomy 9:8

It should be evident (after that episode with Chief and Hank, who were to me then like a pair of ingrown toenails) that, as I've said, no one else had figured it out—about his gift.

The beneficence and the boons he was granting us; him turning dust to water and water into whiskey.

And so as you'd imagine there was then that new smugness about the 302. The low become high and mighty, and it is generally the case that a person will not give success to another when it is so easy to claim it for themselves.

Still: let them have it, I felt.

Even if the kid was providing the steroids that won us the race, we had put in the effort, and it did a heart good to see the home team win. Plus, it spared the boy extra scrutiny.

But I was, then, therefore, also the only weeper who asked the questions.

And not just about his power, but: why that little life of his was broken by such strange goings-on, the trouble he was fingered for, with him habituating those poor places, lurking, transacting those shadowy *layings-on-of-hands*, and it truly kept me up at night, me fretting on it all—the simmering confusion and resentment, such feelings as would lead to those bad hammerings he was taking from time to time.

Well the point is I was worried, but I was also in the dark, as those acts against him happened always offstage and out of sight.

Though actually not really as there was one exception, meaning I only witnessed such as that but once with my own eyes: and so here is the one I meant to tell, the one where him and me both got thumped but good; the one at the church with the twice-struck cross.

As I mentioned, I now am quite familiar with the inside of a coffin, as familiar as one can be without being embalmed and lowered in there yourself, and though you'd think I'd be used to it all, let it be said that open casket jobs are the pits, and nothing shakes me up and drives me inward so much as an actual dead.

It's the thingy-ness of it, by which I mean to say that the deceased is not so much a person as much as a newly minted object, and it is never not surprising to me how quickly it is that we revert from dynamos-of-thought-and-deed to meat. Hard to countenance that what once breathed, shat, crept, sang, deliberated, ladled, trembled, typed, weighed, sweat, groped, pointed, hid, measured, smiled, cringed, dove, savored, scattered, sneered, lolled, hollered, limped, or loved could just go away so completely. I'm not saying anything profound and I know this, but it does go away—the all of it—and for some very confused reasons I cannot figure out, this thought makes the pretense of my role in such events suddenly feel especially shameful. Getting in the line and finally standing there above the deceased (for an appropriate pause; long is creepy, short is cold), my whole thing becomes untenable. And it's hard in these moments not to breathe in; smell things. Get a strong whiff of the embalmed. I mean, it's rarely—except on the warmest days, and we've had a few of these—anything gross, smell-wise; the funerary folks do their best to make sure of that; cologne, perfume, or a special, exclusive air freshener of some sort. But in fact this part is the worst. Though good smells are so aligned in my mind with life in all of its blooming glory, these fragrant bodies only reinforce again the idea that the person is ultimately no more than a urinal with a cake in it.

Sometimes, when I get to thinking this way, I also think about the many ways these corpses can be repurposed; the normal ways—donated organs for instance—as well as those which are not so normal: an example being that rock-and-roller who snorted the cremains of his father along with several lines of cocaine . . . and I think of Mr. Lenin too, in that glass box in the Kremlin, or mummies and other cases of human taxidermy. And then I might imagine that one could just scrumble up a body—scent and all—and make, like, a potpourri out of it. Put it in a drawer in an old bureau, keep your underwear smelling fresh.

Anyway, this particular open casket job I was talking about here took place in a church named after some saint I never heard of who, though evidently graced by God, was not graced by him with vowels; and I knew from that very lack of vowels that the coffin lid would be open, and so indeed it turned out.

Kid there. Got there on his own. For most of it I only saw the back of his head, his collar a little askew so I could see a bit of the dark band of his tie peeking up. Never been the neatest, our kid, his jacket getting ever more frayed at the elbows, though I hate to say that I still found it becoming on him, and I am told by parents that once someone is your child they are always that.

Then and as usual, it began.

People crying, though this time, it wasn't a groundswell, but rather like we all were under the EMT's paddle.

WHAM!

Right in the solar plexus. Crazy.

I could tell I wasn't alone in that—each congregant was experiencing a private breakdown, each driven within themselves, a different tolling bell in every ear, as if they felt then an unbidden and tender call to remember everyone and everything they've ever loved and lost. And I was wanting to arrest the misery he was bringing up. Mourners started looking simply wild-eyed, so I actually tried to stop him—I walked up the aisle and sat right down next to him. I tapped the kid sharply. And as before, was knocked for six, as though I had released something bitter and cold—like the liquid nitrogen from one of those coolant trucks. And it didn't stop. No it did not. A flood tided to the back pews, foaming over, every man and woman wearing that near identical face-of-eternal-sorrows. And it went past all reason, and all hell broke loose. A fight came on; two groups of meatheads pushing toward one another—madder than popcorn on a hot stove. They were pushing the women and elderly out of the way—a whirlwind of suits, square jaws, and high hairlines. Who knew what the particular beef here was, though I imagined it had ancient origins; old-country origins. Yet, despite the sudden rage, they were, all of them, crying as the brawl began, and didn't stop as the packs conjoined; and it was hard to tell if they were grappling or hugging, all of them, in both gangs, sobbing, clutching at one another violently, this sadness-judo which is a kissing cousin to the purely belligerent kind, and so it is with men, and so it has always been, and so it always will be, and anyhow.

A handful of days down the line, I saw the kid walking the strip, going I don't know where, but I also saw that he was heading, ignorant of it, toward three of those same men from the church fight who were loitering outside the Westward Ho; them leaning against its white wall, and as he walked by they looked on him murderously and one of them stepped up and bumped the kid.

I went over there fast then.

—Hold up, I said.

The rest of them detached themselves and one greaseball—thick neck and eyes like the sockets of a ratchet tool—pushed me hard. They came at the boy.

Before I could react, the third man, who must have circled around, rabbit-punched me in the neck, and I was out.

When I came to, they were gone and the kid was lying there face down and unmoving.

—Kid.

I was moving to pick him up when it occurred that something might be broken or ruptured, but he stirred, and then to my great relief, raised himself to his hands and knees.

—I'm getting help, I said.

—Stay, he said.

I put his arm over my shoulder for support—he was so light, barely a presence—and a line from the testaments came to me, and it was: "Even if all fall away on account of you . . ."

The streets were empty, but luckily the proprietor of the Westward had seen, and called the ambulance.

I turned to the boy as the red lights splashed their way toward us, and I will never forget what I saw writ on his face: which was resignation—no, not that. It was the look of a man who had taken a beating as his due. He was smiling. His first true grin. As if relieved to be given something he had been waiting on. Something commensurate.

Of course this had happened. I'd known; long known. Of course: the violence of it. As nothing brings on a souring so much as a person being witness to one's weakness and humanity, especially when one wasn't really ready for that to come out.

As he was stretchered off I had a passing yet scorching notion that I'd round up Johnnie and some of the harder men from the ranches and that we'd find those men and fuck them up but good. But the feeling left me soon as it had come.

Thing of it is: weepers aren't equipped for anger, and so it could not be sustained. I didn't even press charges, and the ambulance guys were upset about that and truly. But charges were just not something we pressed.

The kid was in the hospital for two and a half weeks this time. Rib. Face. Spleen. It was a close thing that he wasn't graveyard-dead, and I experienced his stay there as a frightening what-if. It is also worth mentioning that while he was there, I was visited by a new and strange suspicion, though it was only the merest whisper of one.

I'd been through all of this before.

Sure, the entire dramatic arc was growing increasingly predictable, but more importantly I was sure it was a recurrence. A reenactment.

But I couldn't put my finger down upon it, and it took some real thinking for me to uncover why I felt this way, and then one day I remembered something, and that something was Cornflake; his still forbearance; his demise.

GONE BUT NOT FORGOTTEN

Cornflake was the name the boys gave to the newest lure out at the greyhound track. They had tried a wind sock for a while to keep with newer times, but, though the hounds were chasing it, they were desultory about it and the runs were a good deal longer than before. The old thing they'd had, a dilapidated wool blob which was supposedly once shaped like a bone (name of Yumyum), was just falling to pieces, and people were getting tired of the announcer shouting out "and here comes the bone!," a phrase with little dignity. So Frank brings in a stuffed rabbit which had been the toy of his sister's kid, and just duct-tapes it to the coursing machine. It must have had guide wires inside that stuffing because, up there on the bar, stretched out, legs straining in mid-sprint, head held high and proud, ears flattened against its head, this bunny looked crazily lifelike and not a little bit heroic. If you had commissioned a renowned artist to erect you a statue dedicated to *Hopeless Vanity*, you could not have done much better than our Cornflake. He was, at rest anyway, almost cruelly serene and untouchably dignified: the very picture of a tragedy just before its turning, when things are looking so great yet everyone knows the score.

The very second Frank finished getting him up there we knew he'd found a winner. Of course Cornflake was only a blur from the stands where me and Jeannine used to be sat come a Sunday, but when the race was sprung and those dogs came spasming after in a devil of brown dust, I could imagine Cornflake's tranquility up ahead, him not giving one single shit, knowing he couldn't never be caught, never.

I was friends with the dog men, just like I'd known the jockeys back when I was onto the ponies (I came to dogs as I'd been downscaling my betting, both in terms of stakes wagered as well as in the size of the beast wagered upon; which is to say that I am—if not successfully—in The Program, though in it like someone giving up cigarettes by cutting each one down a bit more each day, until he is merely sucking on a ragged filter; which means that eventually I, with my needing a flutter, will be betting on smaller and smaller beasts than dogs, and though I don't have the stomach for the cockfights down in the basement of the adobe-walled restaurant out by the stripper place, I may just end up throwing my stake down at gecko races, God help), and when I went down onto the oval after a dog run to have a quick beer trackside, sometimes Cornflake would be there, frozen mid-flight, up by the white fencing like our mascot.

He was that, though. Our boy. Our good, good boy.

Once even, buzzed after a memorable win, I convinced them to take him down off his cross, and a bunch of us went with him in tow to the Tap Green, where he stood right up there on the bar watching us drink like he had a soul—a lofty one—while we slowly got more and more hammered and he looked on at us, judgier by the round.

But I suppose the guys never fastened him back again properly, as after that, in the middle of the next day's race, he sprung right off his suspension like he'd been launched from a catapult and landed forty yards up in a small explosion. Those sighthounds went straight at him, where they suddenly seemed to remember they were muzzled, this frustrating them and increasing the bloodlust, and so they started in with paws, trampling, but several of them in this frenzy got out of harness, and began tearing Cornflake six ways to creation; after which they started in on one another, and all the guys had to run in, and it turned into a whole entire thing.

SCRIPTURE READING

If a man vow a vow unto the Lord, or swear an
oath to bind his soul with a bond; he shall not
break his word, he shall do according to all
that proceedeth out of his mouth.

—NUMBERS 30:2

I'M SORRY FOR YOUR LOSS

He'll be out awhile, Francine said, leaving.

And when the drugs started to wear off, it was me on duty.

—Hello, Sunshine.

—Mmmph.

I handed him the pills.

—Francine said take them and I don't want to be on that woman's bad side.

He went back under then and I remained, keeping my watch, because I would not "fall away" ("on account of" him).

But boy I hate hospitals as they remind me of mortuaries and their prospective tenants. Benson County in particular. They had wheeled Jeannine in after her blood had come, the doc saying "we need him out of there," and I'd spun away to leave, but of course he meant the baby. After, Jeannie was pale as milk and not truly present to be comforted and so I turned from her pain to my own, my pain which lay ahead, that is—loneliness and abandonment surely coming for me—which would follow upon what was happening there, definite as death.

But here, with the kid: I abided.

I was there with him every damn day.

"Even if all fall away on account of you" and that there was from St. Peter who said it, and St. Peter was a rock; something I never was, but, late bloomer, might still become.

A rock, but also I wanted the relief of seeing him mend. It also brought me some cheer to watch Francine and those other nurses fuss over him—chide and tut—which is as sure a form of love as any (they were used to those handsy geriatrics at the VA, where they also worked shifts, so having the kid around suited them just fine).

As he slept, I would confer with Francine in the doorway of his room.

—Look at him, I said.

—Go home, Francine said.

—It isn't worth it, I said.

—Being a nurse is easy?

A passing coat said "Catheter in 5," and Francine looked at me all: *see?*

————————————

—You have any of those Popsicles left? I said.

—Plenty, said Francine.

—I'll get him a word jumble. Wheel the kid about the floor when he's more himself.

—You sure do mother him, Ed.

———————————

Another day passed. He lay still and barely woke. He was bathed while out.

—Those scars.

—Hard to miss, Francine said.

—Son of a . . .

—Yeah, she said.

—Ain't new ones.

—That they are not, she said.

—How you think he earned those?

She raised an eyebrow.

———————————

Later, he was sitting up more regular. He never said thanks to me for my vigil. His mouth was bust and he kept turning away to breathe, but that wasn't why.

———————————

Eventually he was sufficiently patched.

There I was again at the front desk, and by then I did wish the kid was actually on my insurance plan as that would be so much cheaper.

—You, the deskman said.

I scowled.

—Need your ID again, and his verbal consent.

—He's not so good in the verbal department.

I wheeled the kid out into the sun. Helped him up into the truck.

—You need to stop, I said to him.

He humped his shoulders, saying in that manner: "Stop what?"

Stop what, and I once again took to looking after him, because I could not help it ("Even if all fall away . . ."), and seeing him crippled, the old habit arose—as it would—and I am reminded that I am built for caring, it being so bred in my bones that I was then like one of those women like that Maureen who are beaten silly by their man and who keep coming back in hope of change, which I think is a very definition of insanity and which lands you on the floor of the Big Box in a puddle of your own piss, yet that's how it was, and don't blame me for it as I blamed myself plenty.

And I knew that no one else would step in. There was a time, after the beginning, when everything was rosy, when the 302 welcomed him, the whole gang ringed in warmth, our adoptive child, but I had come to suspect by this juncture in my tale, with all the smugness I mentioned, that they allowed the kid to stay only for my sake, and only begrudgingly.

I'd seen the lour on them. Still, as I said to Minnie, I vouched. I vouched like a motherfucker and nothing got to him that didn't get through old Ed. And they gave me my ward.

———————————

My ward: I took him back to his home, up those narrow dark stairs up to his place; helped him into bed.

He slept more. Down for almost two days straight. I know because I kept checking up. And I got to really snoop around his place while he was out. I had been right: he hadn't a single houseplant or framed photograph; not one lick of decoration aside from the constellation of nailheads in the wall left over from a previous tenant. A single bulb hung from the ceiling like a suicide.

I had looked in his kitchen and found he drank those protein shakes that are supposed to bulk a skinny man up. I went into the bathroom cabinet (sue my ass) and there was nothing but his toothbrush and paste. I confirmed that he owned but the one pair of shoes and the one jacket. That he was a Capricorn—this from a small calendar on the kitchen table, unmarked but for a single entry; as if he needed to remind himself of the day, or had chosen it himself.

I also got a better look at all of those scars, the likes of which I never saw, that could've been the aftermath of a porcupine fight, or him having fallen into a thornbush, or a bin of nails, his insufficient body pierced through and through.

When he was up again, Chantal and I took him to mine. Laid him outside in a lawn chair. Cooked him a meal. I brought a string of Christmas lights, the moon was out, and the cicadas were plugged in and spun up.

Chantal turned to me and put her head down on my shoulder. We both looked at the boy as he gobbled her potato salad. Then she and me took the dishes in.

—He'll be ok, I said to Chantal while I dried, though she didn't seem to hear me over the sink water, trickle-clanging into the empty pots.

BE PATIENT IN AFFLICTION

Count it all as joy, my brothers.
—James 1:2

That would've been a perfect moment for it: for me to work upon him. Move him off the path. While he was so tenderized, while he had—more or less—remanded himself to my care. But I didn't, and he left.

Then there came a dark night in which—floundering my way again to the can—I stepped on one of those beer bottles lying like traps, and nearly split my cranium. Now who would know if that were to have been the end of Ed, with my brain leaked out and everything? Who would come check? Perhaps the remaining Scottie would find me, my earthly remains, or the park manager would learn of that by my smell; and no one wants their last act to be the expulsion of a stink, though this tends to be the way of it. I don't remember passing back out, but the sleep brought with it strange visions of a world hardened and cracked, Dad the reigning prince of such an infernal kingdom, and when I woke again, face down on my kitchenette tile, it was clear that those constant aches and pains I'd been suffering of late—especially the fevers—were worsening bad.

Such fevers continued for days, and between the bouts of shivering, delirium, and the fervent offerings I gave to whatever regional deity presided over my toilet, all I could accomplish was exactly nothing: lying abed, occasionally heaving myself up to answer the phone, and—in the most resolute terms possible—refusing the company of my friends and colleagues.

But no man is allowed his privacy or dignity ever and of course, and what a noisy flock of terrible gossips.

—Down Canaan Steel.

—Oh yeah? I said.

—Weren't seeing or paying attention to me or fuck-all; another world. He was on the ground; looked real happy and comfortable though.

—What can be said about it, I said.

—Plenty, though, probably, Peewee said.

—Like what.

—Just making talk, Ed.

—He seemed content?

—Bunch of crap there: saggy cartons, old clothes. Office chair. Broom handle, jar of Skippy . . .

—He was using the restroom at Tastee-Freez, Sheryl said.

—Who doesn't.

—Yeah, but a full sink-wash.

—You don't know that.

—Johnnie loves that place. He gets the vanilla with that shell. Cherry dip.

—Well those are fucking great.

—The point is, Ed, I'm up there a lot and I know. A ratty little wreck; damp clothes. And you can tell he tried to blow out his do with the hot air dryer.

—Put it into hock. It's an old man's piece. Worth something *real*; if you know what you're looking at. He went in there. Buy & Sell. One in Benson. Had the watch on and then he didn't. I go in after he's gone; wasn't in the window yet. Got fifty for it. Worth a hundred. Maybe two, Clarence said, and he raised his wrist up and winked at me with that weather-beaten eye of his.

—Barefoot. Right down the goddam sidewalk. Some dirty-ass feet, almost black. He was with that big fucker in brown. Even I wouldn't step up to that, Johnnie said.

—Owes on a month. Minimum, Ed. So no I ain't seen him else I'd kick him in his little ass. Said Dill's cousin Sylvia.

And I tore from my bank book—the one with the pastel cattle on them—a sizable check.

—You look like shit, said Lemon, turning around her cigarette to show me a tarry filter.

Well as you can imagine after that-all, my worry over him became a whole-hog one. And despite my being greatly re-duced, I became dead-committed to getting myself back up to health—bootstrapping my way into it—tracking down the sad little fucker and nudging him from the poor path he had set himself upon.

That much I would see to, one way or another. I had let go of the reins, and it was high time to course-correct. I had a commission. And knowing this, my heart surged. A sacred duty. I felt a weight lift and a power return, and some of the illness recede—such is the power of quests bestowed.

Anyway, what the kid needed, I had decided, was some-thing to cut through all of this low-rent gravity and run-of-the-mill ghoulishness. A new direction.

What he needed was some fun.

—You old fool, Chantal said.

—Never you mind, I said back to her.

I knew what was required. And it was given to me—only me—to remedy it all, knowing as I did how the story could go—and I would therefore rack the balls on the table, cheat-ing a bit, putting the nine ball tight on the corner, such that a simple and decent outcome could be arrived at right off the break.

Of course I'd have to find him first.

Nevertheless it took a full five days until I was back to nor-mal and over my sick—once more a walking, talking, pro-ductive citizen of the world. And on my very first day out of

the trailer, I did find the kid, right away, so it was, after all
that, in fact, very easy. My first job back. He was out front
of the chapel where the show was.

Just over there, on the front lawn like he belonged—with a
bedroll, camped out—which cheesed me, being as I had earlier paid his rent up. He lay on the patchy ground, an old back-
pack in his lap, legs crossed at the ankles, back propped against
the wood post of a sign:

FIRST BAP TIST. PARKING

RES ERVED FOR P ASTOR.

WHOEVER STOLE OUR AC-UNIT : KEEP IT.

IT'S HO T WHER E YOU ARE GOIN G

MATTH EW 13:3 0

—I settled you up with Sylvia, I said to the kid, no
preamble.

—Thanks.

—It wasn't anything, but you have a home and you should
go live in it.

—Yup.

—Ok well, I'll take you back after this job is done.

—Sounds fine, Ed.

—Or, we could, after . . . I don't know. Listen: what you
like to do?

He got up to standing so easy I was jealous of it.

He then pulled on an ear for a bit.

—I mean, do you have regular activities? I said.

—You seen 'em, he said, meaning work I suppose.

—Hungry?

———

I took him to Edna's. We did that.

—Special on the day? I said.

—Same as ever, Edna said, which I knew but it was a routine to ask.

Everything at Edna's did taste the same and only like the griddle and pans of theirs, not washed all that often, if at all, and so the daily special was everything they'd ever cooked all at once.

—Hotcakes, hot sandwiches, cold sandwiches, burger, dog, tamale, hash, steak, baked ham, spare ribs, beef, pork, fried chicken, pie, more pie, short stack and the other, grits, sunnysidescrambleovereasy, enchiladas, chili beans, franks and beans, cheese fries . . .

He ate like a madman and that food went down faster than a fat child on a seesaw.

Full-up, hazy, we hit a flick.

I will say it had been a while since I'd been to a theater, which is not because I don't enjoy them but because these days the pictures are so goddam loud that the entire experience feels more assault than entertainment and perhaps everyone is as bereft of hearing as they are of feeling and what does it take these days to simply *get by*? So we went to the place with the too-grandiose title of the Grande Orpheum, which was in fact a small, threadbare place with few seats and where the screen is warped and dim and the sound is mild and underwater.

During, I looked over at the kid from time to time to see if he was getting into the spirit, but he just sat there, sucking on a pailful of something that sizzled and smelled like cough syrup.

He nodded out from time to time, and when awake, his face held no expression, not even at movie's end where all the action and emotion was, though I did hear an unusual amount of sniffling and hitched breathing from the eight other moviegoers in the audience.

Then we walked like blind men out onto the street and then were back in the truck. I took us both to the Elks where the brethren had a game up and running.

They were wary. Bart, Samuel, Skip. All on guard. Especially Lew—former oilman and my one-time gambling sponsor (we play for quarters, which was methadone to us)— who seemed like he was going to tell me to take the kid and leave, but didn't and surprisingly, it all turned out ok, though it was also more vulgar than our usual game nights, also: stupider, angrier . . . in other words the kid was present and whatever was felt was duly felt.

It took some years off me, and I felt proud to have the boy there by my side as if he were my own.

To the Crown then, and when we got there the weepers were keeping two booths warm. Sheryl and Dill and Johnnie and Chantal and Francine the nurse seemed in a warm-hearted spirit or drunk or both, and so floated the idea of the dance, down Town Hall, where even we old, dignified dudes were eventually shoved onto the line and were carried in the slipstream of it, driven purely by some cumulative life force, taking how many steps forward and however many steps back, turning round and slapping our boots and so on. Then Chantal danced right up against me. Gadzooks. Then people took turns up at the mic to sing old favorites up there with the backing band.

Kid wasn't having anything to do with any of it, and I imagine that if he were to ever hit the floor it would be to shuffle like a pallbearer; and if he were to ever grab a mic it would be only to recite a complete list of the Confederate dead.

I drove him back to the B&G. On the way he asked me a question. Perhaps the day had loosened him. What he came out with was:

—You ever worry about your face.

—What the hell's wrong with my face? I said.

But alone again, puzzling over it, I suddenly remembered that when I was a boy and I'd be in the company of somebody, I'd be anxious that I'd start having the same face on as they did, like, as if I didn't have any natural face of my own. And people would see me doing that—being like that—and think I was making fun and being a smart-ass. Huh.

He nodded and popped out, as usual, without a goodbye. I didn't care. I then stopped off at Chantal's. She answered the door in that Chinese robe.

Next morning I was camped at the window of her place, looking out at the scorched plains.

—Chantal, you ever worry about what expression is on your face?

—Shut the blinds, she moaned. Then she rolled over.

Later, when she was awake again, I said:

—The land is dry, Chantal.

—What?

—Dry, I repeated.

—What? she said again.

—Dry. The land is—

—Idiot, she said, sitting up in the bed, now more or less awake.

—Morning to you too.

—You do not wish to see me in this light.

I lowered the blind a bit, blurry striping her bed.

I notice the sill's dust, an old fly, legs up like a wire brush.

—You look beautiful, any light, I said absently.

—Then what did you say about my face?

I thought of the delicate wrinkles under her lids, peppered with dried makeup.

—Where did all the rain go, I said, rueful.

I heard her slough off the bedding and walk to the mirror.

—I have memories of it, I said.

I added one more cigarette to the flotilla in my coffee.

—Hey, I said, meaning to ask whether I should summon us some Mexican breakfast, but a door had clicked closed. The shower ran in the bathroom for a while, then I heard her flush, run the hair dryer for a minute or two, heard the door click open, then she flumped back onto the mattress.

I squinted still, into the light. Nothing budging in the field.

Congregation of rigs, heads bowed. Hadn't moved in years.

Then the quick snick of a match being struck behind me, and an almost silent sizzle of tobacco.

—Come back to bed. Let me see if you are used up, she said.

CELEBRATION OF LIFE

He had jumped ship again, and so I spent my time on puttering and cowboy poetry and nothing to show for either thing.

When next I did see him, the situation was, to say the least: unencouraging. I drove out to Canaan because of what Peewee had said, and he was indeed loitering alone outside the old steel plant.

—Just look at you, I said.

He seemed exhausted, limp as old lettuce. Also he smelled just terrible.

—Have any cash, is what he said.

He had his shirt off under the mourning jacket; ribs like a radiator. So I drove him back to Edna's.

She came with menus then stopped.

—Not him. He doesn't eat here, she said.

—Edna, what the fuck. He can't, I won't, I said, standing for show.

—Ok then git.

I made him a sandwich back at the mobile.

—I'm making you a sandwich, I said. (I thought of saying "Alakazam, you are a sandwich," but remembered he did not laugh never, and may not have known what a joke even was.)

After eating he slept on the cot I had handy, and eventually I slept too, and whoa Nelly but that night I had another bed-wetting look-in from Pop which affected me for days after, blending with that creeping sense of not-quite-yet-exploded ordnance about the area.

This is the cost of his wondrous acts, I pronounced to my coffee pot, spatula, ashtray, and lucky horseshoe. And, as the man said: "there is nothing done that does not have its opposite done because of that." (Something to that effect.)

It was good fortune then that I found that Plan B quick.

It came to me the next morning in my bathroom, and it came out of nowhere. And it was a decent Plan B, one that would surely help him get straight. Why hadn't I thought of it sooner?

A local gal I knew, name of Belinda, who worked at Joan Hamady's as a junior shopgirl. I set it in motion, cleaned him up, showed him how to brush his suit and shoes. I told him where to go, where to be, and when. He did just that. And it all took so little; passive as a little child.

They went out the once, and only the once (lead a horse

to water, etc.). I don't know (well, I don't precisely know) what went wrong there, but something did for sure.

Then a different one.

I introduced him to a lady I knew worked down at Sepulse County Correctional. After the first date, she reported back that she was reassessing—planned on leaving work at the prison to enter a general studies program she had seen advertised in the *Pennysaver*. It was, she said, *high time she got back in touch with herself.* This was a lady with a thousand-yard stare; one who told me up at the Crown, deadeye, that she once saw a woman in the joint beat another woman to death with a barbell.

Frustrating, sure. Sure. And I was concerned the kid might lose patience though (if, that is, he ever had patience, or lack thereof, or any decipherable feelings whatsoever). But he didn't let on. So.

The next I suggested on his behalf was the young woman, the Sanchez one, that stock girl from the Bow & Gun, whose parents used to live near me out by the mobiles. The girl who seemed excited for a setup until I said who it was exactly, and then she said she had seen the kid, naturally as he lived right above her place of employment, and she was not interested in *no muppet-ass crybaby*, and I quote.

(I won't even mention that whole thing went down when I set him up with that boy from over Benson. Let's just expunge that one permanently from the records.)

So all of those strikeouts and it probably served me right.

But as I've said I am nothing if not constant, and so persisted; my next stab at it being the most ingenious. A particularly crafty idea, the first step of which was to visit my cousin Geraldine, who I hadn't seen in years.

Geraldine'd been lacking for company in the almost two decades since her husband passed (and the several years since her daughter moved out), so me dropping in got her grinning like a baked ham, and she was especially pleased when she saw I'd brought the beers. We pitched up two gossipy chairs in back of the double-wide, cracked the tallboys, and, surrounded by the campers congregated there, caught up about what was left of our local family. After which she began—as I knew she would, without any leading whatsoever—bragging about her Cyndi, still the apple of her eye.

I have only one enduring memory of Cyndi, and that was from when she was just a child, and it was one of the few times (outside of my Granddad's thing) when the whole extended family gathered, albeit grudgingly, and it was for some uncle of mine's service.

If I try to recall anything about her—the then-little girl—now, all I can summon was that towhead of hers, those prematurely pierced lobes, and her strangely inappropriately happy grimace, hovering only just a few inches above the pew as I looked grim death at her. Her mom told her to turn back around.

Who grins like that at a goddam funeral?

Here's the kicker: I knew (this part being the heart of my clever strategy) Cyndi now applied this very same serial and demented chipperness to her professional life. Meaning that she was one of those folks who are hired for celebrations: plants, who get you out on the dance floor of whatever event needs perking up. A "motivator" they are called. And I suppose, like us weepers, they are very much in need, as what events need perking up now is most events.

————————————————————

So Cyndi was a pump-up girl.

Motivation was not so much calling for Cyndi as it was the inevitable result of a defining incident from her youth, in which she caught sight of a televised ballet number up on one of the public channels. To say that the performance she saw then made an impression would be an enormous understatement, and though I don't know much about little girls, if I know anything, it is that they can take to dancing like they are chasing a drug high, and those sweet little fiends will ride this desire all the way to damnation if necessary.

In any case, seeing all that ceremony on the tube—the long limbs, swan necks, those bright accessories, not to mention the pallid gravity on the faces of the dancers—sent her to the full-length mirror hung askew on the back of her bedroom door. She strained up onto her toes, then lifted a leg, experimentally, put it back down again. She bent her knees, let her tush fall a bit, stood again, raised up her arms into an arch above her head, sucked in her cheeks . . .

This then became a routine, and in turn this routine was the gateway to weekly dance lessons; such classes bringing on more rigorous training, which, by the time she was a true teen, her mom could no longer afford. The belt-tightening led to the public school cheer squad, which she captained, which led to, after graduation, her dancing during the seventh-inning stretch under the lights at the local Triple-A affiliate. This led first to plantar fasciitis and then to a knee rupture, which led to an unaffordable surgery and rehab, a rehab which could not be completed because it couldn't be paid for either; which led to her working part time at the Big Box and a bout of cavernous depression, which led to drink, which led to huffing whatever was at hand, and then, for a very brief period, ingesting stronger medicines, which would have led to that shiny pole up onstage at the Stallion Club on State 57, but instead led to a particular self-help title on Aisle 4 (Stationery and Paperbacks), the wisdom therein leading her, inch by inch, back to a modicum of self-worth, which led to studying up on popular dance tutorials online, which led to her teaming up with a local dance crew, which, in turn, led to even more confidence and a few contacts in the world of local entertainment, which led to, at her mother's urging, Cyndi showing up—shy but game—for a call at the party planners in downtown Stanville.

She had lived much of her life up to that point in spandex, her single-mindedness showed, and so she was hired on the spot. She became a motivator, and a motivated one at that.

Geraldine took a breath here from the origin story, and I took that opportunity to cluck in approval on Cyndi's behalf. I thought that she hadn't varnished any of the tough bits for me, but was clearly proud of her girl who had, just like Geraldine herself, come through storms unbowed. The telling of this took time, lasted through another several drinks, pizza rolls from the trailer's nuke. The sky above the RVs had turned creamsicle by the time she took that break, and then, as I caught her up on me, which was a briefer affair (though she interrupted at one point to rehash that whole story of woe that went down with my mom and dad, which I had to nod along to, but which I had known would be part of the fee I'd pay for this visit; an exorbitant fee, the other part being me telling her about my health situation—family is family), the sky became blue and morose, and it then was time to heave-ho. But not without securing Cyndi's new number first.

On the drive back I thought: Shit. *Motivation*.

You think forcing yourself sad is hard, try making yourself happy.

Then I thought about the thrall which the kid seemed to cast on every last person he met, and hoped Cyndi would be equal to it.

———————————

And thus it was on Wednesday I took the kid home from a job, and there was the girl herself, just as I arranged it. Kid gave me a rare look, meaning one that had some feeling to it (it was a petulant one).

Ambush!

Flawless teeth, blond braid like a bullwhip, the threateningly merry eyes of a suicide cultist, single hip cocked to the side, elbow jutted from it.

Kid stepped down from the cab, and she—without introduction, prompting, or observation of social niceties—leapt for him, bouncing on her pom-pom-ed heels, and kissed his blooming, terrified cheek; oblivious to his timidity, or just determined to push past it.

Damn, corralling sullen folks into a line dance must have come like second nature to her, I thought, watching. All that vim just soda-popping through her veins. She was perky as all get-out. Formidably perky.

Detaching herself, she finally seemed to register me, bursting into an almost impossible, wider grin.

—Hey there, Cousin Ed!

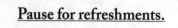

Pause for refreshments.

ON HIGH

". . . out in the hills, just find if

you can . . ."

—"The Old Frying Pan," traditional cowboy poem

In the ensuing days it seemed—if I had been reading the signs correctly—that this setup of mine was a sweeping goddam success. I didn't know this firsthand, being lousy and bedridden once more, but given the reports from the Local 302 intelligence community: him and her were seen on the town and always in each other's company.

I'd picture it. Doing all normal things normal young people normally do. Her: psychotically merry, eager as a cork in a popgun. Him: free of his strange burdens, some color in his cheeks, funerary shoes tied up right in generous loops, lighter in them, him warming to the world and those who dwell in it, a real future ahead, him knowing that.

These tableaux of mine then brought on another image, mushy-ass, and it was an image of a family—if a patchwork one—me, presiding pappy . . . like at a county fair where

Chantal is struggling to hoist some oversized purple gorilla I'd won her through being the crack shot (which I, in fact, am), kids' caramel-sticky hands welded together behind us under the cotton-candy eventide . . . Jesus Q-Lamb-of-God, but what an insufferably sentimental thing—this confederation of misfits, our nuclear unit. But the important thing was that, in my mind, there was no conceivable vision of their future without me in it.

Until he and Cyndi went "up in the hills." *Poof.*

Up in the hills.

And I naturally felt a great soreness about him leaving to "the hills," as who knew if he'd ever be back, and I'd never been to a county fair without having ended up in the dunk tank.

Of course they would continue their courtship without me. As is right. I may be a ramshackle old gooch but I know when I'm not the main act. That-all had nothing to do with me anymore.

But I will admit to curiosity.

I knew nothing, nothing whatsoever about how it was all playing out; I didn't know if the chemistry was there, and if so, was it a good chemistry, successful and such, or if it was maybe a volatile one. And let me say volatile can either be good volatile or bad volatile. Which was it? Dunno.

I didn't know, but I thought about it.

(And I should mention that Geraldine would call to inquire, and I could feel the worry rising in her; my conscience rising up quick to meet that worry.)

—How you think they are getting on?

—Let it go, said Dill.

Ok, and I understood his point of view on this but picture if you will (speaking on chemistry) one of those men of science who, having just dreamed up some test or other that could resolve some important and age-old problem, one we all needed an answer to (like: what do we do about polio?), imagine him being barred from seeing the results of his own experiments? You'd think that state of affairs would drive him completely looney toons.

That wasn't me of course. Believe it. I was *curious*, but *only* curious, and as I said, *curious* in a *normal* way, meaning that I wasn't *too* curious and wasn't going overboard with *being curious* and with that (*regular-sized*) curiosity of mine. I wasn't going to pry or snoop.

A little thanks would've been welcome, for making the introduction between the two of them; the setup.

That's all. Something. You'd think. Right?

Youth.

All of them. The young. Those total dipshits.

The lack of gratitude is simply baked in.

Everything comes at them ripe and ready. And the whole goddam world proffers its soil, moisture—its fruits, that is— with such stupid generosity, with so little dignity, that it comes across as a neediness, the neediness of a fawning parent, and so the whole shebang, that generosity-slash-neediness, is something to be ignored, sulked about, or rejected outright. The very idea of youth taking advantage of the world's bigheartedness—of those absolute jokers accepting (tolerating even) such a bounty, a bounty they should be reveling in, the gift, in particular, of youth itself!—is a fuckery, and will not ever happen, not ever, will not be seen to be happening, not in this generation of young idiots, nor the next, not in any other generation, so on.

And naturally there is nothing an old person like me can do about any of this, the way of it, and it is no use giving council to jackasses; it will make you mad from thwarting—from the rejection of hard-got wisdom.

The good news was, at that moment there I was feeling well again (more or less), and that was lucky because Hector Knox was shorthanded down at his ranch and I was trying hard to put the kid from my mind. I had several days there of handling his broncos for distraction's sake (and because I love doing so). Not to say that this wasn't hard work. But not hard in the same way weeping is, and those majestic, lip-flapping beauties of his acted upon me to some extent the way (what they call) service animals would, in that they helped keep my fretfulness and gloom at manageable levels.

That they did. Though not entirely. The dolefulness would creep back in, and I did wonder how large the kid's broadcasting range was, and if perhaps some of his work could reach all the way to me, out there on that dusty ranch; so far on the periphery that the signal would have to come through busted-walkie-talkie-style, where you only catch five words at a time before the static takes over. Maybe it did extend all that way; from "up in the hills" to "down in the plains."

Which is to admit the truth of it, which was, distractions aside, I still missed him badly.

Whenever I'd be in town, pretty much any part of it, but especially anywhere near that Bow & Gun, I'd have my peepers out for those lovers, the young mortician and his cheerleader.

Dill was as good a companion as a man could want, and he came around a bunch, did his bit to cheer me, or try to. He and me had been together and doing more or less the same activities and having more or less the same chatter since we were seventeen, since we spent our time out in the culvert living on jerky, throwing rocks at other, bigger rocks. Clinging to railway trestles and feeling that thunder above, me spending an increasing amount of time out of the house then, for the usual reasons, those being Dad . . .

Those reasons being Dad because, in my teenage years, my family suffered an ugly succession of misfortunes.

My father ceased being a (real) cowboy as soon as we lost the ranch (though he continued to fancy himself one), but cowboy or no, after the foreclosure he took whatever job he could find, landing finally on insurance, meaning he sold it. Sold policies to dry cleaners, quick-service food operations, down-market rodeos, landscapers, strip clubs, pool maintenance firms, bowling lanes, lube joints, moving companies, wrecking crews, pawn shops, lumberyards, sewage removal, taxidermists, pest control outfits, massage parlors, go-cart tracks, gas stations, brick-facers, drive-ins, to the barbers and the ladies' hairdo spots, the spirits vendors, pet groomers, general contractors, karate dojos . . . whatever small-business interests managed to stick it out through the long drought and downturn, the same one that forced him off his land.

He did not love his new life, it's safe to say, as it is safe to say that risk assessment and liability were not the subjects of his childhood dreams. Horses and cattle were the subjects of those dreams, and the thwarting of them—the daily defeat of unattainable desires—accounted for the serious mean he had on him (the drink accounted for that as well), and by the time I was ten he could be red-faced and despicable all the way from breakfast through bed (we rarely saw him at dinner, but sometimes, late, when I was already tucked in, I'd hear that stammering tread and wince). His unpleasantness was rank: a herd in the parlor, trampling and snorting, squeezing the rest of us into tight places, or flat out of the room.

Then the next drought. And the next slump. A further depression, which was going to happen one way or another, shy of what the insurance people—like my dad once was— would call a Force Major (from Chantal: *Force Ma-joor*), meaning a marvel, or act of God.

Everything blighted, including those local concerns, and therefore, so too the selling of insurance. Money then, always hard for us, became a desperate need, and notices began appearing—first in the mail and then upon the door—at the new place we rented in town.

Then came the death of my mother's sister out east from cancer in her uterus, and then her parents following not long after. And next, as a result of everything combined, such mounting losses, came my mother's discovering Christ.

This was completely out of nowhere, and calamitous. Calamitous for two reasons, one of which was that it drove a wedge between her and me, as though she had newly birthed— and then favored—a whole other son. Soon after, she ceased reading books—once her daily bread—gave up reading them to herself, and reading them to her (true) son, just as she gave up all of those wonderful and various words she tendered to me and only for my benefit. "Impassive." "Wan." "Burnish." "Epitaph." "Susurration." "Cumulative." "Staccato . . ." All language, that is, that wasn't dictated by the Lord.

She also ceased using that sweet voice that she addressed me with, and she opted instead, in my case, for a more disappointed sounding one, as if I was beyond hope.

When had I got beyond hope? I thought.

I had, by then, begun to recognize that when she spoke in that new delivery of hers, she was not in fact speaking to me at all, but to those, generally, who had not, and never would, see the holy light (the condemned, the squirrels, the detergent, the porch, the desert, the sky, the dead).

The second real calamity was that her newfound path mightily antagonized my father, who had always stored up and slung trademarked nastihoods at the faithful, whose ways and manners he took as a personal affront as if they were leveling accusations. And so he would spout off about those who would so collude in mockery of him.

—Hell's better than church.

It was just another symptom of his malice of course. And just as Mom became "raised up," his degradation metastasized into true hate, and he became even more "lowered down." Barely seemed possible then. Though by now, at my age here, I've seen that there's always room in a body for more poison to drink.

He started then to turn up in all kinds of places where he had no business being. He was found in the town dump. He was found asleep in a parked bus he had broke into. He was found inside the car wash on the drag, the one with colorful, riffling little flags. They had almost turned the machines on—the hard, hot bristles, that steaming rubber octopus—before someone saw him curled up down there.

Several times he passed out in a public park and quite a few times ended in lockup.

On a few of these occasions, we were the ones finding him after his marauding. Those were the lucky times.

Mom always cleaned him up after—her expression more satisfied than ever—a look of blushing contentment as she scoured him top to bottom in the tub. This opportunity for greater sacrifice and martyrdom. It puts me in mind now of the kid, lying as he did in the dark street after his beating, and how, despite or because of his wounds, he looked at me like a person fulfilled.

And so we maintained. Maintained through that whole year, until the new minister took over at the church over on Holland: a church which my mother was then just beginning to attend. That's what finally did for us. The start of it, anyway.

We found out about the new minister on the day me and Dad came home early from hunting. My father had expended all his rounds into the dirt and air, having missed every living thing, missed because the sun was too fierce and Dad was too unsteady. He was already in a dark state on the drive home, and I was treated to short bursts of well-rehearsed invective about who exactly should be blamed for his ill fortune, his conclusions on this matter having nothing to do with he himself, but rather focused on a blurry band of cutthroats, teat-suckers, and layabouts who fully intended to rob him blind of everything he had, loved, and, most important, was owed—him being owed everything from his rifle to his undershorts, his commemorative coin collection, his bolo, his brown liquors, slurs and spurs, his gasoline, his Black & Milds, his pomade, the hitch in his stride, the deed on the old ranch . . . At heart, this "owed to him" was mostly (what he saw as) his position at the top of the pile—this bit coming in direct contravention of another lecture of his concerning the importance of *initiative*, an initiative he never showed a lick of himself—a lecture I would entitle Get-Off-Your-Ass, or Where's-My-Fucking-Beer—and why anyone as trainwrecked and delinquent as my dad should be owed a single cent for his lousiness was hard to square. But of course I never said anything about that as it went on and on and on, and eventually we pulled into the driveway. As we entered the house on that day, I heard the muted cadence of pleasant conversation, a thing as strange to hear—as out of place in my home—as hearing an ocean lapping gently at the front yard.

The minister was sitting down to a soda with my mother in our kitchen.

Or rather, he was rising quickly as we entered—in the manner in which polite men might, when caught out alone with a woman. Pushing the chair away, backing up a tick. He even stuck his hands up and pumped his palms, smiling, as if to say "whoa there," a gesture I knew he was unaware of performing.

—I'm Reverend Monroe. I was just telling Eileen about our new ministry.

I'd thought to wonder if I'd ever seen a black man in our house before, but looking at one stood there, I became damned sure I had not.

Dad looked perplexed; truly taken aback. The world took a breath.

—Come join us, my mother said, patting the seat beside her.

But my father's look had shifted. And he looked suddenly, dangerously amused.

He gave a dry laugh, and said:

—It's so kind of you to look in after my wife.

—James was just telling me about his work overseas, said my mother, overly quick.

—James? said my dad, eyes of slits.

I felt then the release of something bitter and cold.

I spun around without anyone even noticing. Went out the front door, and the wind closed it behind me such that I involuntarily jumped over the three steps down to the pavement. I started off east.

I found myself at Dill's. Dill and I ended up going to the minimart for sno-cones and snappers and then went to the parking lot to expend our ammunition. I wasn't home again until the evening. When I did get there, I headed straight for the stairs so as to make safe ground.

My father's voice cannoned out at me from the living room.

—Where is your ma, it said, and I knew this as demand, not question.

So I searched the house, and then went back into the darkening streets and visited the neighbors but she wasn't anywhere. I came home again—empty-handed—and luckily Dad was then asleep on the couch, his back hunched toward me. I took off my sneakers and finally got to my room.

The next day I learned Mom had been at the clinic in town. Dad was by then and as usual: God-knows-where. But there was Mom, back in the kitchen, humming something and wiping down the counter.

She turned and I saw.

A week later, she returned there to that church on Holland. This was willfully unwise. But it was an expression of hope, and at least someone in that disfigured family of mine was drawn to consecrated places.

———————————

Of course there was an aftermath. Another one. A bigger one. And I have decided to let that-all happen offstage, and I certainly don't intend to continue making a big federal-style case out of it. That is just the same old, same old, recounted many times over so there's no news in it, and who gives one dry fart. Except for one aspect of the smackings-around (Mom's, mine), which is this: the sympathy which I feel toward Dad—a prime example of that overdeveloped compassion I have been referring to throughout this whole deal, that is, the ability (need, even) to inhabit the shoes of another. This goes for even wearing the shoes of the antagonist, and such shoe-borrowing can be kleptomania, that is: a disease.

And I'm not saying I forgive. No. I am sure I do not. But anger and resentment do not prohibit my exploring my father's corroded heart, and finding in myself if not love, then some understanding of the hateful engine that drove him.

So: like that.

And thus, despite the unseemliness I feel around it all (which, given that I am a card-carrying commiserative must seem odd, and believe me when I say I do feel embarrassed, and worry that these stories of my youth are, like my poems, too maudlin, even for me: a very duke of mawkishness), begging your permission, I will tell some more of it (if only a little).

Only one more instance, that is, and this was the one when Dad hit me in front of Mom, and because of Mom, and how I did not hit back, and how that—as it were—set a tone.

————————————

I was a little older then—must have been around seventeen—when one day I got an invitation from my teen associate

Marvin Grosvenor, saying that his cousin owned a car which Marvin had been given to borrow, such that we could drive up with Dill to the dog track out in Coolidge.

We did that.

We spent the day there at the dogs, lost some money and won some and lost it again, and after, we had gone to the culvert to shoot our mouths off and shotgun beers.

I had come home pretty late, but it wasn't a thing as Dad was out and Mom had her choir practice. But the following morning, I heard the phone ring and could hear through the floorboards the indistinct sounds of my mother's voice, and hear the pauses between her speaking become longer, and then hear the pitch drop to something lower and more serious. I began to fret. When I came downstairs she told me that Marvin's mother, Mrs. Grosvenor, had called. Turned out the vehicle we took had not belonged to Marvin's cousin, but indeed had been Mrs. Grosvenor's own, and that it had not been so much borrowed as hijacked, and that Marvin, when confronted with evidence of his crimes, had spilled the beans on me and Dill, not just for the joyride but the gambling, the beers, etc., that total rat. And as I stood there under the kitchen's exceedingly bright lights, captive to a litany of my transgressions, I considered the notion that I'd rather be slapped around than see my mother so dispirited in me.

—Shame on you, is what she said.

And I felt it.

That hot shroud of shame.

Still, I found myself muttering, as fatigue and hangover began to encroach upon reason, as if someone else had got hold of my vocal cords (and shame-heat being so proximate to anger-heat):

—It's none of your business, Mom.

(Shame: redoubled.)

It was at that moment that Dad walked in.

—What'd you just say to your mother? he said.

—Nothing, I said.

—Wasn't nothing.

—Didn't mean it.

I stayed still and quiet.

My mother made some small noise.

—Fuck no, he said to her, and she did not say nor do a thing.

Then turning toward me and stepping up closer he whispered:

—What you got, boy.

I looked at the floor, saying, quietly as I could:

— . . .

And the fist hit me on the right cheek .

When I successfully got to my feet again, the thing of it was—not pain, but—the feeling of skin on skin. What I mean to say here is that the punch was shattering, yes, like all the others—I don't think he touched me ever except to hit me— but shattering because of how intimate it was. I had smelled his breath and seen the individual bristles on his chin, the marbling of his eyes, the birthmark above his brow. It felt (I am embarrassed to say it) almost romance-like. A shared secret.

Skin on skin. The rough, hairy ridge of that man's knuckles meeting my smooth cheek.

He swung again, but I had put my arm up, and so it was

more of a glancing thing, and then a grapple, which increased our congress to an unbearable level as I could feel the ambient warmth coming off him, his scent and sweat, hear his heavy snorts.

I pushed away and stood up fully.

—You want more, he said, but gasping.

I realized at that moment—with the fast and fierce intelligence of a furry thing cornered—that if I were to punch back I would score a few hits of my own, more than a few, and good ones, as I was by then big and strong enough, which I think he, in that wild moment, clocked as well, because he looked even angrier then, squared up as if he could have well and truly killed me. And I believe he could have (and maybe would go so far as to say definitely would have), had he had something to swing at me then, anything at all instead of his bare hands. And I don't mean that extension cord or that belt he favored, but if he had:

. . . a coffee cup or a beer bottle or a pipe or the bronze statue on our mantel of the man riding the bucking horse which was a regional insurance award which he had—way back, somehow, and against all reason—won, or one of the two table lamps, or a claw hammer, or a chair, or the TV remote, or one of his guns, or a kettle, or the fire poker, or the phone receiver, or a loose doorknob, or a tire iron, a paperweight, a letter opener, a kitchen knife, a bowling ball, a rake, that old rail spike he kept as a memento of some prelapsarian age, a rolling pin, a crowbar, a baseball bat, a broom handle, a can of soup . . .

That is: I used to do such an inventory of the house, tracking items in it according to their potential use as weaponry.

But though I could see him look around quick (milk carton, dish towel, cigarette pack . . .), he had nothing to hand, and so I was able to duck and slip around him and be out of the kitchen, him shouting hellfire after me, before something further could happen, and I know now that I ran, not because I didn't think I could take him, because I could have, but simply wanted that whole sick, combative closeness to end.

That day of (what was to be) his final attempt on me, as I ran from the house, I looked over my shoulder, but did not see my mother through the diminishing doorway, though caught a momentary sight of *him*, red-faced but also: wet-eyed . . . and I brood over this detail, the detail of the wet eyes, and these eyes have become almost like an emblem of the whole event, a sign for it, the thing it strangely comes wrapped in. That is, when I think back on it, shuddering, I dwell upon his wet eyes.

Those wet eyes, though, I'll think. Those wet eyes.

So I had run. And spent the whole day away from my home, and it turned out that fortune was watching over me careful and considerate, as Dad had become so drunk later that he was sick all the next day as well as the day after that and did not come out of bed, and of course I didn't peek in there neither but kept my distance, and another day went by and Mom wasn't around either; she was with the Reverend Monroe, healing, confessing, atoning, doing whatever it was she did.

And Dad, he left the next week and never came back to live with us again.

(Though he did, in fact, visit the house one last, terrible time.)

<u>Pass the collection plate.</u>

A HOLE LEFT IN OUR HEARTS

Son of man, can these bones live? . . . Dry bones,
hear the word of the Lord!
—Ezekiel 37:4

Would the kid return?

Way back when we lived on our family ranch, one
of the hands owned a dog. She was one of those smiley, ram-
bunctious old gals, wiggling as she went, thumping up against
you (even when she got arthritic and seemed more sawhorse
than hound); following a person around until she affixed to
another man and then back again, looking up, side-tongued,
wet-eyed . . . but the point is that I remember, after she
passed, there was a period in which I would be—not exactly
looking down for her—but extra conscious of the area just
below my knees. Making sure—without knowing I was doing so—not to step on any phantom paws.

Which isn't to say that the kid had been tagging along at
my heels—it was always the other way around: where he

went, so went-eth Ed—but that after he left, at the beginning anyway, I'd pause a beat before hitting the ignition on my truck, as if waiting for him to hop in on the passenger side. Or I'd do a quick scan of the pews at one of those services, after I returned to working again.

So a routine of any kind is (obviously) a physical thing as well as mental, and the hardest part to shake is the part your body has down pat. By the time something is truly on automatic, it becomes clear as day that you are not one person but two: the one who makes a decision to do or feel a thing, and the one who does or feels a thing without you being wise to it until afterward.

Dill, despite his help, had also made it known that he did not condone my preoccupation there, and in this he was just like Rev, and it is amazing to me that when your closest—your road hogs and bosom pals—inform you of a flaw you possess, the same complaint from each of them, you can somehow still manage to be deaf to it all.

There was Chantal of course, and that particular manner in which she and me were.

But we were also, like Dill and me, bound up by our sadness. Being together brought some of that sadness to heel, but it is also the case that two low-grade sorrows may become more than the sum of their parts (as come a darkening evening when the birds chorus the day's final sobs).

Even if that wasn't the case, there'd be no cheering me. I was destined to be on the outside from the kid and his doings—as was right, as was right; I still maintain. But it hurt such that I thought in moments I should go up into the hills as well, scour them, and if he was gone from those, I'd comb the deserts, search the cities of the plains, all the wide-over, and do so until he was located. And in those times what was best was not the company of other people, but rather finding things to occupy my attention: like replacing my water pump, scraping my dishes, buying some new antifreeze (that name being a joke for a coolant), taking my old broken outdoors armchair to the dump, to simply sitting on my steps with a sixer, and smoking from my sawn-in-two cigarette pack. And those were only short respites.

It was when I was at work—standing in the lot, avoiding the gang's solicitous looks, treated with a new and unwelcome delicacy, in my unpronounced and eerie exile; subbed, on the bench, waiting for that young man to call me back onto the field—that I truly felt the labor of my heart. Not that I let on to everyone—and as my mother used to say about our old, broke-down home—"it's too poor to paint and I am too proud to whitewash."

MOURN/REJOICE

Rejoice and mourn with those who
rejoice and mourn.
—Romans 12:15

Yet even with this gloom laid atop my usual one, I understood that the hills were probably in the boy's best interests. Good for him for leaving the path. Hadn't this been something I had said? "You sure you want this?" I had indeed warned him off—check the records. In my unselfish moments, I hoped the two of them up there—in a lean-to, tent, motel, trailer, in possession of their first un-pay-down-able mortgage; the embodiment of happy and the bringer of misery—would rub off on one another. Maybe even cancel each other out.

And when I thought this, it brought on a compensatory pride. My scheme had worked.

Ed, you glorious bastard. You've really done something here!

What I felt was loss and hope both. Confidence and worry both (the worry came in low, more like a question, as when you're eating something good but every now and then, on the occasional bite, you taste it's riding that fine line between fresh and not so, the meal then includes "wondering" on the menu).

For a lifelong melancholic and irrepressible despondent, there is no truly—unqualified, unexpurgated—good feeling. But hey, even happy cut with sorrow is not so damn bad, let me tell you.

Lay tree-est playz-ears is what Chantal calls such mixed-up emotions—and specifically that means something like "the pleasure in the sad." She is more prone to speaking this way after we are close in a sex way, this being for her the feeling of *alone together*, and a decent example of such nice, if blended, sentiments.

Now, conversely, I've always felt my own form of this sweet melancholy when I am by myself—having learned the benefits of being alone as a child, out on walks in the desert or on the old ranchlands, or in the yard on the low, bent, and squeaky aluminum swings, my ass swinging just inches above a little muddy puddle. Or just in my room, door closed, Dad out at the bar or worse, me by myself with my thoughts and the small but ever-rising stack of books my mother pressed upon me.

But it was mostly up in the mesas and buttes.

I went out to the mesas and buttes for solace quite a bit in my youth, still do, and when out there I feel both unmolested by man and joined up with God (which is merely a saying for me and not a belief, mind).

And though as I aged I grew more and more worried—especially after the divorce—that I'd end up like one of those sheeted saints who spend their allotment up on tall pillars, it is also the truth that when I was truly solitary, when I could enjoy the freedom from having to feel anything in particular—meaning not need to follow the strong sway of any other person's thing, particularly those oversized ones like my dad's—I used to feel this time as a relief.

POETRY READING III

BUTTES AND MESAS

Out among arroyos, beneath the steepled skies,
a gray mule grunts and flicks his tail to swat away
    the flies.
He's all alone, there's nothing else reflected in his
    eyes
except the creek that once ran full and now is half
    its size.

E.F.

TESTIMONIAL

You can still see those very same buttes and mesas of my youth. See them easily—see them from the road.

But to really see them in all their glory you have to walk some ways off the asphalt. That's true for the rest of it as well: the dried riverbeds, gullies, hoodoos, and hogbacks. The sky you can see from anywhere, but deeper into the land, it becomes bluer, and the whole shebang becomes just stupidly scenic; like something a cartoon roadrunner would paint to outwit a cartoon coyote.

Meaning death might lurk behind every vista.

My father and I used to go out there together. The "together" being a concession to my mother. A concession granted bitterly and most often retributed upon me.

He'd hunt. Desert mule deer, mostly. He didn't say much to me on those trips. No life lessons. It was mostly us tramping around, him shooting, deer dropping, me bearing dumb witness.

Out among arroyos, beneath the steepled skies . . .

That line came to me once on a trip like that.

On that particular outing, Dad had been worse off than usual even, and when our car wove into the lot and stuttered into park, he listed over, hat falling. I turned the key from the passenger side. The engine pinged awhile. And then it was clear that he wasn't waking up anytime soon, so I got out and began to walk off into the scrub alone.

I walked and walked. The buttes came into focus. Up closer, they were ribbed, like a bunch of lady-giants gathering in their skirts (and I thought up that line then, about "giants" and their "skirts," for later use).

Anyway, back on that hike of mine, I was intent—as I often was—on trying to write something. I had been in church with my mother that morning, and was wanting to say something about the sanctity of the landscape I was then toiling through, and by the time the sun was all the way up I was sitting on a rock in the shadows of one of those behemoth formations, still trying to tie together those themes. I couldn't make it work.

Yet, that day, that time alone, without my dad's oppressive squint and without the silence-splintering gunshots, it did seem that the world had opened itself up before me, and though I couldn't wrangle that poem into anything usable, I was just full of metaphor.

As the sun moved, I moved with it, and I came eventually all the way up to touch the hem of that great butte, where I plopped on down again. Ate my lunch. Drank most of the powdered tea. Saw clouds complete a full passage. The shadow receded. I kept having to move to stay in it.

I wrote some more.

After a while, out in the scree, it occurred that if my

father hadn't woken, he'd be frying in the car, maybe dead. So I put my notebook away, hauled myself up, and went back. I was panting and half-dead myself by the time I got back to the lot.

Car was gone.

I walked home beside the highway—took the whole rest of the day, into evening to get there—tee tied above my charred brow, canteen empty, head swimming, hot metal shrieking past.

That night I had to sleep in a full bathtub, and the pain of those burns didn't subside for a long while.

One thing is but a stone's throw from another, someone once said—this, my shitty translation of that. I knew this from the memory of Dad's wet eyes: how they stirred an understanding in me, one that persisted even throughout the sorrow, anger, and regret.

And so I would think on the past, the way back: when the suit and tie were still new to my father. Think of kindnesses, strewn like a scant handful of seed. Memories of the view from his shoulders. A singalong. Being on our horses together. Before life hardened him. Those moments actually happened.

They stopped of course, and at first, it was that he would teeter between the warm and the violent, and even exhibited the two overlapping, in that he might cry even as he pulled out that extension cord and called for me. I still don't know who his tears were supposed to be on behalf of, but the collision of feelings in him at those moments stuck with me, and made my anger and the mourning of him far more complicated than perhaps it should have been.

I think of Dad, then, as another, if slightly different example of the thin boundaries between opposing feelings,
and in this case specifically am thinking on how anger, abject shame, and love can come together and feed on each
other until they blow up into overwhelming versions of
themselves.

Of course, I am put in mind of horses again, and how
sometimes their shyness becomes fun jockeying, and how that
can turn heated and hateful, and how such a mood can then
spin up a bewildering perversity that devolves into one horse
atop another, and then just as quick, end up in nuzzling.

So, again, feelings of all kinds come in many flavors,
most of them swirled.

Now, I would've been a bit older than the kid (though I
cannot claim to have ever known how old the kid was when
I knew him) when I received the automated message on my
machine that went:

Hello. The _____ *Correctional Facility for* _____ *regrets to
inform you of inmate* _____ *'s recent demise. Our extended sympathy for your loss. For more information, please contact* _____
at _____ .

[Dial tone.]

To this day I do not know how exactly it went down for
him, as I had not cared to inquire.

But now, I do wonder. And I imagine that it would have
been a bad end for Dad there, given the setting, and think
about how, in my nightmares, the eyes of my father became
the frantic ones of those destroyed animals, Scotties and
deer, and I feel bad, but then again, it is he who earned his
end, and I think how, generally speaking, it is we, all of us,

who are our own arsonists of the world, and so with regard to him, I rarely reproach myself for those moments of ill will and nasty thinking.

Mixed. It is all mixed. Which was particularly interesting to me then, as during this period, left alone, I was, of course, thinking on Cyndi, pondering happiness, what it is cut with; motivation, and what motivates it.

———————————

The stretch with those buttes and mesas was once what you'd call protected.

Such protections no longer apply, and now they contain mobile-home communities—including my own, as it happens. You now have to wade through some real bullshit—a gauntlet of wheel-estate, those prefabs and trailers and their inhabitants—to get to a tourist site called, appropriately enough to this-all, "Crying Rock."

This being named after a boulder—about two hours' walk from my door—which lies atop a small spring, such that it appears to cry from time to time. It does so only intermittently, for reasons which are confusing to me but which relate to air pockets in the aquifer or some such.

There was a time when folks from out of town and from all over used to come out here to see it, mostly the religious ones, for the Bible tells of such crying rocks: as in Exodus 17:6, where Moses struck the stone in Horeb, and:

Made the waters spring forth.

And Deuteronomy too, who, jumping on board, said:

Who led you through the great and terrifying wilderness,

with its fiery serpents and scorpions and thirsty ground where there was no water, who brought you water out of the flinty rock?

And Corinthians, not to be outdone here:

For they drank from the rock, and the rock was Christ.

And didn't even Jesus his very own self from his very own sacred lips say:

The stones will cry . . .

In other words the devouts need little excuse to pile into their ATVs and come tick off a box in their holy-pilgrimage book-of-incarnations (incarnations like that weeping Madonna in Salvage which cries, though it's long been proven that she is filled with condensation which leaks out a thin break in her lacquer). Researching "weeping Madonna" it seems there are thousands of these wonders listed worldwide, so there must be a real, precise, collective desire for such to exist.

—Field trip, Dill.

—Sure you're up for it.

—Like old times, I said.

And when we got to the rock-spring, no one was there for a change, and so we just stared at that stupid stone, standing behind the barrier wire, which was only ankle high, and so not much of a deterrent, yet still managed to stop us; and we said nothing, and listened to the babble, which, I thought, sounded nothing like "babble" really, when you really listen to it, but that is how such things are described and so that is how we hear them. When we got tired of the babble and watching that leakage, we went over to a nearby picnic table and ate; two old coots sitting there under the sun quite a bit longer than they should've; neither of them wanting to be the first to get up and go. Result: we both got scorched but good. Not as bad as when Dad left me in the desert to die, but pretty damn sunburnt all the same.

That evening, the new pain upon my skin jumped the fire line to join that earlier one; years merged, and my own youth, and that old outing in particular—all with its loneliness—was there again, unavoidable.

CELEBRANTS

Pay special attention to the elderly,
those with small children, and
the infirm.
—*Funeral Protocol Handbook*, Chapter 10: Ushers

—Dill, Sheryl, Liem, Nancy, Hank, Lemon, Chief, Ed . . . said Regis.

THE LORD SPEAKS TO THEM IN THEIR AFFLICTION

Mercy look what just walked
through that door
—Travis Tritt

And still not a peep.

(Though Francine, visiting her sister-in-law, had seen something up there "up in the hills," which was the kid walking among the squatters in Mt. Cortez—a camp that had appeared overnight on the Common; and what she told me is that she saw the kid working his way through the settlement, stepping delicate over the ragged and wretched like a crane, stopping to speak to those on the ground, entering those shoddy, corrugated shacks, one after another, coming out and going on to the next, his bulging pockets getting smaller, lighter, visit by visit. Francine watched for a while but got bored and kept moving and "frankly had only really stopped in the first place because, Ed, you keep being such a little bitch about him.")

His moving among the people—up high, as down below. I wondered if he was performing his larger wonders up there. Probably was. And yet news of even this was not reaching us. No tears carving rivulets down the cliffs to empty into our flatlands.

You'd think. But no.

Of course I had nothing substantial to occupy my time then, not being anyone's protector or acolyte. I was waiting, sure, but waiting is, at most, a decision made; meaning not a thing but a feeling.

Eventually I did do an actual thing, and what I actually did was haul my ass back into the ole saddle. Work.

Hopalong Crybaby.

I sat and prayed, gigs went ok. Well, ok in the sense that I wept (my modest, normal amount), money exchanged hands, I got drunk, went home, and it all felt like business as usual, meaning: back to blue.

And so my old life resumed; resumed its melancholic

sameness once more. Life just as I'd known it all those years. Day after day, on the path I'd already endlessly trod, step by hobbled step; each footfall sounding my name.

These are the hours, and I have read them.

But during this period of his continuing absence, it seemed that many in Local 302 were changed, as if experiencing a withdrawal. I saw this, though perhaps it was just this "seeming" and nothing more, but what I mean is that I had the notion they were all crying . . . *different*. Different in diverse ways, governed by each weeper's unique temperament, but the exact opposite of that temperament.

Dill less solicitous; Chantal less sultry; Johnnie less intense; and Lemon less . . . Lemon. Hankie seemed less pissy and no longer wore a face like a smacked ass, and ceased to scowl through his crying.

Still, my work—the actual style and production of it—did not change. At least not right away.

At the beginning, it was all more or less the same; and perhaps this "more or less the same" of mine is, in point of fact, my own "unique temperament." Perhaps my unique temperament is a sickening constancy. No matter what sudden miracle or catastrophe might befall me and those around me: here's Ed again, sticking to his fucking row, sure as shooting, regular as rust.

The physical pain and discomfort, however, became worse and more constant. I would wake up on mornings after work and think: *Lord, I am spent.*

I became aware of skull muscles I didn't know I had; itchy eyes; aching teeth, my burlap mouth. Dry. My head turned into the world's worst piñata. If you'd hit me, even once, even gently, I'd lurch open—too easy—spill out a bunch of sand, broken glass, fingernails, a tire, chicken bones, husks. I would imagine, then, children in their cocked birthday hats, staring at my ruined insides and howling.

My eye bags were such that I was rolling my Prep H like toothpaste.

Could the aches and pains also be—I asked myself—the simple way of it? The accumulated aftermath of so much work? The onset of our weeper's black lung; an occupational hazard?

Sure, but also, of course, there were the ones you get from liquor taken in extravagant amounts. The progression of my disease was the big one of course, but stirred in was the consequences of seeing my ex, Jeannine.

—Where's the money, she said.

I shook the hand of the man stood next to her on the street.

—Forgot, I said, which was true, if unusual.

The man excused himself.

—How are things? I said.

—Yeah, ok, Ed. Pretty good now.

—Truly glad to hear it, I said.

I didn't get the same question back. Instead, she leaned in.

—Why can't you ever just sack up and tell me no, she said.

—Jeannie.

—Never had much fight in you, Ed. And don't call me that.

She craned past me to look up the street. And leaving, said:

—No rush on the check.

"She left me for the bruiser," I thought, and surely that meant something. Realizing this I felt there had been a real failure on my part to give her what she desired. Someone in charge.

This added to my general store of woe, and the store had been pretty stocked to begin with.

To summarize: I felt like shit and worse than before.

For two demoralizing weeks, which is how long the condition lasted.

And then, my health and outlook changed. Health for the better, outlook for the worse.

Insult to injury, the tears stopped. Altogether. Came a day when I worked Jesus on the Mount, everything as it ever was, and for the first time in my godbothering life: I could not get it up.

MY HEART WILL GO ON (SOLO FLUTE)

> At the funeral, actors mourned, wearing masks
> known as "imagines."
> —Gaius Quintus

The day of my great impotence, there was a killing temperature, with the land and everything upon it flame-throwered.

Grids went down, ACs went down, the old and infirm

went down. Meaning a lot of calls down at the lot and not enough of us to service them. But service them we did, and the first of those was to mourn Darius Kentucky, up Coolidge.

Pretty standard stuff honestly, except that Darius's memorial was the first of a triple-header. Three funerals; one day. Which is a lot to ask of a weeper. But needs do as needs must.

And I should've at least suspected something could go wrong, which it did, badly, a real debacle. The debacle being that I could not cry. All my tears, dead in their ducts.

Worse, I could not remember at this debacle, for the life of me (and for the first time in my life), what sadness even felt like.

And it had all begun just fine. Took off my hat. Straightened my tie. Took a seat with everyone else; skirts smoothed over knees, pants pulled from crotches. I nodded over to Chantal; her small pillbox hat—its sheer black waterfall—those shapely legs tattooed with lace.

Folded my hands in my lap, bowed my head. Suitably dignified. Absolutely nothing to indicate that this would be but another working day in an endless line of them.

But when service spun up and the minister said his:

We come together to remember Darius . . .

I got to thinking.

It is a bad habit—thinking—and for a weeper thinking on a job is like trying to think yourself to sleep. I am in the feelings business, that is, yet as things stood there I was thinking, and what I was thinking specifically was how—as I said already—I was in for one seriously long-ass day.

Marathon's like that: big ask. A marathon requires regulation.

Thus I expelled a little puff of air and reminded myself that I shouldn't come in hot and wet.

Keep a lid on.

What I'd do, I thought, would be to build gradually, save something in the tank for later. Come up slow on the outer lane.

So, as opening prayers began and we all stood, I found myself trying to measure just exactly how much sorrow I should be doling out and at what kind of rate.

Start with a teaspoon. Sounds right. (Does it?) Tablespoon. How many tears in a tablespoon? But wait, are tears all the same size, and is there even such a thing as a solitary tear? But a drop is a drop, I thought, and a drop is only a drop when it has dropped. Satisfied with that answer I looked over next to me at Johnnie's funeral program and saw that indeed there were single tears spat down upon it as J-Man is fast out the gate—though it was hard to say which of these tears were joined-up tears and which were ones that had taken the solo leap—but still it made me wonder if tears were like snowflakes (uniqueness-wise) and so forth, so, lots of brainless conjecture; therefore I reminded myself what I was supposed to be about, namely: building myself a strategy.

So, maybe just a sob. Not a whole one, of course. Surely not. But then, what does one eighth of a sob sound like—is that a whimper? So what will a mewl cost me? One snivel and then follow up with a whine. Should give me a good thirty seconds of some "moderate sad." Then I can rest a spell.

I looked down at my watch. Thirty seconds. That's a long time. Weirdly long. Has thirty seconds always been long? Thirty is too long. So then, what. Eight?

(Leroy Crawford who loaded freight once told me that when buckles on a track get too out of hand they refer to these rails as "spaghetti," because that's what they start to resemble. Wavy, unmanageable—flaccid. And so did I remember then, observing the first—albeit potentially repairable—buckles in the railway line running between Station-Stop-Ed's-Brain and Station-Stop-Ed's-Tear-Glands, not that I had made it quite to the spaghetti stage then—not so dire—but also I knew that I still had to keep an eye out lest I become the pasta special.)

Darius Kentucky, friend, neighbor . . .

So, as things stood, I would need to keep an eye out on keeping an eye out, and just as I was coming to terms with having thusly tied my mental shoelaces together, I noticed the heat on my face and on my neck. Did the air crap out? I looked around, and people seemed calm as carrots. (Just me then.) Hot though. Very, and getting worse by the minute, me shedding some heavy sweat off my forehead; beads of it landing on my cheekbones exactly where the tears should be setting down (good, anyway, for the look of the thing). But then also running down my neck (not good) and trickling down my spine (bad) all the way into my crack (quite very bad), and there, in that sunless place, having gone as low as the sweat could manage, it enjoined with all my recently liquefied self-confidence, forming a puddle that refused to be absorbed by the shellacked, hardwood pew. But instead, reader, it reversed course—*climbed back upward*—as my trousers acted like a sponge and mopped it all up. It struck me that someone might think I'd wet myself. But if pews are good for anything it is for hiding your rear from those set behind you. (Is this why pews have solid backs?) A quick check confirmed that Johnnie was eyes-front, as was my other neighbor, which was a small boon granted me, but still: I needed this fucking moisture elsewhere (my inner voice piped up in an unexpectedly hysterical tone). Further diagnosis: I have another fever. So it is just the general deterioration of your old boy Ed. Ok, not great, but also, not my fault either.

. . . charitable soul, strong in his walk with Christ . . .

I sat in this: my wet. And indeed, began to sadden from self-pity, and sad is good obviously but it is true that damp plus heat equals itchiness, and so right at this tender (perhaps still salvageable) juncture, a brand-new species of plague was brought down upon me, as if the God of the Israelites was proctoring a complex moral test. And there was this everexpanding itch, pinprick-trauma—one that rattled me but good. It got so bad, so terribly uncomfortable that, unable (under the circumstances) to scratch myself, I began to (and this was super-weird) shiver from it; some rare, secondary symptom, and as I shivered there, gooseflesh rising: my body began to feel cooler, cause and effect jumbled, I had little time to enjoy the new state of affairs because, as with the shivering, it was again such as if my nervous system had begun acting with an authority I had never granted it—an authority to pull the kill-switch on my entire body, which is precisely what happened. So, if before, my itchy skin seemed to be reacting to nonexistent-if-clearly-primordial threats, suddenly, all sensation left me and complete paralysis set in. I couldn't move my legs. My arms. Everything was then so unnatural I could not salivate, began reminding myself to blink, and wondered how it was that my head stayed on my suddenly flimsy neck. (Aren't fingers weird?) I found a new ridge on one of my incisors (had it always been there?) and started worrying that little ruck with my suddenly overly sensitive tongue-tip. Under such conditions, the idea of generating any salt water whatsoever, be it a drop, puddle, or ocean, seemed just impossible (tears of exasperation, I decided, were my last great hope, but even those failed to show). I'd skitter off to the john if I could even move, but (as discussed) 1. I could not move, and 2. the service was then in the middle of its meaty bit, and me, I was in the middle of a long and crowded row, which would mean, by my count: sorry, sorry, sorry, sorry, sorry, sorry, sorry, sorry (eight of them), followed by that shameful aisle-walk. Could I fake a heart attack. Yes. Maybe. No. Why not. No. No. Wait. Now! No, hell no. But . . .

And, departing, left behind for us his footprints . . .

As my seething self-consciousness continued to produce more physical woes, them gathering steam well past the point of viable intervention, I found myself craving the kid's help; his special form of grace; the skills he had lent unto me, and others—those which he spread widely, selflessly. I wanted that contagion, the one made up of sorrows; sadness that would sweep through whatever emotionally unvaccinated gathering he happened to infect. And the Lord knows I hated thinking about him more, thinking about him especially in this particular way—and was ashamed of my need—as it was like a drug hunger; dark passenger. The kid. The kid. But he was gone. The boy. He was gone, and there I was, still there. Right there: a chump. Me. Total failure and complete dingleberry. He was gone and it had been my own big ideas which had sent him packing. (Also, and just, by the way, was I the only one of our number who had gone dry like this in his absence? I stewed on this too.) And then someone sneezed.

(Sneeze.)

Such a small thing.

And yet this sneeze, precious sign, light in darkness, arriving as it did as confirmation that the world, that bounteous, brimful receptacle for geraniums, bedsprings, cornmeal, horse manure, dusk, turbines, cotton balls, elbows, spoons, flags, rope, milkshakes, rhinos, baby blue, peanut butter, rodeo clowns, rusty nails, fool's gold, soy sauce, extension cords, the taste of the hot wind, zippers, bewilderment, candy wrappers, stop signs, ice cube trays, fistfights, grasshoppers, adverbs, radial tires, key of G major, chalk, lust, north, east, up, down, hooves, languor, helicopters, pencil sharpeners, handshakes, gravity, gum, the smell after a sneeze, mist, car wash air-dancers, sarcasm, straw, aluminum foil, rapturous applause, pup tents, sea sponges, waffle fries, fan belts, truck nutz, sneering, four-seam fastballs, whale song, toilet plungers, gall bladders, radio deejays, dandruff, snare drums, escalators, cedar, cider, spiders, spigots, bigots, widgets, wingnuts, frigates, ingots, ingrates, Slip 'N Slides, toenails, skillets, cinder blocks, hand grenades, lecterns, pubes, riding crops, whisks, Chap-Stick, salt shakers, pillowcases, spades, samovars, "Happy trails!," TIG welders, swordfish, the penis, the national anthem, toaster cakes, common-law marriage, game of bingo, boa constrictors, banjos, the fire truck, the cheetah, the tango, the melon baller, and so on, including, most importantly: *other people*—that all of this was real.

Real and distinct from my current predicament. This really goddam perked me up. Let me tell you. And I decided I could rally.

Showtime.

I would reach in toward where those emotions were and brute-force them out of hiding; my mutinous tears. I would try harder, in other words, though "trying" is the equally fruitless cousin of "thinking," as I would soon find out, being as I ended up falling into lazy tropes, meaning I found myself doing something I'd never done ever, which was to sway. Swaying slowly; forward, back, so on. As I said, it was not conscious, but I suppose I was just hoping to get the engine started; provide some kinetic energy. Push the jalopy along the road til the gears catch.

This kind of behavior is fine in the abstract, it's *fine*; but really only if the affair is Pentecostal or whatever because honestly such demonstrative bullshit rarely happens in reality, not with actual mourners, not nowadays, and it comes off as more than a little over the top (obviously I am not discussing the truly gonzo stuff, the hair-rending, the—what do they call it, the throat-warbling thing they do in far-off places—or grave-hole-jumping, so on), though as an aside, I've heard of weepers—mostly out east—who do similar stunts, but these are specialists, independent contractors, and obviously mavericks and outsiders; none of these show-boats in our Local 302

. . . family man, father to three sons and two Irish Setters . . .

and where we ply our trade, even a moderately loud groan is considered amateur hour, embarrassing, so, when I found myself going overboard like that I naturally became even more self-conscious, knowing that no one was buying what I was selling, and I even put my face in my hands (which everyone fucking knows hides tearlessness), and because of all of this infantile theater—this pantomime I had fallen into, driven by sudden impotence—the Grade A shame kicked in.

. . . loving, faithful husband of fifty-two years . . .

You are better than this, Ed.
(Was I, though. Was I? Better?)

. . . hard worker, fair boss, man of the people . . .

Hey, you got this, asshole. Remember the McDonough wake? The Greenman thing? Remember how you killed up at that huge show up in Lemar Hills? I went through the list: how a preacher consoled me that one time; how an imperious old aunt dropped the soft mitt of a hand into my own; how, way back when I was just starting out, a cousin of the deceased took me home after just to fuck the bottomless grief out of me (or me/her; didn't matter).

. . . and we all know how much he loved to be out there in his blind, with his beers and his compound bow . . .

See? There's a track record. Never forget: You're a star. Pro. Come on, buddy. Act the part. Take what's yours. And at that, some of the old muscle memory began twitching. Hope. Grace in darkness. Thank sweet, skinny Jesus. I was starting to ramp up. Taxi out onto the runway.

. . . Darius, we all remember how he was always ready with a joke . . .

Darius was always ready with a fucking joke?

I'd never seen that sonofabitch even smile. Not even a bit, not even once, and he looked like he was perpetually just back from a root canal, slack-jawed and irritable, and knowing this as I did, then, in yet another proof that my body had gone rogue, I sort of chuckled-snorted—the strangest sound you could imagine—one I could not summon again now if I tried; a sound you simply could not believe could exit a man's air-pipes, a sharp, high gurgle; this, in such a time, and in such a place, at which point the head of the good citizen in front of me turned, slightly, about twenty-five degrees counterclockwise, not enough for her to look me in the eye, but enough to indicate that she had heard that unholy emission of mine (remembering it now, it was something like the sound of a broken duck call, or a freshly gelded bagpipe), and this particular mourner in front of me, her disapproval and mild, if irrefutable rebuke—her insufferable probity and indignation made me—me having gone full maniac—want to really crack the hell up; gut-laugh, deep, loud, and long. Fully cut loose. Laughter, that granddaddy of all funerary taboos; and though it is, as they say, good medicine, which is true, if under those circumstances there I had really done the deed I would most likely be forcibly removed, roped up like a mad steer, committed, carted off and away (plus-side of the ledger), and it would be received as a crime against the occasion (perhaps an actual crime?).

But I harbored another reservation, which was that given how ludicrously tickled I was feeling, and given how that weird glee was then combined with the prospect of laughter's sweet release, I began to feel (without putting too fine a point on it): *better*.

If you follow.

Meaning: *not sad*.

And that burp of joy and disbelief I had already let fly had dispelled most of my performance anxiety, which was good, but I had entered some pretty unrestrained and upbeat territory—too upbeat, and that there is what you'd call "overcompensation." I was actually happy in that moment and I cannot emphasize enough how unhappy that happiness made me.

How could I coax myself back to safe ground now, you ask? Impossible. But into that breach again and still I tried to remember my training, regulate my breath. Slow and steady. Slow and steady. Forget where you are and why you have come. Good. Good. Feet of warm wax. Spine of honey. And I let my entire body go limp, and allowed my thoughts to become like unto a summer mist. Gooey. Become one with the pew. Find peace. Melt. Okay.

Then I went for the memories.

I file these bad memories in increasing order of intensity— pet death to child death—though that's just me, and it can sometimes be the other way around, depending on the weeper in question; for instance Crazy Patti from Stanville, who, like all of us, has no kids but dotes on her sugar gliders like they are her whole fucking life, not really having a real one in fact, so for her it probably goes "parking ticket to sugar glider," some shit, but anyway I was in too deep—and so tried to pull my Memory of Last Resort; launch it from out its cold, tight silo.

It is the one I keep for just such moments.

. . . Lest we forget that the memory of a life well spent lasts forever . . .

I'm telling you that I had to recall something just awful that day at Darius's memorial. That's how much stage fright I had to push past. I never told anyone (not even Chantal) what that bad memory was—mostly because it was too hard to say out loud, but also because talking about it (famously) makes it less effective.

But this recollection of mine was terrible. And it should've worked as advertised.

No such luck.

Because just as it floated up, I was becoming aware of Darius's grandson approaching the dais; carrying a flute.

For-the-love-of-all-that-is-holy-in-the-eyes-of-God there is simply no way . . . But yes.

Boy. Flute.

And what would you wager that plucky little lad had in store for us on that dark day? I had guessed it had to be those Sleeves of Green which indeed it had been and a very pitchy rendition of it at that.

Then: Johnnie, who was finally becoming aware of all the sweating, ticking, convulsions—my body still shaking from suppressed jollity—saw the frenzied strain on my face, mistook it for an emotional dam ready to burst, and so leaned into my ear (oh my Lord, so far into it) and whispered:

—Let it out, Ed.

Well I could have murdered him then and there for what he had said to me, and I spent the next bit mentally berserking—seeing, through a red mist—me smacking that huge bastard over the head with the thick black Bible nestled in the back of the row I was facing; imagining I'd hit him until he dropped, until my hands and the good book itself were all slippery with his blood.

———

. . . He could make every person feel like they were the most important person in the world . . .

Meaning that I had cycled through every last feeling (except of sorrow) until I had hit the horror-movie phase of my ordeal, in which the first viewing featured me as bloodthirsty maniac, the second—as contrition set in and yet another wild mood swing took over—in which I was cast as one of those incautious coeds—heading toward the dark wood, climbing the attic stairs, straying too far from a campfire—surrendering to death, accepting the cold, final embrace of a hook-hand; any hook-hand

. . . "Soldier" is a term not appreciated nearly enough these days . . .

a real fright-fest in my mind's cinema, that is, projector smoking, film flapping, screen lesioned with fire, all of it premiering for an audience of one, and then a dizziness came upon me, the world began to tilt, mere seconds before the lights went off . . . out of nowhere

Amen.

Amen—hallelujah. And the service was goddam done. Just like that.

I came to, came to in that way in which—when you faint or are concussed (I'd been kicked in the head by a warmblood once and am lucky I can still speak in words instead of sa-liva), when you regain your consciousness you do so not knowing anything, nor anyone—like Adam suddenly made substance, ignorant in his garden, facing the all of it, the still-unnamed everything.

It took only a heartbeat before I was Ed again, Ed in a church, Ed at a service. And these were congregants, the mourners, and there was Johnnie and Sheryl and Dill, and that I was being paid to cry, and had failed at that, failed badly, and as soon as I remembered all that, I thought how my professional cred was not something I could afford to lose, and even though I still had two more of these services to go, I knew that I could not.

It was clear.

I would not attend the next one. Nor the next one after that. Maybe I'd even quit the game!

People were standing then, and while pushing my own self up, I asked myself if this is what is feels like to be . . . an amateur, one of those total duds who come into the lot and leave just as fast. A busted flush.

I was sure—as sure as God made little green apples—that when I told Chantal of this-all later she would roll those dark eyes and give me the weeper's equivalent of "it happens to everyone."

But this here was virgin territory. Such things never hap-pened to me.

Not ever. No sir.

They did not happen to Edward D. Franklin: cowboy poet, powerful sad sack, five-tool infielder in the winningest, wettest crying-squad in the entire Lower 48.

Didn't happen to that man we all know and love: miserable, cradle to grave.

Weeper by vocation; weeper by birthright.

Yet here we are.

And while it is true that I have, throughout my sorry life, put a few eggs into other, meager baskets, as I've already told it: one marked "poetry," and the other "cowboy"—as I've said, the poetry is mediocre, and though I can pass pretty well as a cowboy with most, it is not like I am a true member of that bowlegged brotherhood.

No, sadness was my thing.

And I would've been sad to lose it.

SCRIPTURE READING

Lord my God, I called to you for help . . .

—PSALMS 30:2

COMMEMORATIVE SLIDE SHOW

So that had been a disaster.

One which should have caused a serious reckoning. A great *taking-of-stock*.

The morning after this display of terrible impotence I duly, gingerly, surveyed my heart, expecting to find it chock-full of shame.

What I found instead was an atmosphere so dull, so bland, it would've disturbed me, had my state not been so tranquil. It occurred to me this tranquility might not have been the result but in fact the cause of what had happened the day before.

The big thing here was, having reached into my heart and got nothing back, I was untroubled by this lack.

—How you doin', Ed, Johnnie said, worried. Sheryl probably having put him up to it.

—Yeah, really great, J-Man.

(*Really great?*)

—Oooooooookayyyy then, Ed, see you soon?

—Looking forward, pal, I said.

(*Looking forward*? *Pal*? Ed, what the fuck is . . .)

I put the phone down in its cradle.

Then I lounged—more than is my usual amount, that is—until I was positive that I was indeed feeling as agreeable as it seemed I was, at which point, I don't know why exactly, perhaps seeking some further confirmation of the change, I pulled my neglected old mirror from under the bed and rested it on top of the dresser. It had been a moment since I'd last taken a good long look at my fine old self, and when I did, I was surprised to see I did not look hangdog in the slightest, but rather seemed to be standing a little straighter than usual. No visible signs of embarrassment or fatigue, nothing abject in my face or posture. And so I came to the strange but undeniable conclusion that I truly did not give one crap about what had happened at that service. Didn't care about any of it, or anything.

I felt, if not quite right as rain, content, limp, as if I'd taken a too-long hot shower. I stood there in front of my reflection for one more moment, turning first this way and then that, and I liked what I saw. Tanned skin, not too jowly, a mustache you could hang your laundry on . . . hairline receding, sure, but on that particular day, even this came off as more rakish than pathetic. And my eyes—my all-important eyes, my professionally wounded eyes—didn't look like they required Band-Aids over them. Not red, not puffy.

I smoothed down my brows with a thumb, pinched the brim of my hat, and winked.

Hello, cowboy.

The morning piss streamed merrily out of me. I zipped with confidence and went to the kitchen area. I hauled the overfull bag out of the can, and though it was one week's worth of heavy, it did not rip. (I also clocked that my knees and back didn't complain as I kicked open the mobile's aluminum door, trash in hand.) Here then, the wakening world.

Hello.

Hello to it all.

All of it . . . bearable?

I did not resent the sun in the sky, those neighbors, the Scottie, the Scottie-leavings (there was noticeably less of it now that the number of Scotties had been halved).

I gave a cheerful salute to the remaining dog, dropped the garbage, skipped on in again, watched the pot percolate with genuine interest, and the coffee ended up pretty damn decent.

I did not fixate on that lethargic light on my aluminum wall. No moping or anything. None of that regularly scheduled Ed programming. Not: Ed-again-begin-again.

A man could get used to such things.

—Wanna fish? Dill said.

It was an old joke between us—he and I both knew we wouldn't find a creek big or wet enough to hold a fish worth a damn but we always had a hoot just hiking around.

Then, I may have gone to the track (but don't get too up in arms about it because I didn't put down too large a wager, so there were no big squanderings either).

Following afternoon, I drove out to the hardware to buy some new flashing for the mobile's old roof. Obviously it was dry as boots up in this region, but it is the spirit of the thing now, isn't it.

I ran into Peewee up at the register buying a bag of thirty-pound nails. Look at us, I thought. A couple of regular guys. I chucked his shoulder like we were sharing a private joke, and he looked at me like he was trying his best to read a book in high Martian.

—You all right, Ed?

—Sure.

We went over and ate burger sandwiches. Ran into the Nguyens, who joined, and Nancy sat right on Liem's lap. We listened to one another chew. Another meal under my belt.

That night, I was blessedly orphaned by my father, and I even wrote a pretty decent poem, hackneyed though it might've been, but I felt my words had lined up, right as rivets.

Was this some sort of remission? Was this, I wondered, what normal felt like?

I thought about this whole "normal" thing more in the truck as I cruised over to Chantal's, where she and me played Crazy Eights until about noon, out under the vinyl eaves.

—What's that, she said, pointing at my bolo.

—Thought I'd mix it up today.

It is a fact that I'd left Dad's tie back at the trailer. That one I was wearing there—which Dill had purchased for me years past—sported a turquoise tear in the center of its silver clasp.

First time I hadn't worn Dad's in years. Probably a coincidence, I thought, and it is quite amazing the tales we will tell ourselves just to keep the world spinning on its primordial and usual axle.

But it did, spin, and I felt, then, that it would continue to. For the first time in God knows how long I was assured of that. A decent future.

And as the world spun, I would embrace being Joey-fucking-Bag-a-donuts; stock character in a stock story. Got myself right. Feeling little, caring less.

Dumb as a hoof.

I'd stay away from the funeral biz, I thought. For a long while anyways. It would do a body good.

I reached over and finished Chantal's beer; she snubbed out her smoke in the tray, turning it as a key in a broken lock.

—You are . . . are you . . . happy, she said.

—Yeah, I said.

—Why.

—Hell if I know.

FORMAL READING OF THE OBITUARY

And so as I've said: those days came and went, one after the other, like the meals of a fussy eater; nothing to distinguish nothing. All was well and every manner of thing was well.

———————————

And then Dad returned from the grave.

He circled with that bantam strut, calling me the usual names. All the menace.

Which I thought I might take as confirmation—as a thermometer confirms a fever—that the kid was back.

Next morning I woke early, having previously enjoyed weeks of sleeping in.

I took my coffee standing up. I found myself staring at my unmarked calendar on the far wall. I turned to look down at the stovetop, its yellowing tin, the sink's gallows faucet. The unwashed pile beneath. I got the kettle, filled it up, and set it on the butane.

The phone rang then and I jumped for it. The call was from Reg. He had a job for me if I was up for it, and I nearly bit his hand off. Might the boy be there? Could I have been right and he was returned and risen? Maybe, maybe . . . I took some deep breaths and straightened up my spine (and ouch to both of those).

So back in the truck. Had to do a pickup for Reg first though, and here's me heading to Soupy's place.

When I got to the scrap heap, it was noisy. Soupy was working his way around a large, branchless tree trunk, out of which was emerging an eagle on the wing. Soupy had his big earmuffs on and so didn't hear me pull up, which was good as I didn't want to startle him and have him lose a digit (there had been many working men on my father's side, and I remember the finger-stumps from the too-casual handling of table saws, oxyacetylene welders, etc.). I have the proper respect, that is, and so waited until Soupy had seen me on his own. Which he did, and let the chainsaw sputter down.

—Howdy, Ed, he said, pulling up his goggles.

We stood there in the sawdust and admired his sculpture for a bit. Then he led me through the mulch-yard to the studio out back, past the bears, cougars, feathery headdresses, totems, bucking broncos, and one giant fist, extending an equally giant middle finger. We went to a walk-in freezer where a swan carved from ice sat on a shelf. I carried it to my truck bed and high-tailed it fast as you can imagine over to the Mason Hall.

When I pulled in, the swan was smoother and drippier than when it had left Soupy's. Still, it had lost surprisingly little of its overall shape and contour, so I got a decent tip from the widow, who told me to leave it with the caterer for after the service.

Saw the whole gang there but not him, and where might he be hiding.

Dill came up to me.

—Who died? I asked him.

—Arn.

—Arn?

—Polsen.

—Arn Polsen, you say?

—Yeah, you gone deaf?

—Just queer is all.

—Knew him?

—Never met the man.

Pause.

—Should I be giving a shit about this, Ed?

—Nah.

But there was something there about "Arn Polsen," and I felt a hazy foreboding, the kind that is a clench in the space between your chin and your solar plexus.

Signs and portents. Signs and portents.

Thursday then, and *Yea* did Cyndi appear up at the chain pharmacy.

I caught her girlish scent before I saw her, a strong whiff of cherry soda—a lip gloss, body spray, something. I was walking down the aisle marked "pain relief" and caught it in my nostrils. I peered around the corner and there she was, little in a baggy tracksuit, squinting at something in her hand.

She frowned as she flipped a small box over to its backside and read whatever was there to read. Stabbed at the help button, and immediately a loud voice came over the whole place saying "help in feminine products," which startled the bejesus out of me. I jumped back into my aisle so quick I dislodged a bunch of power bars and had to swift-kick them over to where I could stack them with impunity. Then I slunk over to my former position by the aspirin. I caught my breath and waited, removing a few bottles from the shelf and putting them back for the look of the thing. I could hear exasperated huffs from Cyndi from the other side, the crackle of gum, even from where I was, even above the tinny music.

I got a better view of her when she finally exited. I was slunk low in the cab of my truck. She had a weary shuffle. No sight of those blinding teeth. Her hair was down-and-out, her face flattened, which made it almost unnervingly handsome. I suppose I mean manly. Also tired.

She looked shitty.

Life does throw a cliché at us, doesn't it. I had believed the one which said "opposites attract." But I was wrong. The boy-of-perpetual-sorrows and the pumper-upper-of-jams hadn't canceled one another out. Cyndi's happy had been no match for his deadly misery. My ruse had been a failure.

Cyndi, wrecked.

What had I done. What had I done?

Yet I had been right: he *was* back.

The kid was back.

—The kid is back, Sylvia said to me (as you'd refer to a tumor).

The kid was back.

Months on, I saw Cyndi exiting the Stallion from its side door. She got into a crumple-fronted subcompact and drove away. Cyndi, once chipper as an ice ax, looked not just sad, but walking-dead. I spared a thought for her mother, who'd tried so hard to keep the girl's flame alight, and now, just look at it snuffed, and I was knocked to my knees by the guilt of it.

What had he done to her?

STAND AS ONE AGAINST DARKNESS

If one suffers, all suffer together.
—1 Corinthians 12:26

So Cyndi.

And that was a hard thing, but it also meant that surely I would see him again. At the lot, most likely. At a job. Outside that grim little apartment. Hopefully not down Canaan Steel (I checked; he wasn't). But he'd be somewhere all right. And back in my purview.

Still, the days went on and on and where was he to be found? I got not a single hint.

You never know when a bad breeze will blow down on you, specially nowatimes; that Santa Ana swooping around; its thermals, the ash from the fires, that yellow smog.

One afternoon I had a visit. I had been home when the feeble knock came on the feeble door.

A young woman I did not know, standing there, arms crossed, hands on her shoulders, rocking back and forth a little, her hair describing the wind. She was skin and bones, wearing a half shirt exposing a hard, round belly. This must be the girl Peewee had seen.

—I'm looking for the boy, she said.

I scowled.

—How'd you get this address, I said, holding open the screen door but not stepping out.

—Man in the trailer.

—Reg.

—I don't know, she said.

—What's it to do with me, I said.

—Trailer guy said you was friends.

—And, I said.

—You tell me where I can find him? she said.

—That I will not.

She came back again, couple days on. Standing out front of my steps, eyes full of want. Stood awhile, eventually melting back away into the dusk. When she came back a third time (and, again, I like to think that I am a kind man and how my first instinct is, generally speaking, to invite someone into my home and hearth), I also saw in that gal her compulsion, and I do not negotiate with terrorists.

In any case, she—getting nowhere with me—started showing at the edge of the lot. Reg, to his credit, let his Rottweilers roam to ensure she got no closer.

Once, even, she came to the Crown. It was when none of us were present. Bartender—the new one—he's who told me about it.

He had carded her and told her to scram.

And the day after that the girl followed Chantal to her home, which ticked me off mightily when it got back to me (though I can only imagine the imperious talking-to that gal was treated to by Chantal).

And she tried me one more time, came round my place

and I told her I'd call the cops, and I actually did that, and they did not come.

I couldn't call her parents as I did not know her name.

So she went on. Looking, waiting. Her presence was a foul gas.

But what was I supposed to do?

Came an evening when during one of my daily drive-bys, I saw the girl was outside the Bow & Gun. Another day I saw her there again but with a thin, bearded man. I thought it was maybe her father but that they were too different-looking. And then one afternoon there was a woman. That lady wasn't her mother for sure. A mismatched family. Each standing apart by the chain-link opposite what was or used to be his window.

Guy with a canvas jacket and cap there too one day, and then sickeningly, that giant misfit in the brown tee from the jail cell was there, shirt brindled with sweat; once again seeming patiently, dangerously amused; secure in some knowledge that his will would—even if down the road, ultimately—be obeyed.

Then I saw some of the kids from the culvert. A vigil? Were they camped out in hope? In hope of what?

It was like this, day after day, me in my truck (stakeout vehicle, me doing my daily patrol), when finally, behold: there he was himself, come back into the light.

Not there though, and not at the lot, but downtown Culpos, in front of the feed store, squatting, back against a wall in a dark rectangle which had to be the only shady part of town that afternoon. There was a smashed forty right next to him, the tendrils of spilt beer reaching almost to the road.

The kid's suit jacket by then was more gray than black. As Johnnie said, he was barefoot, and had those dress shoes tied together and slung over a shoulder. I wasn't too far away but I had become possessed, as at the start, of a strong shyness, and so did not approach further, and a man I did not know came out of the place carrying a sack, and he stopped above the kid, as if the kid was destitute and the man was to give him change. Instead the man put his feed down and bent at the waist to address him.

It seemed that the kid addressed him back. Man listened. His head was bowed.

I had no shade, exception of my hat.

There was an exchange, like a handshake almost. After, the man squatted down too. A bit later I went into Flemming's to escape the sun but really to watch it all through the window. They stayed awhile, then the man turned to walk away. As he left, the kid looked down at his feet again as was his habit.

I came out.

When I saw this man full frontal he so spooked me I almost jumped. Believe me when I say his face was locked in a rictus as ancient as a ritual mask—like he was hurting-from-or-relishing an emotion that ran so deep it made my gorge tickle. That expression reminded me of the cold, dead man in Vince's steel room. Embalmed mouth pinned up to a halfway, lifeless cheer.

The feed-store man worked his way up toward my position. He crossed the road. He looked at me without sight. Then he

stopped right in front of me for a moment, like he had remembered something, and clocking me peering over his
shoulder at the kid, nodded slow.

—You have a good day now, compadre, he said.

Back at Chantal's I could not get that man's expression
off my mind. Went around and around on it; that grimace.
Agony, sorrow. But almost impossibly, joy? No. What was it
though. On that fat kisser? What?

—You just need a lying down, Chantal said.

She pulled some ice cubes from the freezer, wrapped
them in a dish towel.

—They are gathering, I said.

—I worry for you, she said.

—Yes, yes, but . . .

And then she put the ice on my neck.

On Thursday I went shopping for her—whose birthday it
was. And so had gone into that Creations by Lindsay, the
jewelry, scarf, incense, and nice-things shop which is just our
regional version of the same one which exists in every town
in the whole damn country if under different names. I was
looking at the case with the earrings in it when I saw the girl
again, who I thought of as the first of them; first follower,
first in need. She was with her back to me, over by the woven
bags, giving those scant customers her listless help. Shuffling
her feet. She then turned and that grimace again, uncanny
and indescribable. The full-on thing of it.

At which point my mind leapt into those movie scenarios
where a lone hero finds everyone around him to be aliens or

robots, some such. Which brought on a creeping horror, made a whole lot worse by the stink of that place with its joss sticks and pine-smelly candles and so I left at great speed without buying anything. (I got Chantal a succulent at the stand by the road.)

THOSE IN ATTENDANCE

—You see any people?

—What people, Dill said.

The bar barely populated but for us.

—I don't know, just like . . .

—Three fingers, Dill said. Barkeep thumbed-up.

— . . . new people, I said.

—New. People?

—Yeah, I said.

—"Leave ye the presence of a fool": Proverbs 14:7.

—"Shove it up your ass, Dill": Proverbs 6:66.

Dill laughed and this was how we talked.

—It's just that I feel them converging.

Lemon came up then, shoved between us, and ordered herself a mint schnapps.

—Pardon me, ladies, she said, and we were glad for it.

———————————————

Then, another event, a big one happened—an event that seemed a form of proof ("faith," sure, but proof is always preferable to that, so apologies to believers).

And I am just getting to this now—this, only now. For, as it is written: "everything in its own goddamn time."

October the twenty-first. That day was a dividing line, or maybe a new chapter, such that if the first bit of this story could be called "His Early Miracles" and part two could be called "Mysteries and Warnings Unheeded," then this here— a part three—might be called "Revelations."

And it must be filled in because 1. That following of his—those vampires—had awakened then a clamor in me, but also because now, in the now now, I am conscious of the fact that 2. I don't have limitless time anymore, and I can see clearly up ahead the end of my road, meaning, I need to get the important bits out.

So back to the big discovery and here it is and how it was visited upon me.

On a day which made a liar out of the fall and all seasons in general—while standing at the little stove in the trailer— I remembered something. Who knows how these things come to rise up, but often it happens when you are simply heating your beans for supper. I was heating my beans for supper.

What hit me was the memory of when Dill had said the words "Arn Polsen."

I heard those two words when we wept Arn's service, and Dill said them—"Arn Polsen," and I queried Dill about it and then let the matter drop because I was not sure at the time why it surprised me so to hear his name ("Arn Polsen").

But at the stove that evening I remembered—though I had never met this "Arn Polsen" when he was among the living—I had seen his name prior to his death and interment. I had seen it quite a while in fact before that funeral.

I had seen his name back in August. Outside the police station in the kid's notebook.

Listen: certain truths have been established here, and I'd like to think that anyone attending to all this would have, by this juncture, come to know me for what I am. I do not fight tides; lean into gales. I am not a man of action; my way is the way of the lament. Also let me say that I live by what you could call an ethical code. I am a decent man. Maybe not entirely "good," I would not go so far, but again, I could be called, with some confidence: "decent." Yet there are just some goddam fucking moments when you know down in the reinforced toes of your socks that something in you will go rogue. Though it is written that *prying is wrong*, and that *what is private is—and should be kept—private*, it was clear to me then that I would open and read that fucking thing. I can also say that this particular trespass of mine was inevitable, meaning that I seemed to have no say over it, and the whole matter felt like life expressing itself in that way it can: seemingly haphazard, but with total certitude. Not to absolve myself. It is simply the facts. And so I admit now it was, my hand guided thus, that I cracked that notebook of the boy's open and was surprised to see it was pencil-writ in a neat, level hand—so unlike my own, which looks like an attempt to write upside down and backward with my poor, aging penis. But his handwriting was clean, finicky. Weirdly so. Yet the meaning of what was said in there was not a scrutable one but very much of the other kind. Whatever the kid's intentions were, whatever this writing meant, it set something to work in my heart, such that I told myself I would have to confront him on it. Though once again and as was the pattern back in those days: I did not. Instead, I had just buried that-all. Buried the whole incident as I had buried all the others that were of a dark, enigma-like nature. I buried that-all, and by the time I was not fifteen minutes gone from the station and heading out into the desert's furnace, I had managed to bury even the burying itself. A coffin inside of a coffin.

But of course, that which is buried will not stay buried and instead will punch a gangrenous hand out from the ground, haul up its crumbling frame, and lurch away wanting brains to savor, and here it was, and I remembered everything about what I saw when I had peeled open the kid's bedeviled diary.

Revisiting that moment, let's begin with first impressions:

First off, I had seen that the boy's inclinations were stranger than I could have thought—meaning that I would not have taken him for a hoarder, but clearly he was.

> Pepper Troutman
> Cleon Hill
> Winona Purlieu
> Jeb Sullivan-Weeds
> Clint Greenjacket
> Redondo DeLicht
> Reuben Bland
> Mandy-Line Barnett

Lenny Turcotte

Greg Big-Savings

Cooter Wilhelm

Angel Concepcion

Roy Lester Finch

OK McClatchey

D'Martha Mae Lenwhich

John D'Leux

Martiale Laureen

Kade Whittle

Jango Montgomery

Adelaide Penelope Fender

Jack Denizen

Lawson Shulevitz

Barney Leferts

Iwan Rasmussen

Imogen Boneparty

Diego Mandelay

Oakley Sandoval

Kiara Bush

Mary-juan Scottsdale

Macauley Walls

Emma Dowager

Jannette Hodgeling

Dathan Underwood

Melifornai Duffy

Jordanne Cecelo

Yash Bradshaw

Cleo Adkins

Freya Branch

Orla Fuentes

Ibrahim Archer

Bobby Frenchlink

Fergus O'Dohertella

Verlyn Malonski

"Gonzo"

"'Hot' Gonzo"

Elysia Orozco

Hamzah Johns

Rhea Kemp

Franciszek Blaawsen

Rosalie Muhrlé

Russell Petty

Mitchell Burnrouge

Kadie Saundlidj

Deborah Deborah Delgado

Gianluca Dillon

Ayesha Barking

Siena Pham

Dennis Buckaroo

Kelsie Heytha

Lacey Randall

Dhruv Del-Everett

Angelina Vauxhall

Sammee Camilo

Theodore "Ted" Theodore

Lincoln Jefferson Garfield

Carl Combs

Hiram Buck

Charlemagne St. Pierre

Lance Digest

Roman Lilac

Scooter Fontenelle

Tammy Wa'mammy

Marla Callaport

O'Shea McClay

Bertha Brandywine

Melvin Todd

Hankleroy Henrysson

Honeybunch Editburg

Eugene Hogwatch

Ed Herdy

Daisy Axlegrind

"Little Boot" Lenny Ludwig

Stewey Von Benson III

Sheriff Robb Cobb

Crazy Patti

Rosemary Budders

Sly Batonne

Sprig Waggleman

Lass O'Leary

McGill Haggardly

Father Dom Brisket

Rumor Wilcock

Jervis Wily

Charlene Focantacon

Kermit Swirl

Kaylum Jenkins

Wyatt Cockburn

Kaylee Haley

Luqman Richardson

Morleson Key

Milan Deblink

Habiba Laundry

<u>Arn Polsen</u>

Kymeera Decker

Abel Moyette

Larry-Earl Navarro

Katerina Meadows

Bernard Cheeks-Kilpatrick

. . . Et cetera and et cetera.

So, a log of each and every service the kid had worked since the day he had roamed his way out of the nothing and came on through Reg's gate.

———————————

There are (famously) two flavors of persons with regard to the question of remembrance: there is the kind that says "Never forget," and then there is the kind that says "Carry on, life is for the living, always look forward." Both tend to proclaim their positions noisily and publicly, as if running for office on an attitude-toward-the-dead platform, which bothers me no end, and so I feel sheepish about saying which group or the other I would fall into. So let's leave it.

Anyhow so the kid was a hoarder, and big deal, except that—during that moment at the stove, while my beans began to sizzle and subsequently incinerate—I remembered something else.

The names in the notebook did in fact belong to people we had mourned, and "Arn Polsen" was there too. All the deceased—mourned and interred.

But sweet flaming Moses: I had read that notebook while Arn was still alive.

I checked the other names. In that careful, clinical hand of the kid's, there were—if only a few—mentions of folks *yet to pass* at the time of writing. Who were not yet dead when his pencil was set to paper. What was this shit.

The kid had known?

SCRIPTURE READING

Surely I am only a brute, not a man; without human understanding.

—PROVERBS 30:2

DO NOT SUCCUMB TO FEAR

But some doubted.
—Matthew 28:17

There were those many nights when I went to sleep in a heavy sweat and that night was one such. And as was also even more regular again at that time, cometh the sleep, cometh the father. Though his behavior in this dream was new.

Up and until that moment, the dreams of my father had been felt as premonitions: of resentment, hatred, wroth, devastation (all of which did indeed arrive at the close of it all, which we will certainly speak on later).

I thought after one such vision, this might yet become a calamity, not sure exactly what was meant by this, except that the dreams did seem to . . . *bode*.

And as those days of autumn flew by—the kid within touching distance yet still untouchable—such dark premonitions became more frequent, but also my dream-father had become ever more tyrannizing; his admonishments louder, clothes more decrepit (pants unbuttoned, sock stuck to shirt, stains spreading like tumors), and those thin wisps of white hair; as if he had walked, bald, through a room of cobwebs. His skin too was crepe-ed and spotted, his eyes bruised darker.

But this next one I am recounting about was (as I've said) something else entirely.

My father's expression was not knotted with fury or flat with disdain. It was imploring.

Brows sagged in regret, eyes glistening ("and I dwell on this detail of the wet eyes"), his chin stretching very slightly up and forward in supplication, wanting . . . absolution? understanding? I could not stand this—this more than anything preceding it.

Then, I saw he had my mother's dress—the faded and flowered one—draped across his outstretched arms like he was carrying an unconscious body. He held it out.

Take her. Take her.

———————————

—I'm telling you.

—It's fucking moronic, Dill said.

—Right here in black and white, I said, showing him.

—You got the dates wrong.

—I did not get the dates wrong and know how to count.

—Anyway that book there does not belong to your sorry ass, and have you considered returning to him that owns it? Dill said.

—I know how to count, I said again.

Exhausted pause.

—People keep diaries, you know, he said.

—Nothing in there but names.

—Maybe he was thinking of starting a paper route?

—Hilarious.

—Census?

—Fuck you.

—Process serving?

—Dill.

—Bounty hunting?

—Quit it.

—Here's the thing, nitwit: when it comes to the health of people, sometimes the writing is just on the wall. Mr. Lamont, remember? He was—for months—close-to-gone. Everyone knew. *You* saw it on him. You did. Told me as much; and all due respect but you are not the most perceptive scout in the troop. Maybe the kid helped him along?

He gave me the look of a man saying a thing without saying it.

—Was Arn also . . . ? I said.

—Liver cancer. In pain. He was yellow as corn, Dill said.

I know when I'm licked.

GRANT US THE SERENITY TO ACCEPT

Except that I don't, and Jeannine had said it, and I didn't want to hear it, but she had been right: it was time to god-damn sack up. I knew what had to be done, which was that I'd ask the boy about his book. Just ask him. Not so hard.

Except that scamp knew how to scamper. And so, for yet another goddam time in this terrible tale: I had to sniff him out.

Meaning I had to canvass the community in order to get even a whiff. A community that had, to say the least, become pretty damned jaundiced about the boy.

—He's baaaaaad news, Ed. Why do you care? Maybe he goes to the Oasis Wash-and-Fold now, said Nancy.

—Johnnie don't know neither, said Sheryl.

—C'mon, Ed, please, said Dill.
—I'm easy-breezy. Don't you fret.
—Do something else. Solitaire, skeet shooting, jerk off, for chrissakes.
At that I was silent.
—You'll make things worse. I know you don't believe that, but you don't have to believe something in order for it to be true.

—You know I tolerate you . . . said Hankie, letting his shitty implication drift down the line.

—Don't be a homo, said Lemon.

—No, Regis said while hanging up.

—Suck my balls, said the kid by the Culpos embankment. He ground to a stop on his board; a little too close and stared me down. Then hopped back on and skated around me in a neat little circle before rolling away; leaving me alpha-dogged by the runt of the litter.

—Narc, the girl in the shop said, and slouched on back behind the register.

(I did see the man with the brown T-shirt then but could not ask him for fear, as he most certainly held some subtle and malevolent sway over the boy.)

—Making a complaint? the cop said.
—Just trying to find him.
—File a missing persons.

Tuesday Wednesday Thursday Friday then finally.

Lo and behold but he was back in the lot again. The crew'd had enough of him, but Reg had always been a free thinker and a greedy bastard.

So the kid was alone under that locust—our place—looking like a scarecrow who has been fed through a thresher. He was surveying the land like the story had begun all over again. The whole rest of the gang: huddled as far from him as they could be.

After the initial shock, his presence there, then, felt almost disappointing, so normal, and some of the gravity and drama deflated.

Still, I had decided to do what had to be done, had

decided firmly, and had been toting around that notebook with me for that purpose basically everywhere.

—You invite him? said Nancy to me.

Johnnie glowered, and Sheryl looked sullen, as a waitress asked for a fresh pot of coffee fifteen minutes from the end of her shift.

—I had nothing to do with it, he's done nothing, and whatever happened to kindness.

The trailer door opened and Reg came out having heard us bickering, only to chuckle in spite.

I left them all there.

Almost exactly halfway to the kid I realized I'd left the book in the goddam glove. Jesus, Ed.

By then he had seen me though and I stopped, totally stuck, rooted like a turnip. But there was no way I was going to one-eighty and go get the thing, so I started walking again, straight on; man on a mission. He walked toward me too and I saw that he was favoring his left leg. (We had that pained gait in common. I was gimping like an idiot then for those reasons all my own, and of course I gimped my way through the rest of that year and am gimping far worse now, when I am able to walk at all, that is.)

Anyway we gimped, and then I was right there in front of him.

—How's tricks, I said.

—You know, he said.

—I do not know, and where you been? I said, at which point he raised his head and I saw his weirdling eyes. This time, I was reminded of the eyes of those lizards you see gargoyling out upon the hot wasteland rocks. And I felt for a moment like I was in a place that was not that place, and then the old dizziness came over me again, my knees buckled again, and I fell on them as in prayer, just like when the kid and me first met. He reached out a hand, but I didn't take it.

—Uuhng, I said.

And then Reg called the names and, just as I knew he would, called the kid's.

The 302ers looked murder, but Reg don't care. No one said another damned thing in any case and they all got in the work van.

I was no longer chauffeur or anything else to him, if ever I was.

Dill had chosen not to go work, instead hustling over to me, having been the only one to have seen it.

—Like I told you, you need a new hobby, Dill said, but looking troubled.

—No shit, I said, shrugging off his hand too, and, very slowly, levering myself up.

Later that day I went (for a change) to the Badger Tavern, to be alone, and to take the edge off what had just happened. I did this using several doctor-prohibited drinks.

After, I pitched my way back toward my truck, which I had parked in front of the pharmacy, several blocks from there. The woozy walk took me past the faded, pastel row-houses, trimmed in white aluminum—sorry ice-cream cakes in a supermarket fridge. The evening was as hot as they were then, and are, and there were people out front of these houses in lawn chairs, chawing and more or less doing nothing but hoping to catch a stingy breeze, even a lukewarm one. Bikes let to lie where they fell, multiple ATVs per driveway, kiddie pools set out in the dirty, grassless yards, cans of beer bobbing in them.

—Amen, brother, came the shout down from one of the chairs.

I looked over and there was the man from the feed store (this time he was wearing no shirt at all) smirking at me once again like we shared a secret. I kept walking.

But then I changed my mind and circled back.

—Praise be to him, he called out as I got close, lifting his beer in a toast.

The whole town was in a miasma of heat, and it cast a distortion in the air.

—"The child came to us," he said.

—Fuck off.

—"He shall feed his flock," he said.

—He doesn't have no flock.

—Accept him into your heart.

—Keep him out of yours.

—He's got what we *need* . . . he said, and sat up straighter, not smirking a bit anymore, and making to stand up fully.

I turned and started walking away.

—Let the boy be, I said over my shoulder.

He laughed, and his laugh hung in that ponderous air.

Again, my father. His need and longing. His pain. Again, holding the dress.

In that way dreams have of—not shifting exactly, but

presenting new material as if it had always been there—I saw
a figure standing behind him. It was only a charcoal smudge
of a person as everything was dark, and the figure was hidden by Dad's shadow. He was, of course, thin. His shoulders
were wide and wilted at the corners. The shadow-kid placed
his hand upon Dad, as if to urge him back into the murk.

———————————————

"He's got what we need," the man had said. So the kid was
dispensing, but dispensing what? Sadness, sure, and some
respite from boredom or suffering; but perhaps even some
kind of obscene pleasure?

Dill knew a cop down Sepulse city who told him there
was then some heat on the kid.

—It's my fault, I said to Chantal.

She turned off the tap.

—All of it, I said.

I could hear her wipe her hands on the dish towel.

—"I'm bored," I'd said. "I need new things," I'd said.

—Let's go out, she said.

—Prayed for *a change.*

—A film. Something, she said.

—I don't know.

—*Sherr-ee* . . . she said.

—Maybe it was going to happen anyway.

—Dance hall.

—It was all so dead. God, the prospect of more-such.

—Picnic. *Deenay soor layrb.*

—"A hole needs filling," I'd said.

She looked at me with what I can only call professionally astonished indignation. My, how her selective hearing and poor English could be weaponized. Her unique and powerful way of changing the subject.

—I'm being serious over here, I said.

She came close, and her thighs pressed up against my leg.

—Me too, she said.

—I'm feeling real low.

She bent back, took her heels off one at a time.

I looked at that spiny birthday plant, erect on the table, and then back up at her.

Why wouldn't any of my nearest and dearest lend an ear and take it in?

Everything had changed and the globe had tilted when I put him on that first job. Only then. His coming.

So shouldn't I have deserved a little condemnation? Been held to the fire for it—for Cyndi? For his rabble? For having forgot—in my need—that some miracles bring on the dark? That there are both good miracles and bad ones?

And here comes a real sermon because I would like to talk about that now.

SERMON

And he will change our body to be like
his, according to the working whereby
he is able to subject all things to himself.
—Philippians 3:21

Miracles; here's my two cents:

To begin with, some miracles—and probably most—consist not of magic, but merely of a change. A change from the regular. A new thing. Fresh manner of being and of seeing. And so miracles are good and necessary, because over time a man grows used to what he knows, and holds every single one of his assembled facts close—so close in fact, so tight, under such immense heat and pressure, that they all coalesce into a hot and gooey tar, at which stage this asphalt is in turn slopped on down, steamrolled, and then it paves the immutable way of the world. A man will henceforth take these roads everywhere, always, never deviating from them, and it becomes impossible for him to imagine that there was, or could ever be, any other path to travel.

So taking, or even being shunted into, a detour becomes as hard as could be, virtually impossible. But a miracle then is that: a sudden rerouting; opening of a new terrain; a sudden and new way of viewing the world afresh.

But of course, there are other kinds of miracles too.

———

There once was this guy I knew who used to pour drinks for us. He gave them out in a cheery way like he was manning an ice-cream truck.

We never saw one another outside of that place. But liked one another. He got himself sober finally and quit the bar and got some bottom-rung position working in one of the big glass office towers in Byron. When he left bartending, his place at the Crown was taken by a guy who everyone uniformly found to be bad. Stingier even than the manager required him to be.

I wanted that old bartender back.

Anyway, that guy I'm telling you about moved to the big ole city and jumped to his death.

After the man's service, I had a smoke outside the church with someone who said that this bartender had got up from his desk on the ninth floor at that new job of his and levered open one of the big floor-to-ceiling windows. It was one of the windows none of the others in the office knew even opened. They-all just watching him do it, no one knowing what was required of them, and you could see them looking around at each other like "this cannot be good . . ." Then the old bartender surprised everyone by walking away from the window and down to the Men's. The gusts were bothering everyone's paperwork, and just as one of them got up to close the damn thing, the former bartender came out of the bathroom with an odd expression on his face, not looking at them or anything but straight on. His hair had been newly slicked down with water, and his shirt was then neatly tucked in, and for some reason he had taken his shoes off, and he strode down the aisle separating their cubes and it suddenly became clear, and he didn't stop at all until he reached the window, at which point there was no downward look, but only a final, slightly bigger step, as if he were casually stepping over a curb, and he went plumb out and down.

Just taking a walk.

I wept that bartender's funeral and did ok. Back in my place, I began to write—in my head—a poem about him, thinking I should expand my repertoire beyond cattle drives and campfires. Next morning I committed it to paper.

It was grandiose in the basest way. More importantly, I knew I hadn't worked hard enough at it, and that I wouldn't. But also I mean more importantly that I could never fathom this man, this suicider. I could not reach into what I knew of him and take from those facts something larger, and thus could not imagine him right. Lacked the true talent. Could not feel that-all.

I suppose this is to say that with words, as with weeping, the real triumphs are arrived at in such a way: getting down deep. When you do, and can, it all simply comes out correct. Real McCoy style.

Such work pays off, even though it must be said also that there are limits, and, in the end, it is all still guesswork.

Unless . . .

. . . you just see it. From the get-go. See in. Deep. Deep through the brainpan to the all and all and all and everything, until you can see no further, having reached the vaporous, roiled, and sparking core of another person's real self. That far-off milky clump of stars that regular vision cannot make out for trying. Seeing so well, far and deep, that you can even see not only the now, but the becoming.

But, that way of seeing: you have to be born with it, and

that is genius. Not something achieved, but something given.

Miracles: there are those that confirm and corroborate; those that are calls to action; those that help, heal, inform, delight. But there also exist those miracles that divide, confuse, instigate.

And also there is such a thing as one miracle too many.

I mean, how many can a body take?

I had wanted my fill; more and more. And when remembering that bartender who suicided I think about the kid's works, and how, despite his deep vision and understanding, perhaps they were not quite like those on the side of the angels—marvels which serve as demonstration of divine grace and that lay that grace upon all of us. I say this because miracles, especially the kind he dispensed, should be used only in compassion, and again, Rev's: *suffering beside.* Not suffering *at, from, above,* nor *below.* Not *causing to.*

Because we weepers do a very specific job: we get things going. We do not heap onto the general pile of sadness. We allow others to find their own. Abet, coax. We help them to reach what needs to be reached. We do no more, no less.

The kid broke this particular rule, broke it making of normal sorrow a new thing—chaotic, keening, cataclysmic. Ugly. Unseemly. Not encouraging the tears as much as fracking for them.

So he was adding, and (another rule broken) more importantly, usurping.

The feelings of others are not—no matter how we might shepherd them along—ours.

Usurping. The Code of the Weeper forbids this sin in particular.

So robbery, I'd decided. That was his miracle.

READING OF THE EPITAPH

And as it happens, next, there was indeed a robbery, and a real-life one.

The day the robbery went down happened to be an important one for the 302. An annual observance.

There is, here in our country, a day—the same day every year—called, I shit you not, National Planning Your Epitaph Day.

(Of course no one knows about this day, just as no one knows about National Systems Administrator's Day, or National Alien Abduction Day, or Lost Sock Remembrance Day either.)

This particular observance is, according to its creator, "dedicated to the proposition that a forgettable gravestone is a fate worse than death." Which I dispute. I hope my epitaph is merely a name and two dates, meaning duly inscribed "dullard," remembered as I lived. (As "a dullard.")

Stupid as the whole thing is, our country does *not* observe a Take Your Daughter to Mourn Day, etc., so this was as close as weepers get to being men and women of the hour.

There's no parade or anything, but on the morning in

question, rather than work, we (just us lifers; not the fly-by-nighters or Larry-come-latelies and most definitely not the kid) meet in the old cemetery and Dill brings the barbecue. Eat, talk, and walk the graves.

I always love seeing those old tombstones, worn down to molars. Inscriptions especially. There's one marked RANDOM, for a man conceivably named thus. Another is called WEED, which will crack me up always, even knowing it is the stone of Samuel Weed, the famous abolitionist. My favorites though are the ones marked merely HUSBAND, or WIFE. It is so touching that folks would want to be remembered in such a way. But also I find it funny because WIFE also reads to me as a cause of death. (As does HUSBAND.)

So we do that, read the old epitaphs and think what our own might be.

But had I had some inkling of what was going on at that very moment, I would have known my epitaph to be "Injured Party," because my property was burgled.

When I got to the trailer after the get-together, I saw my door was flapping around in the breeze, which is no big thing as often it'll just swing open on its own. It was always so flimsy you could unhinge the fucker with one hand.

Going in, I closed it after me; went in the bedroom for a lie-down. It's tiny, and there's precious little in it. Calling it a "room" is giving far too much credit where none is due. There's a bed which is essentially a cot, a shallow dresser, a few books, a framed photo of my mom on the wall next to that certificate I won in my high school writing contest (this left everyone flabbergasted, me having been a steady C student). So there was basically nothing in there, and thus my eye went immediately to the spot where something was missing.

It was (or rather wasn't) my dad's tie.

When I wasn't actively being strangled by it, I kept that tie hanging from a knob on my dresser, where it was, at that moment, decidedly absent. And though it's true that it could've been misplaced, especially during one of my unsober spells, I doubted that. I just couldn't lose that thing for trying, though there was many a time when I wished I had (a man simply cannot be absent-minded on purpose), so I felt that perhaps my luck was changing. A random stroke of fortune. I'd *gotten rid*. Perhaps someone else would now suffer that perpetually pinched and monotonous ghoul instead of me. And then I found that other things were gone too.

1. Coffee maker: a vintage, off-brand "Señor Café." The bottom of the pot was permanently rimmed with brown, like a drained lake or an old toilet. Worthless.
2. Boots: two pair, one leather, one snakeskin. One previous owner, high mileage. Worthless.
3. Four porcelain dinner plates, the ones they used to give away at tollbooths as part of a municipal giveback. Each had a different local attraction on them, chipped and faded. 1. State's biggest organ pipe cactus ("Ole Prickles"). 2. Sepulse Crater. 3. The Crying Rock. 4. The old Quantro uranium mine. Pretty much worthless though I don't keep up with the prices for vintage plates and such.
4. Several bottles from my medicine cabinet. I suppose that when I say I didn't own anything valuable it was

because I forgot about the medications. Those pain-dulling ones in particular. These were *quite* valuable actually, more valuable on the street than the price I paid for them at the pharmacy. So valuable that I always got evil-eyed by the pharmacist when filling the scrip.

5. One carton of my browns. For some reason this one made me madder than any of the other pilferings.

6. All my booze bottles were empties on that day so fuck that burglar for the scrote that he is.

7. The bottle of cologne Chantal got me once. I hated the smell, and only used it on those rare times when we'd go to a fancy dinner because she insisted on it. In the meanwhile it had been evaporating in the heat and what was left had consolidated into a green goo smelling of men's room soap. Good riddance.

8. A milk crate. Not a loss per se.

But excepting that this crate contained my mother's paperbacks, her yellowed favorites, including the heavily underlined dictionary and thesaurus. And I couldn't, and still can't bear to think of their loss. The more time passes the more valuable they seem, and I hope that if I encounter her in the beyond (perhaps soon even), she may recite them all to me. Perhaps she would've had it all committed to memory—every book she'd ever read—during all that time cloud-sitting. Heck, being as she was, she might have also memorized everything that ever transpired period; each instant of every day, every inhale and exhale, so on, all of those moments which would of course include everything in the way of love between her and me, and that especially. Perhaps we too shall all remember everything that ever happened to us when we get up there, and that's just part of it. If so, heaven would just be a form of living our lives right over from the start, and maybe this is what people mean when they say their lives flashed before them and eternity might be continuous reruns. I of course do not like this idea, and would consider this scenario not a heaven, but in fact quite the other thing.

(The fucking books though.)

Anyway, that was basically it in terms of items gone. There may have been others but they would've been too small and insignificant for me to remember and were therefore not worth a damn to begin with. Who would've bothered with me and this sad trove of bullshit? I'm not a famously rich person obviously.

It was while taking inventory that I noticed a circle of light playing on the Frigidaire.

It wiggled and shimmered. I stared at it, then turned around to see the spoon or watch that was doing the reflecting.

Instead I found a neat hole halfway up the wall. Around an inch high and wide, its lip bending in toward my kitchen. Exit wound. And there was another, about half a foot lower.

I went back outside and saw nothing at first but then saw the lone, remaining Scottie. Lying on the ground across the way like a bloodied decorative cushion. It didn't take a goddam Sherlock to know what had gone down there, meaning that most likely, one of those upstanding neighbors of mine—

seeing a stranger on the property and thinking that the much-discussed, ever-expected government incursion had finally found its way to the outskirts of Los Culpos—reached for a rifle, ran outside, and tried to no-scope. Having no skill or knowledge, they capped their own dog and also my mobile.

I walked over, looked at the pup. Little guy was blown to smithereens.

I heard my neighbor say from behind me:

—You some kind of *animal lover.*

He leaned, one arm high up against his doorframe, asshole wife peering from under.

I stared at them, rageful rejoinder stuck between my tongue and palate, but then I swallowed, turned, and walked away, leaving them to do what needed to be done. If they could muster the energy. Dog was over their property line.

Once back inside mine, I went to my toolbox, pulled out a Phillips, and tightened the hinges and lock on my door as tight as could be.

Later I learned about how no one else in the park had been hit, and so the crime struck me then as deeply personal. Further to that it did also seem because of this that the deed may have been done by someone who knew I would not be at my home that day.

Someone who knew it was epitaph day.

Though that was quite impossible, truly.

—Stay at mine tonight? Dill said.

—Why would I want to do that.

—Case you freaked.

—I am not freaked.

—Good. You snore like a backhoe.

—Thanks all the same.

—Have another, it'll calm the nerves, said rancher Hector Knox, who was downbar but close enough to eavesdrop.

—Don't, said Dill.

Hector there knew, as a rancher, that you're supposed to give beer to horses when they are holding their sweat. The holding in of things makes them overheat, and the beer gets that out. But I didn't need to get anything out, didn't want to be more inebriated, and so got up for air; past the Men's; through the dark and narrow passage out to the scrubby lot behind the building. There was a single klieg. I stood there looking at the x-ray of a big cottonwood. After a while Dill came out with his beer and was there for a bit before going back in. Some woman came and left. Bartender too, who was on break.

Then I was alone again.

And I was thinking how this moment between worlds would be prime hunting grounds for Dad, yet there was no sign of him. I waited awhile. Maybe; maybe not.

It used to be that when I wore that tie at night I'd feel him scrape around like a scorpion trapped under a drinking glass. But having lost it, I could not ignore the new feeling: that creeping sense that he too was leaving forever. I felt it was true. Felt it deep in my nethers.

Had his abiding spirit been held there in that bolo tie like a saint's relic—finger bone, etc.? Seemed too simple.

One more beer then and Dill came and got me and we folded ourselves up like a rusting clutch of umbrellas.

<u>Take up your neighbor's hand.</u>

SUFFER NOT ALONE

I listened to the steak-sizzle of sand hitting the RV's aluminum. The mirror was where I'd left it and I looked in it: things were pretty fucking glum.

One glum chum.

In the kitchen I looked through my new peephole and saw the dog was gone.

Then I went outside, where the neighbors had pegged up one of those wilted cardboard red-white-and-blue LIBERTY! signs out front of their patch. Christ, I thought, nothing makes a fascist quicker than being shown up as a chickenshit, and I guess the intruder had done that to them.

I took my coffee back into the trailer and parked at the table. On the radio was a man reading local news:

CULPOS "HORSEMAN OF THE YEAR" KILLED OWN HORSE WHILE SHOOTING AT WIFE (AUTHORITIES TELL US).

That sad tale was it as far as local color, but then came on a man's furious haranguing, him being yet another organ-grinder cranking out the pitchy tunes of a political death cult, and it didn't help that I was already angry, but after listening then it was as if someone had sneezed a great rage onto me; and so I changed the station, but another version of this man was on all of them, and why was I listening to the damn news in the first place? Pissed as I was, I thought: I should do something about that damn sign next door and that something was uprooting it and tearing it into mulch. But I did not.

So it was I also had my own cowardice to consider.

Cowardices. Various:

That I abided throughout that long stretch of my numb living of course, in attendance to nothing but the daily offices of my dereliction, but mostly I never did ask the kid *what*, nor *why* about a thing; ask him not outright and in so many words. I remembered how I did not inquire—that time once when I saw him set on the steps outside Town Hall—about why the kid had been in there, about birth certificates, social security numbers, driver IDs, hell even about hunting licenses. That had been a real perfect moment for it; some background out of him. And neither did I accost him when I saw him on the street directly after the whole prison to-do—out on the street with the man from the jail, the huge one with the brown shirt and the rolling waves of fat. Cowardice, there too.

And just then, as I was making a list of my cowardices various—as if in a parable—the kid stepped out of the fog.

———————————

The fog came in sudden, and I saw it first from the mobile's windows, cloaking the park, carpeting the ground, and I said out loud: Holy Shit; as this was a marvel—miracle of miracles, precipitation at last, and rain will surely follow, will fall—but it wasn't until I raced my ass back out the door and smelled the smoke that I knew it for a brush fire (it was a bad one), and he walked from that white wall, strode out, from whence I knew not, as if he was not of this earth—for what purpose he came I could not divine—and he came to me and we did nothing except stand there. Having kept the habit of kicking the ground he had bloodred dirt from the desert on his shoes, and dropped the kerchief from over his mouth and said:

—How's about this.

And I said:

—Yeah, Jesus.

—I come in? he said.

—Course.

—Got anything to drink? he said, and I thought he meant alcohol.

—Wait, I said, and got water from the tap.

And we sat, nothing inquired about what he had been doing roaming out there, as I did not want to ruin the moment. But he was slumping in his chair so precariously, I had to go around his back and hoist him by his armpits and he was terrible-badly.

—Stay, I said.

—I got places.

But I knew of course why he had come and made him lay down on the cot again and he did so and was quickly asleep.

————————————————————

Those days were the most intimate we ever spent, and perhaps this is because he could not leave for the aches and pains on him, and it was as if he was performing an uncanny imitation of me. Was it all for my sake, I thought, seeing him suffer his version of what I suffered, which was surely cockamamy, but I did think this then, seeing how he shook and vomited and scratched and was generally in the throes. And when he wasn't, he was nodding out.

Then one morning:
—I gotta go, he said.

And there was no arguing as he was already putting on his ruined shoes, and he would've walked on out same as he had walked on in, so we went to the truck, me yelping at him constant, me propping him up, and what a sight me and him, like in a war mural. And I drove him back to town, leaving him at his, and later found one of my dresser drawers wide open.

(So you see, Francine was right about me being "such a little bitch." A "bitch" about the kid, but also in general.)

LOOK NOT BACKWARD, BUT FORWARD

Naturally I was especially softened at that time. Frail of body, but also I should not have been exhuming my past, my father, those old poems of mine.

Brought things up, such poems, not good things (I still see in them my heart on my sleeve, rather than locked in its cage where it properly belongs).

What a wet fucking blanket, me. My poetry is sappy, no

doubt, but, well, maybe it isn't always totally terrible, even despite the forlornness all about it. Sad, sure. But also: not altogether lousy.

And (welcome now to *Poetry Corner...*) by the by, you'd think the things you make by-yourself-and-for-yourself—poem, ship in a bottle, hole in the ground, even, God bless, a real-life account of something bad that truly happened—well, you'd think you would have real authority over that. But even such things as these will not come out as intended and bend to your bidding.

What ever does? In the case of my poems though, my lack of success is not simply down to "the general way of things." There is a true reason for it, and that is that I cannot, no matter how hard I try, reconcile two distinct voices—my mother's high-flown talk and my dad's flat, down-home ugly one. Her milk, his tobacco juice, at war in my mouth.

Nevertheless, I can, every now and then, still eke out a decent piece of writing, one I'll consider passable. Poems like my: "Final Roundups," or "Light at Old Bluffs," or "A Rooftop of Sage," and "Canyon Stray."

So it always comes as a surprise to me when one of my poems works out; though perhaps it shouldn't. Some people collect hubcaps or shells on the beach or sticks to whittle, but I had always collected words and phrases, which I have always shoved deep into a pocket, until that pocket overflowed, at which point I started in on another pocket, eventually having to spill them out into jars. Jars to barrels . . . and now it is like I own, out behind my trailer-home—an in-ground pool of language. It is green with gunk for lack of cleaning; really should not be swum in.

And I can, on occasion, see something in there that might be unexpected—something that catches the eye, like, say a commemorative silver dollar, often all the way at the bottom, down by the drain, glimmering through a small window between the moldy leaves, saggy floats, and drowned prairie dogs.

When such a thing occurs, I dip a skimmer in deep, and pull whatever that shiny thing might be out of the slime. Which in turn would mean that those words of mine will sit up for me just right. Most times they don't of course, but there was always the chance of it.

It also helps that I stick to the cowboy shit. Its tone and subjects. Deserts. The long rides. Coyotes, etc. As it's easier, the language and form of it; its cookie cutters.

And I take as my examples those poems like Ferret Johnson's, who is famous for those homespun, humorous anecdotes about life on the trail; those of Fletcher Smalls, whose poems tended toward the tragic—death of horses, cowboys drowning while fording rivers, the scrub-fire destruction of ranges, etc.; like Big Jimmy Wallace's, who ventriloquizes an old prospector's confusion about—and antagonism toward—modern life; Sam Brownyoke's, at whose feet I once sat, and whose elegiac poems about the long-gone life of trailheads and bitterness regarding the loss of the "old ways" are a frequent warm-up feature on the rodeo circuit. Each and every one of these Stetson-wearing professionals, myself included, did a hardscrabble stint at some point in their youth and have earned the longhorn buckles, and know and love a life in the saddle.

I know a cowboy is now, mostly, a mere notion, and often

a terribly misused one at that. And yet we need such cowboy poems, if only as reminders of the territory before it began to shrink and the range became more idea than viable career choice. And so it is we who commemorate, and should, as we love that life in a way that can only spring from acquaintance with a fallen Eden.

So maudlin or no, cowboy poems are what I've chosen, and at least there's a genre there, with a particular style attached; which means, on some level, such pieces as these are supposed to be (well, folksy, but also) a little bit nostalgic, a whole lot corny, and as purple as the heart Johnnie got from the army.

And poems are hard and I'm not a real poet and boo hoo.

The thing I do have a natural, God-given talent in—one that does not take so much labor, and one that makes my tears possible and weeping a viable calling—is *regret*.

POETRY READING IV

I think on rides—if never rode—
that would've spared my horse.
If only Lucky never drowned;
that river changed its course.
Each day I'm saddled with: *what if*;
bridled with: *but, why.*
I wish I'd shake my blinders off
And let my dead horse die.

E.F.

DO NOT CAST YOURSELF INTO REGRET

And the Lord regretted that he had
made man on the earth, and it
grieved him to his heart.
—Genesis 6:6

Regret: I am very fucking good at that, and just in general get caught up in the ruing of things. Things that needn't have been, if only I'd have done my bit differently. Regret—that particular, hindsight flavor of grief—which comes as spill-off from the central artery which is called: *things, good and bad, may always be otherwise.*

Things may always be otherwise is the sole dominion of human beings—available to no other species—the cause of our ascendancy and the seed of our ruin. When we think of all our advancements—from these reading glasses to what's in my drip; from my truck's internal combustion to the gadget which revolves the wieners at the gas station; from the U-bend on my toilet to the happiness tablets which Jeannine took . . . even the very words I spout—I think of how someone somewhere looked out at the world and thought: *nope*, and then *maybe*.

When my dad would bring down those bucks, and they would not be dead but almost that, they would sprawl there staring up just like that wounded Scottie; and in their black and bulged eyes was never regret, but rather pure panic and agony. I'd turn away then, of course, unable to bear that-all; being encompassed in those eyes, and Dad would shout some mean, shitty, and spiteful garbage—mock me for this, or worse—and he'd make me do the mercy itself which would end the suffering (and to force my hand would prod and worry the animal with a boot; stepping down so the blood would gout), but later, I'd think on such events (with regret) and imagine, for such creatures as these—God's innocents—that life is riding a quick river; tugs of current, with no time or ability to plot a real course. They attempt, where possible, to avoid peril, but immediate peril only. Such as: danger, here. *Now. Right now.*

So real pain and fear, but also real peace. Each thing what it is. So.

But we: we are cursed with the "what if" of it all, and this—as I've now said already—allows for all we have by way of dominion, but also all that anxiety, remorse, and disappointment.

It is worth mentioning that regret, as I experience it, can also be, perversely, just a general feeling—meaning devoid of such specific, personal content; unallied to special or individual disappointments.

I feel this species of regret from time to time.

It is periodic, as if the skin on me thickens and thins with the wax and wane of the celestial bodies. And in such times, the times of this feeling, without knowing why, all at once, that regret seems to have flavored the world, and everything has a strange tang to it; as if I was then receiving life like drinking water from a tin cup.

I feel this way now.

Maybe these recollections have put me off.

Or maybe it's a passing car on a sultry day, and the wash of someone else's music going by, or the heat-wave clouds, massed way off. Maybe it is nothing, as usual. The thirsty yard from my window, the chide of the hopeless sprinkler, the hum of the fridge, the groan and whine of a toilet, coming through the wall from the patient next door . . .

So much work to keep us cool and damp. So much work.

When I still worked before the sick got me well and good, I'd drive past those irrigation units out by the old highway. Large grids of thin, sagging pipe. Useless. But once used to water the—what is it—*alfalfa*.

I'd think how it is that I now feel like one of those machines too. And I wonder why they leave those out there, as those fields have been sterile forever.

And I regret the building of them, as they have ended up dilapidated like me; just another leaky pipe which served its time and was left to ruin.

SCRIPTURE READING

Weep and wail upon that day.

—EZEKIEL 30:2

ONE OF US

The night after the kid left my care, my dome hurt like a strongman squoze it. There were the wobbles, and once again my hands shook. My state was worsening undeniably and it got so bad by then that, in the ensuing weeks, at the end of services, Dill would have to come up to my aisle and take my arm and walk me up those rows like in a reverse marriage ceremony (a funeral is in some ways a divorce, I suppose).

But because of my quivering mitts, the next morning I had a very bad shave, cut myself all over, and had to throw my only towel out (once white). My razor is a straight one, inherited too, and no comment upon that. Anyway, I needed to be clean-cut for the next job, which I was not going to miss—pain or no pain—as it was for Crazy Patti; Crazy Patti, retired weeper, who was called on home.

(Yes: we die too.)

What I mean is not only do weepers pass on, but we also have funerals.

This always seems to surprise people, as if we aren't human beings—perishable in our own right—but more like official equipment in the funerary-industrial complex; an urn, a shovel . . . And when we pass it is always the same confusion and everyone acts like they just found out their dentist had a tooth pulled.

Anyway, the important thing is that in mid-November, Crazy Patti was gone. Coronary infarction. She was found in her house four days after the event, her sugar gliders shivering and goggle-eyed with hunger.

I offered to help clean the place and direct her belongings however they should be directed—which was nowhere really, as Patti never had anyone. But then a distant cousin (so distant you'd need a telescope to find him on the family tree) screeched on in from out of state, I suppose in the hope that he would find something of value there. He was to be sorely disappointed value-wise, yet still took off with anything not nailed down (Patti's pets were not nailed down, and though he did not take them, they were loyal to the last, swirling around, dive-bombing and strafing this lowlife as he struggled to get the cracked Hummel figurines and tarnished aluminum silverware into cardboard boxes).

And so there was nothing for me to do but find a new home for those pets of hers, which I did, and, of course, to attend her service.

The 302 met before, down at the lot.

Crazy Patti had retreated even deeper into herself prior

to the heart attack that got her, rarely working and rarely leaving her place at all, which I suppose is not that uncommon with weepers. There seems to be two ways of it when it comes to prolonged sorrow: 1. It drives us toward others, and the comfort you hope can be proffered. 2. It drives us to shun others (and a hermit, among other things, is a person without anyone to mourn). Meaning that the prospect of ridding oneself of loss can seem more and more attractive to men and women predisposed to meditate upon it constantly.

So Patti being of the latter type, we had essentially all but forgot she existed. But all who work 302 are family and so we were a plenary session. Exception of the kid.

The boy's weird (and increasingly weird) would simply not do for Patti's remembrance, not one bit. So when I say it was all of us there, I felt it was; even Reg agreeing that the boy brought more potential trouble than the money was worth. Thus was he struck from the rolls. Excommunicated. That was the end of him as 302; the final chapter in The Book of the Kid; Professional Mourner.

That aside, as usual down in the lot we smoked and jawed, standing in the dust, before circling up, waiting until someone would step forward and say something appropriate, assuming it to be Dill or me, but then Reg, ill-advisedly-and-totally-out-of-fucking-nowhere gave a botched little speech. We bowed our heads because what else the fuck were we going to do? Reg said:

—Petulla, who we all knew as Patti, was a strange lady; boy did she love those little fucking sugar bats of hers. She was always on time, put in the effort . . . anyway, screw it.

Good enough for government work. Reg walked away then to feed the Rottweilers, and we disbanded to the vehicles and off to the service.

Which was touching, with only us in attendance. Some good, heartfelt tears. We had splurged on a big sashed wheel of flowers and a blown-up poster-board photo of Crazy Patti set up there on an easel, her staring out crookedly at us all in a blessing of the lifelong mutual idiocy we had all signed up for.

Overall, a decent send-off. The final words of it were given by Dill, which was correct and as it should be, as Dill is always very good and fatherly at such things. There was no formal passing of condolences afterward with no one to pass them on to except one another, which we did, shaking hands and hugging.

We were done by noon, and I wasn't going to the Crown, being so generally feebly to begin with. We all went off toward the Burger Mr. Papo, which was over in Fort Cuervo—a mere dot on the map. I was the first, and when I got there, the town was totally empty. I saw a toppled paper rack, an empty, sun-warped ice tray on someone's windowsill; a condom in the street. Something scrabbled. Chafing wind.

The kid had been everywhere and nowhere and suddenly there he was in Fort Cuervo, standing in the empty street like a lugubrious gunslinger, looking down to the turnoff as if waiting.

—Hey, he said, opening a conversation like he did that regular.

—What are you . . . I said.

—Dunno, he said.

We walked to the curb in silence.

I looked him up and down, taking his measure anew; for a suit or coffin, and . . . Oh-help-me-Rhonda but wasn't he just wearing my dad's tie.

He played with the strings. Not shameful. Looked back at me.

I saw the thing as I'd never seen it then, the delicate veins of black running through the turquoise. So close up and clear. I fell into it, sucked in like into a vacuum.

Inside that stone I spent a life, in a green sea, summed in its currents of time and memory, then receded back out, and I drifted into voided space as an astronaut sees the diminishing earth, hung in the black by strings of stars, and felt a serenity all over, as he had granted me this extraordinary thing, which was, getting down to it, a piece of goodwill: a charity. The removal of a great burden.

Gang wasn't far behind, and everyone upon seeing the kid was primed for umbrage, and Chantal was the first to come up and so was the first to see the thing he wore, and was moving to rip it off of his delicate neck but I took her arm.

—A gift, I said to her; smiled and nodded. She pulled her arm away from me forceful. People trickled over.

Outrage can feel good to a soul, and even decent folk can

be reluctant to let it drain off. Dill began to raise an objection but I nodded "fuck off" and he nodded "ok, ok." Sheryl had put her arm around Johnnie's waist as he is always the first to action and last to peace.

—Ed, you rube, Hankie said.

The boy didn't look like any of this mattered to him particularly.

—Can we have a goddam moment? I said to everyone.

They-all crossed the street and collected there.

—I have your book, I said to the kid, which was dumb because he knew, and I knew he didn't give a shit.

—You want it back? I said.

God he reeked. But also he had got even skinnier, which hadn't seemed possible—face shrunk and had begun to look far older than his years, such that what came into my mind then was the bony gentleman who poles the dead across his river.

I had plenty more to say then, many words, almost all of them rising up as questions, the rest were words of gratitude—a thing I could never be able to successfully explain to anyone, though the truth is that I knew that this particular theft had been a great act of mercy, love, and sacrifice on the kid's part. But a squad car was already pulling up.

Cop got out, kid patted down.

Chief had taken it upon himself to call it in.

After, I turned toward my truck and saw, standing next to an idling van two blocks away, the man in the brown tee—watching, before turning around like a destroyer, getting into his ride, and then he was gone.

———

—Slap on the wrist, Chief said to me at the Crown.

—Asswipe, I said to him.

—Lockup, no big thing, Peewee said, trying for comfort.

—It's where he was headed anyway, said Sheryl.

—It wasn't for money, and that had nothing to do with it, I said.

—You're a dunce, said Hankie.

—You going to try to educate me, Hank? I said.

—You know already, said Nancy quietly.

—Every-bo-dy, please . . . said Chantal.

—He's a fucking junkie lowlife, said Lemon.

Johnnie grunted.

—But balls of steel, Lemon added admiringly.

—Tra-fucking-la, said Hankie.

(I'm not a dunce, and sure, he's a junkie—*but what kind?*)

—All he does is dope, deal, and hide; it's like you were just born, Ed, said Chief.

—Ed knows more than all of you rednecks put together, *apologies to Chantal*, Dill said.

—Apology accepted, said Chantal.

—It's not your fault, Ed, but you got carried away, Johnnie said.

—Leave it, Dill said.

I shook my head to them all gathered round me, knowing my headshake might be the final piece in a rite of expulsion, like the closing words in a St. Michael's prayer.

—I'm going to go get him, I said, but didn't.

I drove for a bit and then pulled into the parking lot of the nail salon and dental practice, parked, put my forearms up on the wheel, and closed my eyes. I then sent out a brain wave: thought it out deep, in widening concentric rings; out, into the recently hushed beyond.

And "rest" and "easy" are the words I sent there. "Rest easy," on all the frequencies. I sent that "rest easy" specifically to the star of the one-man show I'd been forced to attend every night since I was nothing but a kid myself. I hoped those words might find him.

Then I went to Chantal's, and she made my favorite con carne. Eased me into the lounger, put the game on. There was a beer in my hand. She worked my temples. Pulled a stray thread from my shirt. How I was tired.

I could have drifted off except for that something rustled in me. I asked for pen and paper.

After, I thought perhaps I had made an ok thing. That I felt I had pinned something important to the page, at least in my own, simpleton manner.

POETRY READING V

SUNSET (RIDING OFF INTO THE)

Through the desert, westward ho,
Where the colors gallop to.

A bigger herd than it began,
Because all of those colors ran.

E.F.

WE COME TOGETHER AS ONE

County jail then:

My painkillers would've been in his pockets, him clearly having rumbled the medicine cabinets.

I wondered if those priors of his would mean a bigger bail.

But I had hoped, after I got him out, whatever came of the boy, that I would no longer give a shit. That I'd be free of that-all too. (Hope being a thing with blinders.)

—The kid you're holding back there: I'll pay his release, I said to the cop.

—Someone beat you to it, the cop said back to me.

Sprung.

Sprung, I thought.

So he was sprung; and perhaps the word is "sprang," which would be better, the sound of it, because I imagined him standing on a big spring, compressed beyond tolerance, that would violently release itself and him, and *sprang!* the shit out of the kid, far into the air, up and out of the county in a perfect, miles-long arc.

Anyway who sprang him?

It had been one of *them*. I was sure of it.

They indeed were gathering. The cult of him. Weird-beards. Coterie of mental patients; unabashed, and gravely committed. Come an evening I would picture them kneeling at his feet, else ringed round him, as you would around a bonfire in unholy dance, indulging in whatever foul pleasure they might take, glancing at one another in sly collusion, not a collusion with the boy, but with one another, in on each other's game, and: how many would they become?

Man in the Kenworth, lady who'd taken the place of Brenda down by the railroad crossing, the skateboard dickhead and the rest of those Junior Scouts, man with the rattle-skin half shirt, the "wraith," the weeping willow of a girl, brown tee of course, then another one who I called "The Leathern," the young man with a cane (too young for a cane), woman with the cough, pencil-man from the lot behind the filling station, "Cans," the guy whose head craned so far from his shoulders it may as well have been perched on a phantom walking in front of him, "Some change, brother-man?," "Grainy-face," "Street Sleeper," Sammy's eldest daughter, "the delirium twins," Ranch hand 1, "Coconut," Concepción, Ranch hand 2, "On His Knees to Beg," "The Scream," "In Her Sunday Best . . ."

. . . . and so as the needy were drawn unto him, so too were amassing those on the side opposite. Animosity was rampant.

—Have you heard this shit on the radio? Dill said.

—Nutjobs.

—Stay off the streets.

—You'd think God would not have dispensed so many small penises in a single county, I said.

—You'd think, said Dill.

THEY WILL BRING A MOB AGAINST YOU

"This is America still is it not," and it being America, we pledge allegiance to the biggest, loudest, angriest grievance. And I'd go so far as to say these are—these days in America—the days of fury, with such "fury days" (and "days of grievance") celebrated each and every day, at least by some group of shitheads somewhere, meaning that you can close your eyes and throw a rock (a thing you would do in such "days of fury and grievance") and are likely to hit someone who was already killing-mad at the very idea of you.

Of course these days are also, as already told, days of numbness, and these two types of days ("fury" and "numb") are really all that's on offer, though fury is perhaps the stronger of the two feelings, meaning that blind rage may have the power to break through even the general deadening, and soon, I think, there will be no more numbness, and all we will be left with is fury.

The violence.

The violence though. Common as cancer and regular as rent, and what Dill and me were talking on then was that *huge* shitshow of "American" "fury" that began outside the city hall down Los Regardes; that militant show-of-force. The very one at which the kid performed more of his magic, that flaring and wondrous magic—another miracle, that is, perhaps one of his most astonishing.

So, a real snake roundup, squirming and corkscrewing— all that heartfelt hissing about the homeland, imminent threats to it, collective birthright bestowed and stolen (just as my old man had believed, him a real trendsetter in this department), values held dear—values which not one single oily and twining patriot there could define or explain the inherent worth of, but which the entire nest would be willing to drain their fangs to defend. And that's all I have to say in the way of snakes and let's discuss people now.

(Though there is nothing even to say that isn't already known about such lowlifes—their opinions, their ways—not even much to say about the way that particular thing went down on that particular day, as such things have a usual and generic form, down to all their finest details, the "American" style of "fury" in such "days of fury" tending to manifest as a line dance, same steps each time, the final step of which is always a barbarism.)

And here they come, marching toward the mini-mall, hitting the Wash-o-mat, sure, hitting it hard, because of some bruise—throbbing deep in their collective and delusional historical memory—a bruise blamed specifically on the Nguyens (who had been brazenly making off with those aforementioned birthrights and eroding those aforementioned values and them being prime example of those who would take illegitimate dominion over every last possible thing), and the mob set on breaking the Wash-o-mat's big front window and were walking toward it with crowbars and bats when Liem Nguyen runs out to remonstrate and is immediately and predictably pepper-sprayed.

This was right before we arrived.

Rev had been doing his laundry (robes, collars, cassocks, whatever the fuck) when they crowded their way into the parking lot, and Rev had hit the pay phone and called Dill such that we came running, and arrived to all the shouting and posturing and gloating (they hadn't got to the window yet), and Liem was laid out in front of his family's laundromat in tears of agony (by the by: different tears—pain, sorrow, anger . . . are made up of different chemicals, which is known science), and Nancy comes out the doors with a double-barreled, yelling some really fantastical—foreign, strong, and heartfelt—obscenities and well, all of us 302ers stood there agape (we were minus Johnnie, who was otherwise occupied and who, if he had showed, would've stopped those skid marks cold in their jackboots as his camo was earned and credentialed; would not have shied away for a single second from taking some of those dumpy, untested eunuchs to the mat and in the most brutal manner imaginable, but he was not in attendance, and so), we just stood there, and now I think back on that day with Dad when he hit me and I did not hit back—when, in fact, I learned that I could not hit at all or would not ever, not hit outward, but could for the rest of my life only hit inward, the enormity of the wound perhaps greater than or equal to the enormity of the rage that might've ensued, and maybe all weepers have an equivalent to that-all—though there was some vague attempt by us fellas to at least step in front of our weeper-women so as to protect, while knowing perfectly well that Chantal, Sheryl, and Lemon would have gone in there the hardest; Lemon especially, who had been dropped off by the disability van and so was riding her old-person mobility wagon, and you could just see her gearing up to ram someone and probably would have, and gotten away with that as who was going to fight a sweet old lady like Lemon, but meanwhile Nancy is shrieking, swinging that shotgun side to side, the men circling, their weapons already drawn (drawn since birth), and it was clear a *very bad thing* was about to happen, inevitable, when:

The kid, formerly at large, emerges from that alley next to the place, as if he had simply been waiting there for exactly the right moment to stroll back onto the set. Or was cued. There he was, right there, look at him as he walks straight into a surefire beating—one meant for the Nguyens; offering himself up in their stead as substitute victim, Abraham's goat, an offering sure to be accepted by this mob as equal-to-if-not-greater-than the offering they were actually planning on receiving (the Nguyens), this being because the region had more or less unanimously declared that it was clean-up-the-streets time, the kid being by then pretty much synonymous with them ("the streets"), and so as he continued that idle walk of his you could feel larynxes being primed, hear knuckles cracking, see veins popping, but still he came, the kid, untroubled, riding that line of his between vacant and pregnant, ambling toward the Main Man, him with a

head like a beet and a mouth tight as his own asshole, spear-
head of the crotch brigade—a man who, wait a minute,
seemed, suddenly, to recognize the kid, and, as the kid
walked right on and up and into the man's zone, whereupon
this fucker became, visibly, caught up in a (what must have
been, given what I'd seen of him thus far, uncharacteristic)
moment of confusion and indecision, as if this kid's auda-
cious act, this kid's indifference, meant the kid *had* something on him, something that made the man shrink an inch
or two before willing himself up back into a ramrod. Was
the man dangerously blackmailable? He certainly appeared
ashamed; perhaps at seeing his own moronic reflection in
the kid's still, depthless eyes, and it was thus that the man
and the kid ended up nose to nose, not in aggression, but in
assessment, Main Man's eyes rapid-fire scanning the
kid's face, frustrated to find nothing there, while his mob—
not possessing the subtlety of mind to realize what was
happening—fanned out, ringing them in a "fight, fight,
fight" circle, believing this to be like two generals of the
ancient world adopting single combat as a means to stop a
wholesale war, at which point all I could see were beefy
backs and no more.

The 302 stood rooted, scared, sure, but also (at least speaking for myself) recognizing the fragility (and perhaps sanctity) of that moment, how the kid, despite the danger, might
have had the whole scenario all in one palm like a pinless
grenade. I'd seen it before, and hoped.

But then, as they say:

"Cue the waterworks."

———

A real, crackerjack crying sesh, just as in those past, thunderous days. Tears begetting tears as yawns encourage yawns. Jesum Crow, I thought: these things, if they should happen at all, should go down in houses of worship, not out in front of a mini-mall, though I wasn't complaining, definitely not, as that very mini-mall desperately needed a miracle and boy did it get one. Those beefy backs began to heave, heads lower—fuckwits over there hit the hardest.

And as it got wetter and louder, I knew that the parking lot would begin to feel to them like a grave, those once furious men abruptly finding themselves strapped to a rickety lowering-truss, slowly descending six feet deep—ten feet, twenty, a thousand—convinced the gravitational pull from this light-swallowing hole might just *shhlllluuuuupp* them all down to oblivion, into that chasm (we weepers knew, always, all along, every man and woman alive was always loitering by), and now observe their fright as they back away, the circle breaking up, their choking sobs, looking down at hands which they were convinced would soon be crossed over their own chests, collectively moaning like a rack of organ pipes. It was a relief that we 302 could once again see the kid, and he was standing there, casual. I imagined a long piece of straw dangling from his mouth.

Peewee had shouted: *"it's going off!"* and he had been simply stating the obvious, and we all knew from experience that these men had crossed the invisible meridian which establishes a point of no return, like in a sexual congress, when, at a certain juncture, even if the roof were to cave in, or one's grandmother was to walk into the room and sit down in a chair with a tub of popcorn and a coke, sure as shooting one is going to just have to keep going at it until the deed is done.

And so they wailed, clinging by their toenails to the edge of that vacuuming ditch, and just as it became unbearable it stopped.

Like: *stopped*.

Pulled up by reins. All feelings expunged in less time than it took for a tear which was already leaving a man's eye to hit his cheek.

Voided of thought and emotion, dumbstruck, silent. And I remembered then that it was exactly like what had happened with the kid and those dogs at the kennel—and I had forgot the dogs (and didn't you also?) and how that barking and moaning was snuffed. I looked over at the kid, but he was already vanished.

Then, the sniffling leader of the idiot brigade wipes an eye with a forearm, walks over to help Liem up, gives him a pat on the back, the way a child will apologize—mechanically—when commanded to do so by a parent. Nancy running to Liem, Chantal running to fetch some water and a cloth for Liem's eyes, that mob in ragtag retreat—a bunch of war reenactors playing out a conflict their fathers, uncles, grandfathers had lived their lives in umbrage over—and then Dill very, very slowly removes the firearm from Nancy's trembling hand . . .

And fuck if the kid hadn't just handled it, and the only thing that was robbed that day was a rabble's self-righteous anger.

We shook our minds clear then, and took off quicker than a prairie fire in a tailwind. We all practically raced to our cars. At the Crown there was a scrum to get served first.

Strength of habit, the soothing muddle brought on by the consumption of alcohol, the cleansing effect of a supernatural amnesia, perhaps all of the above . . . but soon, nothing at all had happened at the Wash-o-mat except for a gang of angry men showing up, a rampage of idiots who turned out to be all hat and no cattle.

But me, I thought: *as he giveth, so he taketh away.*

GOD'S MYSTERY

Seriously though, how else can you explain what happened except to call it by its true name? "Miracle." One I thought was to be his last.

(Wrong.)

The family have had their disagreement, all families do: Cousin Jervis, Cousin Carl? But today, we cast such enmities aside.

TEN-GUN SALUTE

So that was what had happened at the Wash-o-mat, a marvel and no doubt. His diffusing it all, fending off the violence, his sucking and spitting it harmlessly aside.

Have you ever seen such authority, audacity, supernatural sway exercised by anyone, let alone a young man?

But just because that act of his there had been a boon and for the greater good, it did not mean my worries were lessened, and one skirmish does not make a war; as it turns out he made himself scarce once again, and things around town just went from bad to worse.

—Where's Shitburger?
—Gone. What'll it be, Edna said, impatient in her apron.
—Gone to where.
—How'm I supposed to know.
—He's always in front of here, I said.
—That makes me an expert on Shitburger? Edna said.
—Should do.
—You gonna order?

It was almost December by then.

I finally heard the truth of Shitburger after a gambling meeting. I still attended, though I had in fact started wagering anew and with even greater abandon—was back as a fixture at the OTB and spending down my savings on lotteries and dog bets. What did I have to lose? Money? Money wouldn't help where I was headed. No, I went to the meetings for the reason that a regularly scheduled event keeps you from anguish, and I've always needed to put one cowboy-booted foot in front of my other. That is.

But on this occasion, my sponsor Lewis held me back after, having heard a thing or two he wished to share.

—What happened, I said.

—Some men. Don't know who.

Some men. Some Men.

Some. Men.

Some men did for Shitburger.

(Some men.)

And no one gave a fuck. "Streets cleaned," and so on.

But there should have been a statue erected to SB—instead of that big bronze statue of town founder John Singlet; famous genocidal maniac and scourge of the indigenous. Shitburger was more part of the place than any other citizen living or dead; how he lived out there in the open and you might once have thought of him as you might a street, square, roundabout, or park. Something to expect, to navigate by. He was hard to countenance, you bet, but that was not his fault.

A terrible thing, "some men" doing for Shitburger, but as I said the atmosphere was turning toward it.

—It's simply wild out there, said Dill.

For instance, as if to push the general awfulness point home, even more of those brush fires had come from the north and put an acrid pair of sunglasses over all of us. No one, weepers nor townsfolk, felt there was any control to be had anywhere anymore. The land and sky were filled with currents, wild ones, whipping up all kinds of dirt, dirt so small you wouldn't see it in the air, but only later would it appear, dark and cloudy in my phlegm. And we felt an unspoken fear, that our paths, individual and collective, were being determined for us by some force; fearsome, darting, and ill-omened.

And so (the Dyer City groundskeeper told me), the cremains of Shitburger were hauled out to some dumping ground with neither attendants nor ceremony.

Most days at the lot, Reg would slink out of the trailer to say:

—No. Nothing.

Some days he would not come out at all (probably in fear of Lemon and her tongue).

There were so few services then. Few and far between, and we hoped this state of affairs to be temporary.

(It was not that we had fewer folks dying—that kept on as much as ever—it was just people were avoiding one another and the dead kept close.)

Our tears had stopped catching on anyway, and what events there were turned out to be low-rent, small-scale, hasty affairs, something to get through just to say you'd done it. Maybe things would improve. But it seemed unlikely. We worried about Reg shuttering it all up.

Then:

—I'm cut, Johnnie said.

—Not possible.

—Totally possible and totally true. I'm out. Sheryl's in a rage. It's cute as hell, Johnnie said.

—I'll talk to Reg.

—Ed, don't bother.

—Shouldn't be you, I said.

—I was done with it anyway.

—Hell you were. I'll convince him.

—Not worth the cost of the phone call.

—He knows how good you are. We all do.

—Won't change a thing.

—He listens to me, Johnnie.

—Not on this.

—Trust me, I said.

—Trust *me*, he said.

—Why are you so sure? I said.

—Because you're out too, Johnnie said.

—You can't even walk right, Reg said.

—I have my good days, I said.

—It's out of my hands. Your whole thing is making people sad, Reg said.

—I'm a fucking weeper, douchebag.

—You're supposed to make them cry, not make 'em depressed.

———

—A trip, my darling.

—Where would we go? I said back to my Chantal.

—Out from the smoke, she said, taking a long, quivering drag on her skinny cigarette.

But no way, no how. I wasn't going to take it all lying down. Reg or no Reg I was going to go on what jobs there were and would not be told. Who was going to stop me? I'd just find them in the obits and ask around like a ghoul.

"Who was going to stop me" and so I kept weeping, coming on my own, coming for free. And again, what did I care as I was never paying back on those medical bills and had no descendant to inherit my debts.

More importantly, as the Book of the Cowboy says: "Above all else: *look after the cattle.*"

And so it was that during this moment I snuck into an interment.

INTERMENT

A job. If not a legitimate one. Technically speaking. Not for me.

This one was for Wyatt Cockburn, who was a signals man, and who had been hit square in the face by a large, unsecured bolt off the top of a speeding diesel train (closed casket).

Sheryl, Lemon, Peewee, and Chief were there when I arrived, and having seen me, there was no lid batted nor word said. The family didn't complain either as they didn't know our roster from that which did the road work on I-20, and it only seemed like a bonus to have paid for four of us and received five.

The stone and plot was a family one, and it had been there since the days when great-great-granddaddy Cockburn had driven his steer into the region in hope of ample water, grain, and *just a little goddam peace and quiet.*

There was a sepulcher, chiseled with the numbers "1815" and the words: COCKBURN; FOREFATHER. Though it actually read: COCKBURN; FORESKIN as someone spray-painted over the last bit.

The bright paint had been washed but only half-heartedly and traces remained. The widow was incensed of course, and there was a great hubbub around getting the cemetery attendants to come back and scrub it more, which eventually they did, though could not eradicate the joke entirely as it was now also chiseled into our minds. But, though we were a little tickled, we were also pros, and thus settled in to the service.

And the thing went as they do: prayer for the dead, words from the Old Book, "for God so loved the world that he gave his one and only Son, that whoever believes in him shall not perish but have eternal life," and a reading of poetry, this being from "A Cowboy's Prayer":

"I seem to feel You near . . ."

Everyone pretty much loved Wyatt as salt of earth.

We cried.

At some point, above the black silhouettes, I saw a figure up on a small rise—holding himself away and above the thing—in front of some other vault like a guard at the tomb of the unknown soldier. Yup. I had wondered if the kid would ever show at a service again, and of course it made sense that he would, and would keep doing so (on his own, ineffable schedule of course), and when a man has such a large, unignorable, unrivaled gift, no matter how dangerously high-octane, he is compelled to the use of it. It becomes inseparable from him, just as the word "genius" describes a person and describes his talent, both.

Anyway living with death just gets into a body and quitting this, it turns out, isn't easy or simple. For me neither.

He'd be back for all the services, I thought. Had no choice, and thus he'd be back in better company.

Not that I cared. I only cared a little.

———————————

And yet when I saw him next it was in town in the front yard of the feed-store man (*He shall feed his flock*), the skinny girl was there too, and the kid—heavy lidded and slouched— they had their feet in the man's kiddie pool, green hose snaked into it, coiling between their legs.

TESTIMONIAL

Put my tears in Your bottle. Are
they not in Your book?
—Psalms 56:8

But I was wrong and he did not come back to mourn after that, and I continued to be the only funeral crasher. Though

I'd still get a sighting every now and then, just as it was, as in the beginning. I would not approach him. Me, the man who'd built the foundations upon which his church was erected. And yet still, sick and demented as I was, I continued to watch and write his ways. And the kid moved through the streets, haunting them, squinted against the low sun; drifted, pulled in some current like the mast of a dark ship. He's out back, and then he's on Main, past the cars, finding shadow under the eaves, in the lot, alone, passed by, past, anonymous, by the trash bags, in the gutter, in the aisle, the dead park: trash caressing sad trunks. What did he study, learn by heart; dark boy. Who'd forgotten more than we ever knew. Tracks and service stations and truck stops and bus stations, cardboard boxes; erect, crouching low, always there, always gone, not a creature of habit—a habit himself. Did he swing in the wind; soliciting the occult, slip past lit windows, mistaken for the sinister, penniless, graveyard shift, and he must have been taking blows and weathering all that came at him, and what had come to him, or not. Grist for it. Sacrifice, sacrifice . . . the longest-running show, but shut down after a night, his jewels of thorn. The asphalt was always hot. Piss. Beer. Improbable? The sky is always red and we earned that. Where is he? Standing at home plate like an exterminator. Won't someone help him? There he is. Here: he's not. Born. Gone. Original. Last resort, pitfall, demise. Hitching on the shoulder, and when I passed him I'd have put my foot down a little harder on the accelerator but did not notice that until after.

And he could be in company. I saw him once slip into the man with the brown T-shirt's Thunderbird and they peeled out leaving a roar at their back.

He was bad, and worse and really worse, and I saw him curled up by the gravel depot under a sunshade made of plywood and old bedsheets, and this other time I saw him walking with a bunch of birds and he must have been feeding them as they followed him around like an unruly rug.

That time with the birds, his communion with them— and I am prone to tenderness around animals—even in my new philosophical, less sentimental state, I cried just a little, two tears let's call it, involuntary, and speaking of animals I was reminded of those crocodiles who the old Christians thought would cry (after taking down a gazelle or whatnot) as if they were crying from the guilt of the thing; which is where that saying about crying crocodiles comes from. Though of course lizard-*tears* are just lizard-*instinct*: eating food makes their eye glands water. Simple. Nothing but a mechanism, as far from feeling as a factory line.

No matter what you've heard, there is no animal which cries. Not a one. Only us chumps. Nobody knows why we do, why we lament in our wet way (those of us who still can), which is quite a significant gap in our collective knowledge when you think about it, after all of those years of scholarship and study.

Anyway, I thought that this was the last time I'd ever cry for him, though I'd continue to see him luckless and blighted in his descent—see that he'd taken the place of Shitburger and picked up some grubby mantle.

My throat was always sore then. A man may fall asleep over his oatmeal. His feet can swell and he can forget to pay his rent. He may never forswear the bottle. We can all agree that his temperature is high. He can find honesty at last and christen himself dying.

The few numb cohorts left became more and completely anesthetized, and the multitudes of the angry became psychopathic. Most of the taco stands were packing up. Joey shuttered up his shop as did Flemming, and Lindsay packed up all her "creations," and the menu at Edna's got smaller and there was nowhere to buy an appliance (liquor store doing fine business though). "Howdy" was no longer a thing. Can't remember there being any weddings, and babies weren't a phenomenon either. School attendance fell off a cliff. *Culpos Gazette* says "AW FUCKIT" though the radio continued to scream to high hell. Screen doors set in front of shut ones like an extra coat of paint. We move from this to emptiness and wreckage. We wanted for the demolition crews; at least there'd be a fresh start. Did we always have buzzards? No one came in from the reservations much, and there was a general hunkering. I was reminded of those same conditions which set my father on the course toward degradation and then savagery. The foreclosing of options with the foreclosures of houses and land, and the meanness that this gave rise to, and without being a total twerp about it anymore, I should say:

That even though Dad possessed exactly zero sense of symbol and metaphor—when he killed his wife, my dear mother, it was with a book.

He had wrenched that big, hardbound black Bible from her hands and smacked her across the face with it so hard she fell like a tree such that when I imagine it as evidently often

I must, I can hear the whipcrack of breaking bark; though in fact what was cracked was her skull, and on that kitchen tile.

———————————

Now: did I see it happen? The apocalyptic event?

No.

Was it me who found her?

Yes.

Were there any of those "wet eyes" on my dad afterward?

I don't know because I never saw him again. Other than on those many fevery nights of mine, deep in my slumberings from March into the last convalescent weeks of fall.

PALL BEARERS

People also ask: What is a paw bear?
—Google

We're screwed, said Regis. Go home.

HOMILY

C racked," and things were cracked and cracking and one of the things cracked was, finally and unsurprisingly, the Nguyens' window; its plate glass flaring into atoms, machines vandalized, ugly words dripping down walls (you'd think Nancy and Liem would've left then, as I would have, but they stuck it out, at least from what Dill told me). For then there was a true violence that put the earlier ones to shame; oh brother was there violence.

Shootings, beatings, hellfire, tornados, blood-rain, and locusts . . . you just fucking name it, not just saber-rattling but saber-using, and the region was all-in on one single outcome, and that outcome was everyone paying dearly and everyone participating in that payback.

The diocese of weepers had shrunk over time to a mere parish, then to a single congregation, then to only one or two parishioners. Then no one. Other jobs were sought. Few found. The ranked pews were emptied: harrows cut into dry earth, never to be seeded again.

Remembering that great gust of feeling that first came on with the kid's arrival: I mourned its loss, even more in its most extreme version; that gnashing, rending mania of sorrow and scalded cheeks, those orgies of grief, the halls rollicked with wails, rimed with saline, a sadness which was almost like the violence that beset us after, but which to me came as a great exhale. Others remembered, but remembered that different, for that is how the mind may work and most often does. And though my mind still worked, my body was throed in a violence all its own, which, as in Culpos, was a violence that could not ever be stemmed. I couldn't go out much and could do little of anything except for to remember everything as is my wont and holy duty.

Dill goaded me toward recalling only those other, less tortuous, and more happy things:

—Remember the quarry? he said, seeking toward such better moments:

—Remember Jenny Fitzwilliams and the tight jeans?

—Remember that fucking rodeo with the goring where you puked nachos, which looked the same coming out as going in?

—Remember the pinball in Baneros that was free to play by accident and nobody cottoned on to it for days?

—Remember . . .

The event is running long, and life is for the living, so I'll try to wrap things up quick as possible.

EULOGY

Don't be afraid to show emotion.

—H. A. Kebbel Funeral Home, "How to Write a Eulogy"

Trembling Hills.

Where everyone walks on six legs or rolls on two. I knew it well, mostly due to that Mr. Lamont, and I knew the stink of the air—smell of orange soda mixed with used toilet water fermented in a gas tank. I knew the endless squeak of the white sneakers on the orderlies. I had seen that mural of forced jollity many times, with its sinister and utterly redundant sun. And I thought about the time my father spent behind bars. The folks at TH were not exactly *behind* bars but the place was rife with them; bars running the length of the corridors, on the sides of beds, in the shower, next to the shitters.

Hell no. Not for me.

—You'll be better off there, Dill said.

—Not going, I said.

—Look on the bright side, if you just haul your ass to the Home, you'll miss the entire thing going on out *here*, Dill said, pointing through the window to the world as a whole.

Francine smiled the only tender smile I'd ever seen on her face.

—I'll leave this mobile when you drag me out by my testicles, I said.

They did not (drag me out) though the illness up in me dragged on. And I knew these weeks were to be, in many ways, my last-chance spittoon. What would I use them for, I wondered? I knew the answer, which was putting the story down on paper. And so I started with that and dug on in.

302 began a rotation of visits to my trailer home again— Dill, Francine, Sheryl, Rev, Johnnie, Peewee, and even Hank once. I always asked them the same question, and they would not reply to that, and I believe—in those times—it was because they truly didn't know the answer.

Except for Rev, who did.

—It hurts me to be the bearer, he said.

—Christ knows you're always bearing things to me Rev, I said.

—Comes with the territory.

—Have you considered all that bearing so many things could be bad for your back, I said.

—Simmer down, Ed.

—And he'll be around again, I said, knowing the kid's ways.

—I know you loved that boy.

Loved.

Well shit. Maybe I did. That could've been a true thing I suppose, though sometimes a man can fall for the crowbar he thinks will pry him from the life he's been leading.

But perhaps love. Who knows. Love: present tense.

The news came in earnest, and from everyone.

He'd overdosed to death up in Ojares. They found his corpse, pruny and open-mouthed up behind the supermarket, nothing on him but that funeral suit.

In another he'd been kicked to death out by the campground restroom. Someone stumbled on him there and he had, it was later determined, been dead two weeks. As is always the case when the destitute pass away out in the open, people walk by, thinking them asleep or high or just think exactly nothing at all. So he'd been gone for a while when at last he was discovered as deceased.

There were others.

Arms strung up on a cattle fence to die of exposure. Set alight with kerosene. Mistaken for a mule deer and brought down, another loud *crack* in my litany of such.

Bitten by a rattler (this was, in my opinion, the happiest of the bad scenarios as it did not implicate mankind; mankind being so dead set on implicating its own self).

Didn't matter because I refused to believe all of it, and shy of seeing the body pulled from a morgue's drawer or exhumed from a pauper's grave: I don't think I ever will. Though, whether he yet breathed or had ceased in that, I did finally submit, then, and only then, to his never coming back.

And eventually no one raised it to me anymore.

I was getting hints of an oncoming amnesia in the area, and began to conclude that when you cease talking about a thing, soon no one will remember it—perhaps even old elephant Ed, prodigiously memorizing as I am, might lose such recall, and that's just people and how we do. Which is why I continued to write it all.

Though, maybe I was wrong about that then, and maybe such a chronicle as mine would *not* be necessary. He would be remembered by one and all. He might live on as local legend, like a chupacabra, skunk-ape, moth man, river monster, or some such. Maybe even seekers would come, like those who visited the Crying Rock. Would look for brogue-prints in the dust and speculate on his origins. Hadn't he cured the sick and fed the beggars? Would he be inscribed in history for his sufferings, the way he was broken down like a shotgun, horsefucked by the world he was so intent on saving? Or would it be that his legacy would be that he had terrorized the community and brought on its damnation. We tell tales about such things too, but remember that nothing gets so eagerly devoured as stories about outlaws, as bad folk can be folk heroes. Especially them.

Canonized or demonized, there might be some who would await his return.

I would not be amongst them. He was gone, I knew. And without him, I saw it come to pass that a tear—whether from laughter or sorrow—became a delicate and rare thing. I wished it were not so. I myself had, in my time, tried to tap the earth for what springs there were, and had sought to bring down what meager drizzle I could coax from that stingy sky. Tried, best I could.

He was, I'd thought, our last great hope. And I believed in his goodness, despite all the excess and troubles.

A good kid, badly used.

There is no turning back the clock of course, and the way things were going, I did wonder, kid aside, if maybe this thing of ours was simply the way of it; the unerring and natural order of it, meaning that perhaps that was just how all things come to die; with a weak breath, a final parched exhale.

But I also couldn't help but wondering if I mightn't have been wrong about that too.

I wondered if maybe we might have been able to—gingerly,

adoringly—siphon and save what we could of these scarce and scattered drops. Tear by precious tear. If we mightn't have pooled them in our palms; shielded them from the sun's greedy heat.

What if?

Could we have, if we had truly rallied, eventually, devoid of supernatural assistance, gathered enough to drink from? If only a single swallow?

POETRY READING VI

WITHERS

Wither? Wither?
Wither? Wither?
Wither? Wither? Wither? Wither?

E.F.

CALLED ON HOME

It's goodbye time
—Conway Twitty

I was eventually pulled out of my trailer by the testicles, by which I mean I finally did relent to the chorus, and was remanded into the care of that dread and godforsaken place, Trembling Hills; home of drool.

(Too young! I thought moronically.)

And it was as awful there as I knew it would be, for sure, but: "a man can get used to anything." Which is true and what I eventually did (get used to it). Got used to: pills, drips, canasta, watercolors, so on. Even the truly bad stuff, though I made sure the worst of the humiliations (sponge baths, changings) were well and over before Chantal came to visit, and she would visit every day except on the ones Dill came by or on the rarer ones when someone else might.

———

—Hold still, she'd say, trimming my mustache.

—I'm trying.

—Don't you look handsome.

—Don't you need glasses.

She would never agree to become an actual widow—not on the dotted line, that is—despite it being the role she always dressed for, and we celebrated no eleventh-hour wedding. Of course not, as she and I both still had some goddam fucking dignity. This did not mean that Chantal wouldn't (and quite often did) run that mascara of hers, though on such occasions it would be for love rather than money.

—I'm not gone yet, I'd say to her, and she'd always end her time with me in the late evening by kissing me on the mouth in the sexy way, taking her time doing it, making sure not to slide into anything that might be mistaken for comfort.

And Dill of course. The Seagram's he would sneak in (which helped with my pain, and was, to me, preferable to the pills on daily offer in the Home, rattled from those little paper cups, the total anesthesia they brought on); Dill telling me the gossip, us reminiscing about the times when we'd be free from our houses and lords of junkyards and creeks (when there still were some). I'd ask every now and then about the 302, and it sounded like there were still zero jobs and he was ready to retire anyway and just commit to his land. (Though God knows what he'd do on it—"maybe I'll get me some of those fucking llamas," he'd said, "put up some chicken wire. Grow some sorghum." But I could not picture that.)

—Anyway I got my hands full-up with you, dickhead, he said.

He really did do his part, that much was true, and my best days were when he'd kidnap me, and I'd submit to his carrying me to my truck, which I'd bequeathed as his ("call it a loan," I'd said), and we'd drive out to Hector's ranch. He'd set me out in a chair in the shade to watch the horses crop, and this was soothing and it was as if it was me being fed. But eventually I'd move my gaze over then to watch the horizon beyond the fences, where the land ends. I'd bring my dad's binoculars just in case there'd be an interesting bird out there (or was it, in fact, me searching the scorch-plane for some sign of a young man?).

And sure, that's a summation of what Chantal would call something like the *day-new-mont*, but hold on, we are not done, because I did attend one more service.

SCRIPTURE READING

Write in a book all the words I have spoken to you.

—JEREMIAH 30:2

RECESSIONAL

Well in point of fact it was not a service but my birthday party.

Normally no big deal, my birthday, excepting that (this being the "pointiest" part of the "point of fact") I knew this particular birthday would be my last.

I wasn't expecting to celebrate at all and usually don't. But old Dill, persistent, said he'd haul me out to the Crown, where him and Chantal would grab a booth for us. (Dill also said he'd make me a cake for the occasion—a thing that seemed to me as improbable as a snowfall, and we will just see about that, I thought.) So there was no choice really, and as I've said I'll take any occasion to escape my residential penitentiary.

So at the duly appointed hour, Dill arrived at the Home and gathered me into the truck. He collapsed my wheelchair, and the sound of its snapping metal startled me. I was suddenly reminded of Soupy's brother, who died out at the automobile graveyard near Gejónda, having fallen drunk and blacked out in that enormous compactor they have. Waffled flat, was Soupy's brother.

Which of course reminded me of Dad laid out in the car wash that one time and how he barely escaped being drowned and scalded to death, and got me thinking, generally speaking: whooeeeee, Ed, but there are far worse ways to go than in a hospital bed.

Alone in a campground . . . bound to a cattle fence . . .

The roads were entirely empty.

When we arrived, Chantal was already in front. Through the doors of the Crown then, we three, and (of course) surprise surprise but wasn't there just the whole entire gang standing there: 302, keepers of the dampened flame, hold-outs, paladins of compassion, defenders of the better, unimpeachable sentiments, those feelings that bind; "those feelings that bind," and there were some things weepers could be counted on to do hell or high wind, and those "feelings" that were "counted on" to "bind" were all good-hearted ones.

So there they all were and everyone back-clapped and saluted me and I felt pretty good for that, though I worried still, through all the smiles and such, about how I had become so fleshless and severe; the memento mori at the feast. I did not want to bring down an occasion that had been organized on my very own behalf, and so affixed an absolutely crazy grin to myself, in an attempt to offset whatever morbidity I imagined might put the gang off, and really I felt just like whirling the fuck around and spinning myself off into oblivion. But of course I could not as we all began to move deeper into the Crown, toward the back tables, inexorable, and I was mulling over this retirement party of mine; severance package, gold watch, etc., thinking more on embarrassment than gratitude ("if my bladder releases now, it is game over"), and then I saw that back, brick wall, and there was my picture all blown up on an easel just as Crazy Patti's had been at her last rites, and there was a big old banner hanging from the smoky ceiling.

It read:

HAPPY SWEET SIXTEEN, ED, and I expected balloons to drift on down. (They'd have to be black ones of course, accompanied by a sudden surge of gloomy doves, cooing like ghosts.)

But the last of my self-consciousness and worry vanished completely upon seeing that-all, and everyone looking so damned pleased with themselves about it, and so . . .

Dill and Chantal took me to a booth and helped me sit.

The soft rumble, like pews being settled into.

There was a spotlit, stand-up microphone there. God help me.

Rev walked up and tapped it twice.

—We gather here today to celebrate Ed Franklin . . . he said.

—Do we have to celebrate his fucking poetry? Johnnie said, and everyone roared.

(Commence roast.)

They took their turns.

A lot of mockery about my hundred-dollar words. Easy

mark. I turned around, shrugging "guilty as charged," and everybody liked that too and seeing them behind me I thought about that cheerful waving of handkerchiefs such as once accompanied a ship's leaving harbor. Best wishes and safe travels to foreign shores.

Dill got up and told a few amusing stories from long ago including but not limited to that barfing rodeo one, and basically summed me all up to everyone as a massive chucklehead. But then, he started in on saying all sorts of sappy and sweet words about me, kind things, unusually kind, and I noted how strange life is that Dill and me had come to a moment where we would have to try, so damned hard, for once, *not* to cry.

I love him up until the ends of the earth but when he finished it was frankly a relief to us both.

Others then.

Jokes about my hat. My gambling. My drinking.

Horse jokes. Many, many horse jokes.

Peewee had written a limerick. That was rough.

Nancy and Liem—who I hadn't seen since the violence—did a toast from their land, in that language of theirs.

Hankie went too but it was so obviously begrudging that he was merrily booed offstage. Yet he still put a hand upon my shoulder as he passed on his way back to his booth, and there is humanity even in those who are the stingiest in giving of it.

Chantal, of course—she performed a whole sexy "Happy Birthday, Mr. President" thing, but in French, wearing the hat she had snatched off my head, one of my own browns jammed into the side of her bright red mouth, and the whole act was goddam *drole*.

We took a pause to eat Dill's cake—the saddest-looking swayback you've ever seen—but having guessed at just such an outcome Sheryl had gone ahead and brought a big old cake of her own, one with my name and the idiot words "save a horse—ride a cowboy" piped onto it.

Paper plates and plastic forks bussed and then our master of ceremonies Rev got up to the mic again and bade us:

—Y'all rise for the hymn.

At which point Lemon, that absolutely glorious old bitch, stood and sang not a hymn but my famously least favorite song of "Danny Boy" (exception that it was "Eddie Boy")—her voice sounding like two cheese graters wrestling for prize money.

And I gobbled it all up. Couldn't help myself.

Jesus, I thought as I looked at my mug up there on the easel. That pic Chantal had taken when we'd first met in the aftermath of Jeannine. I was smiling in it, believe that or not. Though as usual it was hard to tell what the hell was going on beneath my worldwide-celebrated mustache.

But my eyes told the truth of it.

My happy, wet eyes.

———————

After Lemon had (strenuously, noisily) made her way back to her seat, Rev came back up there for the final time and then says:

—Anyone else got anything?

Didn't seem to be any takers, so he said it again, just for the form of the thing.

—Anyone?

The microphone feeds back.

Feeds back in a whine; in one long, pure wail, as if it's just discovered grief.

A keening cry.

In the silence that followed, melancholy whorled around us, tender and hushed as a mother's bedside recitation. *Plangent*— which is what people say about music and poems—shot through with nostalgia like a bitter blessing; delighting as it wrenched, joy and sorrow hugging one another tight, a most "tree-est" of the "playz-ears." That silence.

Bittersweet, that is it. Bittersweet is what you call it, the best word for it.

Bittersweet and we were held in that "bittersweet," its prayer, sustained in it, awaiting each successive moment like an expected note's rise or fall; a *now*, always a now, now, now, but also that now's yearning for the next now and what it might bring, which we knew would be some resolution to the previous one as well as some setup for the one coming after.

It sounded like *oh!* and felt like *sigh*, and we knew that though everything outside those walls was on fire—going to shit in a shitbasket—we were safe.

Inside of our holy lodge we were safe, even though, perhaps, we comprised the whole weeping world.

And each member of the 302 would later report to me—leaning in toward my hospital bed—that in the silence following that microphone's complaint, their names were spoke, privately, to them alone, and that there appeared a boy before that microphone. The real memento mori, but one who offered irrevocable recognition and solace.

And I reminded each of them that I was there too, and could affirm it all as such.

I was there too and when it was over I looked around at my friends and they at me, and we looked at one another in knowledge—otherworldly understanding—for though he was gone, we knew that he had come down on that day and taken for himself a place. Still amongst us (and perhaps it was notable only to me that what he had bestowed was not the old scathing grief, but this softer thing, as if the kid had discovered mercy), still amongst us and ready to fill up what needed filling, ready, just as were we then ready—dead-committed to form up a line, a bucket brigade, him at the rear, him, first to dip into the well and pass his blessing to the next in line, man to man, woman to woman, this line, our line—and there was not one body in that church that doubted it.

And he finally had true apostles.

Praise be to the kid. Praise him up in the hills, meaning: on high! Or down low, or in whatever his new place he might be "on," or "in."

Praise be.

Praise fucking be.

We staggered out to the vehicles.

Chief's enormous Cadillac, Sheryl's Lincoln, Johnnie's Hummer, Lemon in the passenger seat of Hankie's bust-ass wagon (both of them immediately lighting up with all the windows up), Liem and Nancy got in their subcompact, Chantal hitched a ride with Peewee, and out in front of it all, driven by Dill, me in shotgun, first out of the lot, exorbitantly rented from Vince, nuptial-ed to several dragging cans, was an actual, goddam, fucking *hearse*.

My ride.

Everyone turned their headlights on, and our cortege snaked slowly through the hills under the buttes and mesas— through canyons—as an old passenger train would; curves of sandstone softly lit by soft lines of soft light: lit, darkened, lit again, darkened, lit again, darkened, lit again, one by one the vehicles shunted onto new rails—my stop being the terminus; and finally the whole stage was left to blackness.

Back at Trembling Hills, Dill helped me up into my bed, night nurse came in and lowered me, the blinds rang closed.

The blinds rang back open again in the morning to wake me late, and I looked out on the mesas and buttes (buttes and mesas) as I always did, and I could imagine being up in them, and imagine it clearly.

In the afternoon I watched a program, got bored, got irritated, ate the rest of my corn pudding, and tried to write a new poem. Failed. Passed out.

Next day I woke and tried poetry some more.

And then even more lousy poetry. And I tried again further that night. And the following day. At some point, I thought: one of them would truly work—it would, I was sure; and I'd be at it, attempting poems until such a time came.

Get it down, Ed, before it all blinks out!

Or, is it "winks out"? Well, "blinks" or "winks," when in the entire history of eyes did one ever wink (or blink) shut without its having blinked or winked back open again? It's in the meaning of the words. And thinking on this, I feel a kind of serenity come over me, a calm, and a feeling close to what you might call religion. For this particular blinking (or winking) back open is an interesting case, you must agree, and we could say here that each and all faiths are built upon this premise—the promise of "back open again." And though

I expect no fluffy clouds and no virgins and no nearness-to-his-throne or other such incentives, it is possible that there may just be something after, something to open your eyes to.

The next day was much of the same. Poems again and failure again. And the following week it was like unto the one before that.

And so it was, and over and over and none of the poems did yet work, and nothing indeed has changed, and the poems will not come, and I know now that so shall it be until the end of an age, and I believe this failure at poems is now due to my thoughts being already disclosed, such that there is nothing left to tell. And if that's so, if I'm right about that "disclosed," now, I may finally—if I'm lucky—become clear and unhindered and thus lift up my hands.

A Note About the Author

Peter Mendelsund is the author of seven books, including the novels *The Delivery* and *Same Same*, as well as the nonfiction works *What We See When We Read*, *Cover*, *The Look of the Book*, and the memoir *Exhibitionist*. A former designer and a recovering classical pianist, Mendelsund is also the creative director and a contributor at *The Atlantic*.